W9-ADQ-587

The Sea Wall

The Sea Wall

by Marguerite Duras
Translated by Herma Briffault

With a Preface by Germaine Brée

Huston - Tillotson Library

FARRAR, STRAUS AND GIROUX
New York

PQ2607
.U8245
B313

Copyright 1952 by Marguerite Duras
Preface © 1967 by Farrar, Straus and Giroux
Published in France under the title
Un Barrage contre la Pacifique
© Editions Gallimard 1950

Library of Congress catalog card number: 51–10420

All rights reserved
Published simultaneously in Canada
by Ambassador Books, Rexdale, Ontario
Printed in the United States of America

To Robert

Preface

In the late twenties, French authorities opened up for cultivation the undeveloped lands of the Mekong delta, east of
Saigon, in what was then known as Cochin-China and is
now a part of South Vietnam. They built roads into hitherto
unpenetrated territory and, in order to promote food pro-
duction in a region dominated by hunger, they provided
settlers, made land-grants, offered loans and other incentives
to the agricultural development of the area. The sun-baked,
salt-soaked coastal strip just north of Saigon, an area perennially invaded by the July flood tides of the Pacific, is the
setting Marguerite Duras chose for her third novel, *The
Sea Wall*, more specifically entitled in French *Un Barrage
contre la Pacifique*. The Pacific is one of the forces that ruin
the settlers' hopes and the sea wall is the quixotic attempt
of a settler to tackle the problem singlehanded.

Marguerite Duras was herself born in Vietnam and lived
there till she was seventeen, thence perhaps the intimate
feeling for the land and the people that permeates the novel
and the atmosphere that gives substance and life to realities
which fail to come alive in the more technical works on
Vietnam that our involvement in that country's fate has
elicited. *The Sea Wall* would be well worth reading for what

37865

it lets us glimpse of the timeless native round of existence lived at the level of bare subsistence, yet infinitely human. It also gives a brief but pungent view of a large, Westernized city—Saigon—with its different sections and different layers of population. Seen through the eyes of the poor white settlers, behind whom stands Marguerite Duras and from whose viewpoint the story is told, the book is an indirect comment on colonial administration. There is no doubt at all as to where the novelist's sympathies lie, although she never intervenes directly. Her point of view is inherent in the setting and characters she has chosen and what befalls them.

If *The Sea Wall* may be read as a document, it makes no pretense at literal accuracy. Ram, the small settlement which is one of the poles of the novel, is a composite, not a specific place. Mme Duras does not even identify as Saigon the large modern city, the other pole of the story at the end of the single paved road that is Ram's only link with the outside world. What makes *The Sea Wall* fascinating as a novel is the masterful way in which setting and situation are reflected through the characters, giving the ones and the others an intense specificity. We look out at the settler's half-built bungalow, at small, remote Ram, with the casual intimacy of seventeen-year-old Suzanne, for whom they are the most familiar of settings, neither exotic nor startling. And so the stark geographic and economic conditions of existence on the plain come to life. Suzanne, with her twenty-year-old brother Joseph and Ma, a widow and former school-teacher, has been six years on the land when the novel opens and they all take for granted the discomforts and hardships this entails. So does Mme Duras. She asks for no tiresome commiseration for her characters. She describes things as they are, however grim some of the details may seem from the stronghold of our own secure lives. We too are in the habit of building dikes against certain basic truths about human existence in less favored circumstances than ours.

The family's region is meager, overrun by a starving, diseased, and kindly, indigenous population of peasants whose children are born with dreadful regularity, grow up for a few years like the hordes of semi-wild dogs that follow them around, sickly children always at play in roving bands and who die inevitably like flies of the hideous ailments that beset the perennially starved—a misfortune which haunts Ma but which the peasants accept as one of the givens of life. The salt-ridden coastal strip is adjacent to a narrow band of arable land, realm of the rice paddies, backed against the higher forest ground towards which the sleek cars of the wealthy hunters from Saigon speed, a jungle peopled by shadowy mosquito-riddled mountain tribes. There is no issue for the natives, as far removed as if they lived on another planet from the city-life of the hunters or of the wealthy rubber planters further up north. For Ma and her children, when we first encounter them, the land promises nothing but a monotonous paring down, a slow absorption into the ambient age-old misery of peasants living on impoverished, arid land.

Their plight is classical in its banality, a story familiar to many other settlers in many other lands and which we soon piece together from odd scraps of conversation. Ma, a Frenchwoman, whose ethics and view of human relationships belong to the democratic France in which she grew up, has been cruelly despoiled in the colony. The land granted her, in which her life's savings are sunk, is, for the most part, irreclaimable, invaded every year by the July flood tides. She cannot meet the requirements of her contract. The corrupted land agents who made the deal need now only apply the letter of the law. Ma, struggling against debt, faces the loss of her concession after the loss of her money, a sizable part of which lines the pockets of the land agents, along with similar takings from her predecessors on the land and, presumably, her successors. In one of its dimensions, *The Sea Wall* is the account of Ma's refusal to be despoiled; of her feud with the land agents, a feud as quixotic as her struggle against the Pacific. Her point of view is fully set out in the last of the many letters she has addressed to them in her sleepless nights, an illusory paper dike against the inevitable. All the poor settlers' misfortunes are depicted in that letter which her son never mails, but also Ma's personality and outlook, a wonderfully vivid and persuasive character creation that dominates the book.

Thus summarized, the novel may sound grim and dreary. Yet, out of this material Mme Duras has fashioned a resilient, robust novel in which all the characters, even the most incidental, live with a kind of elemental gusto and genuineness. The techniques she used in the creation of her small universe—and a universe it is, and not so small at that—are familiar to American readers. She wrote *The Sea Wall* under the influence of what the French call the behaviorist American writers—Erskine Caldwell, the Steinbeck of *Grapes of Wrath*, and, more especially perhaps, the early Hemingway. The first incident, the death of Joseph's old horse, plunges the reader directly into the atmosphere of disintegration and the stream of events that lead to Ma's death and put an end to the lifelong dream that has foundered in the silt of the plain. The events are reported dispassionately, without comment or analysis, mainly as seen through the eyes of Suzanne, yet told impersonally and liberally interspersed with dialogues that give the characters a chance freely to reveal themselves. The episodes move rapidly, often giving the impression of improvisation, of fresh informal spontaneity.

Through allusion, association, reminiscence, and flashback, a total picture of Ma's life emerges, intertwining past, present, and imminent future—Ma's death—into a coherent pattern. The dominant strand in the pattern is not recrimination or despair but the shared family legend, with its bitter realism and excitement. Better than could any commentary, it communicates the zest for life, the capacity for enjoyment, the bonds of respect, solidarity, and love that hold the family together.

In family lore, things and events assume semi-epic, semi-burlesque proportions. Ma's building of the sea wall and its crumbling in a single night is her fall of Troy, a defeat too terrible to be endured. Joseph's routing of the land agents is a glorious vengeance that enhances his aura in the family eyes. Objects, like Joseph's old car and his gramophone, or, in contrast, the "sparkler," the diamond bestowed on Suzanne by her luckless suitor Mr. Jo; animals like the old horse, the worms in the thatch, or the panther triumphantly brought home by Joseph; the whole expedition to the city in search of a buyer for the "sparkler"—all these fall into an epic alternating pattern of unexpected triumphs and unvoiced defeats. A picaresque epic realism runs through the book, counterbalanced by the intrinsic candor and human sensitivity of the characters involved.

Marguerite Duras obviously took immense delight in her characters and has created them hardy enough to stand on their own and elicit our sympathy and respect, but not our pity, of which they have no need. She most effectively accomplishes her task as storyteller by skirting and avoiding the expected in one episode after the other. Moreover, seen within the novel's perspective, Ma's life is far from being a series of defeats. It culminates in the fierce authenticity, the untrammeled and proud capacity for living with which she has endowed Joseph and Suzanne. Her children's triumphant defiance of defeat is the measure of Ma's triumph over the engulfing Pacific.

Remembering perhaps her own seventeen-year-old self, Mme Duras has bestowed upon Suzanne her imaginatively perceptive gaze, her matter-of-fact acceptance of things, moods, and feelings as they are. But both Suzanne and Joseph are also primarily adolescents emerging into adult life. *The Sea Wall* owes much of its humor and freshness to the uncompromising candor with which they confront the people and events that come their way. They have learned, by watching Ma, the real ethic behind the façade of colonial respectability; they are quite without illusion in some respects, but they have their own high standards, which they apply rigorously and efficaciously. Their reactions to Suzanne's rich and inept suitor, Mr. Jo, may seem, like Joseph's own love affair, singularly amoral in conventional terms. But within the context of their own experience, Joseph and Suzanne instinctively follow certain basic rules that work toward their happiness and preserve their dignity.

Basic in the emotional build-up of the story is the relationship of the two young people with Ma. Mme Duras avoids the commonplace "conflict of generations" theme, and does not indulge in the snide cerebralized neo-Freudian "generation of vipers" attitude that has so tiresomely marred a number of contemporary novels. The bitter outburst of grief and anger with which Joseph greets Ma's death is a monument to Ma's place in her children's affections. Of the many events in the novel, the most sensitively handled are those that reveal the quasi-physiological bond linking parent to child—one of the most constant underlying themes in all Mme Duras' work. Most moving, perhaps, is Ma's tacit and humble relinquishing of her authority, her recognition of her children's new needs and of their right to choose their own way toward self-fulfillment and a certain self-sufficiency. In the novel, both Joseph and Suzanne achieve a measure of understanding of themselves and of what they fiercely demand from life, an understanding untainted by self-pity or recrimination. They refuse to accept the wreck of Ma's dreams as their own, but they are deeply, compassionately, unsentimentally aware of Ma's human worth. They are free human beings with a passionate integrity.

One may sense, behind the figure of the indomitable old woman in her run-down bungalow, the defeat of an Old World optimism. Ma's solidarity with the peasants, the fight she puts up against the forces that oppress them all—human rapacity and the untamed forces of nature—suggest that she has built into her life an inner barrage against resignation. It is in Ma's name that, as he leaves the bungalow after Ma's death, Joseph prepares an eventual mass revolt of the peasants against the land agents, their oppressors.

The Sea Wall is an absorbing, readable, many-faceted novel. Its many latent implications haunt the imagination. The third of Mme Duras' novels, it was published in 1950, six years after *La Vie tranquille* (A quiet life), which preceded it. It heralded an intensively creative period during which Marguerite Duras emerged as one of France's most talented younger writers. Since its publication, she has written seven other novels, a book of short stories, and she has made a name for herself on stage and screen. Two of her novels— *Le Marin de Gibraltar* (The Gibraltar sailor) and *Moderato Cantabile*—were successfully filmed and, besides, she also furnished the dialogue for a couple of films, one of which, Alain Resnais' *Hiroshima, mon amour,* was widely acclaimed. The successful adaptations to the stage of another novel, *The Square,* and of one of her short stories, *Des journées entières dans les arbres* (Whole days in the trees), point to a capacity that is abundantly apparent in *The Sea Wall,* the capacity to convey character and mood through dialogue.

The Sea Wall has the complex thematic richness which is the hallmark of Mme Duras' writing. Yet, because of its concrete pictorial vividness and directness of approach, it is more immediately accessible to the reader than her later, more experimental work. Like many of the mid-century novelists, she has put much thought into the development of new narrative techniques, of new approaches to mood and character creation. They have on the whole been musical rather than pictorial in kind. In their formal and thematic diversity, all her novels make fascinating reading. And all in some way are related to the basic symbol Mme Duras established in *The Sea Wall*. Ma's unequal battle is waged, in different mode, by all Mme Duras' characters. Her struggle symbolizes the never resolved antagonism between human dreams and the limitations of human life. But in the case of *The Sea Wall* the solitude in which her other characters must, of necessity, wage battle against the inevitable and confront themselves and their truth is tempered by the unvoiced but unquestioned understanding that unites Joseph and Suzanne to Ma, and, though more superficially perhaps, to the unpretentious people who surround them.

Much has been written in our time about the "novel of derision" and the "dehumanization" of literature. *The Sea Wall* shares with all Mme Duras' work a compassionate, comprehending approach to human beings. And it is, besides, permeated by a youthful vitality and humor that set it apart and give it its quite particular appeal.

Germaine Brée
Vilas Professor
Institute for
Research in The Humanities
University of Wisconsin

PART ONE

1

ALL THREE OF THEM HAD THOUGHT IT WAS A GOOD IDEA TO BUY
that horse, even if Joseph could earn with it no more than
his cigarette money. To begin with, it was an idea—which
showed they were still capable of having ideas. Then, own-
ing a horse made them feel less lonely, for it linked them to
the outside world. Thanks to the horse, they could still manage to get something out of that world: not much, in fact
pitifully little, but all the same something that had not been
theirs till then, and they could bring it to their isolated piece
of the salt-soaked plain, to the three of them soaked in boredom and bitterness. A great thing, the carrying trade! Even
from a wasteland where nothing would grow, it was still
possible to squeeze out something by ferrying across this
wasteland people who lived elsewhere and were part of the
living world.

This state of things lasted only a week. The horse was too
old. He was much older for a horse than Ma was for a human
being. As far as a horse's life was concerned, you might say
he was a centenarian. Faithfully, for a week, he had tried
to do all the work required of him, but it was much beyond
his strength—such strength as he had had for many years.
And then he died.

They had been so disgusted over the whole thing, so thor-
oughly disgusted at being once more without a horse on
their corner of the plain, in the same old deadly solitude,

9

that on the very night the horse died they had decided to go next day to Ram, all three of them. In Ram, they could try to forget their troubles by seeing people.

And it was at Ram, the next day, that they set up an acquaintance which was destined to change all their lives.

Which proves that an idea is always good when it accomplishes something, even if you start out all wrong, with half-dead horses, for instance. An idea of this kind is always a good idea, even when everything fails woefully, because at least you end up by getting tired of your lot, as you would never have been if you had mistrusted your ideas from the very beginning.

So then, it was for the last time that Joseph's carriole creaked homeward late that afternoon towards five o'clock. They heard it when it was still a long way off on the highway, approaching from the direction of Ram.

Ma shook her head, worried.

"It's early for him," she said. "He must not have had many fares."

Soon the cracking of the whip and Joseph's shouts could be heard, and then the carriage appeared on the road. Joseph was sitting in front. In the back were two Malay women. The horse was moving very slowly, dragging his hoofs along, rather than walking. Joseph was whipping him, but he might as well have lashed the road, which could not have felt the whip less.

Joseph drew up in front of the bungalow, where the two women passengers got out and continued, on foot, towards Kam. Jumping down, Joseph took the horse by the bridle, left the road, and turned into the narrow drive which led up to the bungalow. Ma stood waiting for him on the raised strip of ground in front of the verandah.

"He won't take another step," said Joseph.

Suzanne was sitting under the bungalow, her back

propped against one of the wooden piles of the foundation. She got up and went out towards the terrace, without leaving the shade.

Joseph looked very hot as he began to unharness the horse. Sweat streamed down his face from beneath his cap. When the horse was unharnessed, Joseph stood back to study him.

Only a week had passed since he had had the idea of earning a little money this way. He had bought the whole outfit—horse, carriole, and harness—for two hundred francs. But the horse was much older than you would have thought. From the very first day, once unharnessed, the horse had gone off to the seed bank where he would stand as if rooted to the spot for hours, his head hanging down, nibbling the rice-shoots from time to time, but absent-mindedly, as though momentarily forgetting that he had vowed never again to eat. Aside from old age, they could not imagine what could be the matter with him.

The night before, Joseph had tried to whet the horse's appetite by offering him some rice-bread and a few lumps of sugar. But after sniffing at them, he had gone on with his ecstatic contemplation of the young rice-shoots. Doubtless, in his whole long past existence, spent in dragging heavy sawlogs from the forest to the plain, he had never eaten anything but the dried and yellowed grass of the clearings and, at the stage he had now reached, he had no taste for any other food.

"Eat!" Joseph bawled at him. "Eat!"

The horse would not eat. Joseph started to say something. Could it be that the horse was tubercular? Ma disagreed. She said the horse was like her, he was tired of living and simply wanted to give up and die.

All the same, until that day, he had not only been able to make the trip back and forth between Bante and the bungalow but, in the evening, once unharnessed, had managed to go by himself towards the seed bank. He had had that much strength left, and had gone of his own accord. Today, though, he stood on the earth terrace in front of Joseph, not budging, only lurching a little from time to time.

"Goddam it!" said Joseph. "He won't even take a step!"

Ma came forward now. She was barefoot and wore a big straw hat pulled down over her eyes. A thin braid of gray hair, held with a section of inner tube, hung down her back. Her loose, sleeveless, dark red dress was made from a *pagne*, a square of native cotton cloth. It was worn thin over the breasts, which were pendant but still fleshy and visibly swinging free beneath the dress.

"I told you not to buy it!" she shouted. "Two hundred francs for this half-dead horse and this cart that's ready to fall to pieces!"

"Shut up!" said Joseph. "Shut up, or I'll leave home!"

Suzanne now came out from under the bungalow and went up to the horse. She, too, was wearing a straw hat, from beneath which locks of red-brown hair showed. She, like Ma and Joseph, was barefoot, and she was wearing a blue sleeveless blouse with a pair of black Malay pantaloons reaching not quite to the knees.

"And how right you'd be," remarked Suzanne, "to run away from home."

"I don't ask your advice," said Joseph.

"I give it, free," said Suzanne.

Ma lunged at her daughter and tried to slap her. Suzanne dodged away to safety, returning to the cool shade under the bungalow. Ma began to whimper.

The horse's hind legs seemed to be half paralyzed. He did not take one step forward. Joseph let go the bridle by which he had been trying to lead the horse and gave him a push in the rump. Staggering jerkily, the horse moved as far as the bank and, arriving there, came to a halt, burying his nose in the tender green seedlings.

Joseph and Ma and Suzanne stood stock-still, looking at him hopefully. No, he was not eating; he was merely caressing the seedlings with his nose. He lifted his head once, twice, then again let it hang down, heavy and motionless at the end of his too-long neck, his thick lips resting on the tips of the green rice-shoots.

Joseph hesitated, turned, lit a cigarette, and went back towards the carriole. Then, after stacking the harness on the front seat, he dragged it underneath the bungalow. Usually he left it standing near the flight of steps, just barely under the bungalow. But that afternoon he put it far back, underneath the central wooden piles. This done, he seemed uncertain what to do next. After looking again at the horse, he went back towards the tool shed under the bungalow. Only then did he seem to see his sister, who had returned to sit against the wooden piles.

"What the hell are you sitting in here for?"

"I'm hot."

"You're not the only one."

He went into the tool shed, took out a bag of fertilizer and emptied it into a tin box. Then he went to put the bag back in the shed. Returning to the box, he began to crumble the fertilizer with his hands. He sniffed the air.

"What a stink! It's the deer carcasses. Must chuck them out. How can you stand the smell in here?"

"The carcasses don't stink as much as that fertilizer of yours."

He stood up and again went to the tool shed, carrying the box. Then he changed his mind, went over to the carriole, gave it a kick in the wheels, after which he resolutely mounted the bungalow steps.

Ma had gone back to her weeding. It was the third time she had planted a border of rad cannas between the rice-seed bank and the terrace. Regularly the drought killed them, but she never gave up. In front of her, the Corporal— as they called the Malay laborer—busied himself raking the ground and sprinkling it. The Corporal was getting harder and harder of hearing and Ma had to yell her orders louder and louder. Near the bridge, towards the highway, the Corporal's wife and daughter were fishing in a *marigot,* where they had been squatting in the mud for a good hour. For three long years they had all eaten the fish, always the same fish, that were caught each evening in that same pool beyond the bridge.

Under the bungalow it was relatively cool. Joseph had left the door of the tool shed open and a current of cool air came from it, smelling of deer carcasses. There were five of them hanging in there, four does and one buck. Joseph had shot the buck and one of the does two nights before; the others, three days ago. Those two had stopped bleeding; but the others still bled, the blood dripping out of their open jaws, drop by drop.

Joseph often went hunting, sometimes as often as every other night. Ma bawled him out for wasting his shot killing deer that only had to be thrown away at the end of three days. But Joseph could not bear to return empty-handed from the forest. So they always went through the motions of using the beasts for food, hanging them up under the bungalow until they were rotten, then throwing them away, casting them into the mountain torrent—the *rac,* as they called it. Everyone was sick of eating them. For some time now, they had preferred eating the stilt-birds that Joseph shot at the mouth of the *rac,* in the great salt marshes that bordered the concession towards the sea.

Suzanne waited for Joseph to come for her before going for a swim. She did not want to be the first one to go out towards the river from the bungalow. Better to wait for him. When they were together, Ma didn't yell so much.

Joseph came down the steps.

"Come quick," he said, "I won't wait."

Suzanne ran up the steps to put on her bathing suit. She had not finished when Ma, who had seen her, began to scream.

Ma did not scream to make you hear what she was saying.

She just screamed to scream, yelling out anything, things utterly unrelated to what was happening at the time.

When Suzanne came down the bungalow steps there was Joseph, indifferent to Ma's yammering, again struggling with the horse. Pressing with all his might against the animal's skull, he was trying to force its mouth down to the seedlings. The horse submitted, but did not touch the green shoots to eat them. Suzanne drew near.

"Come, Joseph."

"It's the end, I think," said Joseph sadly. "He's going to croak."

Regretfully he left the horse and, together, they went towards the wooden bridge, where the river was deepest.

Swarms of native children were playing on the highway. The minute they saw Joseph going towards the river, they stopped playing to follow him and to jump in after him when he dived into the water. The first ones plunged in as he did. The others let themselves fall, bunches of children at a time, into the gray foam. Joseph usually played with them, lifting them onto his shoulders, making them turn somersaults, and sometimes he would let one of them cling to his neck, much to the child's delight, while he swam down beyond the bridge to the edge of the village. But today he did not feel like playing. In the deep and narrow part of the river near the bridge he turned and turned, like a fish in an aquarium. On the bank above the water he could see that the horse had not made the least movement. Standing there on the rocky earth in the hot sunlight, the horse had the closed look of an inanimate object.

"I don't know what's wrong with him," said Joseph, "but one thing's sure, he's going to croak."

He dived again, followed by the children.

Suzanne did not swim as well as he did. From time to time she left the water, sat on the bank and watched the road which went in one direction towards Ram, in the other towards Kam and, beyond that, much farther off, towards the city, the largest city in the colony, the capital, which was eight hundred kilometers away.

The day would come when a car would at last stop in front of the bungalow. Suzanne was sure of it. A man or a woman would get out to ask something, or to have her or Joseph give them assistance. Suzanne could not very well imagine what information they could ask for: in the whole plain there was only one road, this one, which went from Ram to the city, by way of Kam. So you couldn't miss the way. All the same, the future might hold something, and Suzanne kept on hoping. Maybe one day a man would stop because he had seen her sitting near the bridge. Why not? Possibly he would like her looks and would offer to take her to the city. Few cars, apart from the bus, passed that way, though. There were not more than two or three a day, and they were always the same cars, carrying big-game hunters to Ram, sixty kilometers away and, a few days later, the same, passing in the opposite direction. The cars went by at top speed, honking their horns to chase the children off the road. Long before they appeared in a cloud of dust you could hear their horns, muffled and powerful, in the distant forest.

Suzanne knew that Joseph, too, was waiting for a car to stop in front of the bungalow. The car he was waiting for would be driven by a platinum blonde who smoked English cigarettes and wore lipstick and rouge. She, for instance, might begin by asking him to mend a flat tire . . .

Every ten minutes or so, Ma screamed and shook her fists at them, raising her head above the cannas.

As long as Suzanne and Joseph were together, she never came near them but just took it out in screaming. Ever since the collapse of the sea walls, she began screaming every time she tried to say a word, no matter what. In the old days, her children had not worried much about her fits of temper. But since the crumbling of the sea walls, she was a sick woman—dangerously sick, the doctor said. She had already had three epileptic attacks and all three, according to the doctor, might have been her death. You could let her go on yelling for awhile, but not too long. She must not be allowed to get into a towering rage, for that might bring on an attack.

The doctor traced these attacks of hers to the crumbling of the sea wall. Maybe he was mistaken. So much resentment could only have accumulated very slowly, year by year, day by day. There was more than one single cause: there were thousands, counting the collapse of the sea walls, the world's injustice, the sight of her children splashing in the river . . .

Ma had certainly not been destined from the beginning to attach, towards the end of her life, so much importance to misfortune that a doctor could now talk about seeing her die of it, die of sheer misery and despair.

The daughter of peasants, she had been so bright at school that her parents had allowed her to go to college. After that, she had been a schoolteacher for two years in a village of northern France. That was in 1899. Occasionally, on Sunday, she stopped to gaze at the Colonial propaganda posters in front of the town hall. "Enlist in the Colonial Army!" said some. And others: "Young People, a Fortune awaits you in the Colonies!" The picture usually showed a Colonial couple, dressed in white, sitting in rocking-chairs under banana trees while smiling natives busied themselves around them. She married a schoolmaster who was as sick as she was of life in the northern village and as victimized as she was by the maunderings of Pierre Loti and his romantic descriptions of exotic lands. The consequence was that, shortly after their marriage, they made out a joint application to be sent, as teachers, to that great Colony then known as French Indo-China.

Suzanne and Joseph had been born in the first two years after their arrival in the Colony. After the birth of Suzanne, Ma had stopped teaching in the State Schools, continuing to

earn a little money by giving private French lessons. Her
husband had been appointed head of a Native School and,
according to her, they had lived well, in spite of the burden
of their children. Those were undoubtedly the best years of
her life, years of happiness. This remembered past was like
a distant dreamland, a happy island in her life. As she grew
older, she talked about it less and less, but when she did, it
was always with the same desperate eagerness. Then, each
time, she recalled new wonders and perfections, new qualities in her husband, a new ease of life which they had
known, and which tended to comprise an opulence of which
Joseph and Suzanne were a little skeptical.

When her husband had died, Suzanne and Joseph had
still been very young. Of the period that followed, Ma never
willingly spoke. She said it had been hard, that she still wondered how she had managed to survive it. For two years she
had gone on giving French lessons and, since that did not
bring in enough, piano lessons. Then, since her earnings
were still too little, as the children grew up she had found
work as a pianist in a moving-picture theatre, the Eden
Cinema. She had worked there for ten years. At the end of
ten years she had saved enough money to apply to the cadastral government of the Colony for a concession of land.

Her widowhood, the fact that she had once been a teacher
in the Civil Service, and also the dependence upon her of
two children, gave her priority rights to a concession. But
she had been obliged, nonetheless, to wait two years for it.

She had now been on the plain for six years. It was six
years since Ma and Joseph and Suzanne had arrived there
in that Citroen car, which they still had: "the B-12," as they
called it.

At once, the very first year, she had put half the concession under cultivation, hoping that the first harvest would
enable her to pay off the greater part of the expenses on the
building of the bungalow. But the flood tides of July had
made an onslaught on the plain, drowning the crops. Be-

lieving that she had been the victim of an unusual occurrence, and against the advice of the people of the plain, Ma had begun all over again the next year. And again the sea had risen. So then, she had had to admit the truth: her land was irreclaimable. Each year the sea invaded it. True, the sea did not rise to the same extent each year. But it always rose enough to destroy everything, either directly or by infiltration. Except for the five hectares of land bordering the road, and in the middle of which she had built her bungalow, she had thrown her savings of ten years into the Pacific Ocean.

Her artlessness was incredible and her misfortune was due to this. The ten years she had passed in complete abnegation at the piano of the Eden Cinema, living on a minute salary, had shielded her from the struggle and the abundant injustices of the world. She had emerged from that ten-year tunnel virginally innocent of any knowledge of the powers of evil, desperately ignorant of the blood-sucking proclivities of colonialism, in the tentacles of which she was helplessly trapped. The arable concessions were not generally granted except for twice their value, of which half the sum went into the pockets of the agents in charge of distributing the land developments. These petty officials really controlled the market in land concessions and had become more and more insolent in their demands. So much so that Ma, had she tried to assuage their devouring appetite—which could not be tempered by any particular considerations of any exceptional case—would have had to give up the idea of buying any concession, supposing she had been sharp enough to refuse the irreclaimable tract of land that had been assigned to her.

When, a little late in the day, Ma grasped the situation, she had gone to the land agents in Kam, to which town the concessions of the plain were dependent, and had been so naïve as to insult them and threaten to complain to higher quarters. They disclaimed all responsibility for the error, saying that the responsible ones had been, no doubt, their predecessors, who had long ago returned to the metropolis. But Ma had continued her attacks upon them with such perseverance that they had been obliged, in order to get rid of her, to use threats themselves. If she kept on, they said, they would take back the concession before the legal lapse of time. It was the most telling argument with which to silence their victims who, of course and naturally, preferred to have even an illusory land concession to having none at all.

The concessions were never accorded except conditionally. If, after a designated period, the totality had not been put under cultivation, the Land Survey department would seize it. None of the concessions on the plain had been accorded a definite title; these were the concessions which easily enabled the land agents to make a considerable profit on the others, the real and arable concessions. The choice of attributions was left to them. The agents of the Land Survey reserved the right to distribute, according to their own best interests, immense reserves of irreclaimable land which, regularly attributed and no less regularly taken back, constituted in a way their reserve of capital. On the fifteen land concessions of the plain of Kam, they had settled, ruined, driven off, resettled and again ruined and driven off perhaps a hundred families. The only claim-holders who had remained on the plain lived by traffic in opium or absinthe, having to buy off the cadastral agents by paying them a quota of their irregular earnings—"illegal earnings," according to the agents.

The righteous wrath of Ma did not spare her, two years after her arrival, the first inspection by the land agents. These routine inspections were merely a visit to the claim-holder, for freshening up his memory: he was reminded that the first trial period had elapsed.

"Nobody in the world could make anything grow on this concession," the claim-holder would say.

"That's strange," the agents would retort, "our government does not usually allot land that can't be cultivated."

Ma, who began to see a little more clearly into the mysteries of their peculation, showed the agents the bungalow. It was not finished, but all the same and incontestably it represented a beginning towards development and should make them concede her an extended term of tenure. The cadastral agents succumbed to the argument and gave her one more year.

That year, the third after her arrival, she judged it was useless to renew her efforts, so she allowed the Pacific Ocean complete liberty. As a matter of fact, even had she wished to plant crops, she would not have found the means to do so. Already, to finish the building of the bungalow, she had made one or two demands for credit at the Colonial banks. But the banks acted only after consulting with the land agents. She had secured a loan only by mortgaging the unfinished bungalow, and it was precisely to finish this that she had borrowed money. For, as to the bungalow, it belonged to her, in full ownership, and she congratulated herself each day on having built it. Always, in proportion to her growing destitution, the bungalow, to her mind, increased in value and solidity.

Following the first inspection, there had been one other. It had taken place that year of the crumbling of the sea walls, in the very week after the event. But Joseph, by that time, was old enough to assert himself. The handling of a gun had become familiar to him. He had brought out his gun and had brandished it under the nose of the inspector who, without insisting further, had gone off in the little car which took him on his rounds. From then on, as far as inspection was concerned, Ma had been left in relative peace.

Strengthened by the delay accorded her on account of the bungalow, Ma had informed the agents in Kam of her new projects. She was going to ask the natives who lived

miserably on the adjacent lands to construct, with her, a
barrier against the sea. It would be profitable to all of them.
The dike would follow the seacoast—the Pacific coast, she
called it—and would ascend the *rac* up to the highest level
of the July flood tides. Surprised, the agents considered the
project a bit Utopian but made no objections. She could go
ahead, draw up the plan, and send it to them. In principle,
they asserted, the draining of the plain could come only
within the scope of a governmental plan, but no ruling, as far
as they knew, forbade a settler to erect a dike on his own concession. The only conditions they laid down were that she
must acquaint them with her plan and have the authorization of the local cadastral services. Ma sent in her project
after having spent nights on end drawing it up; then she
waited for the authorization. She waited a very long time,
without becoming discouraged, for already she had become
used to this kind of waiting. Such waits—and they alone—
were obscure links which bound her to the powers of the
earth upon which she was dependent soul and body: powers
such as the cadastral agents and the banks. After having
waited several weeks, she decided to go to Kam. The agents
had indeed received her project; they had not acknowl-
edged receipt because, decidedly, the draining of her concession did not interest them. Nevertheless, they gave their
tacit authorization to build the dikes. Ma left them, proud
of this result.

The Ocean-barriers would have to be buttressed with
mangrove logs. Naturally, she alone must assume the expense of procuring them. The bungalow, unfinished, had
just been mortgaged. She spent all the mortgage money to
buy the logs, and the bungalow had never been finished.

The doctor's diagnosis was not completely wrong. It was
possible to believe that everything began just there. For
who, taking into account the loving care expended on the
building of that sea wall, would not have been seized with
a great anger and distress at the sight of its collapse? Hun-

dreds of the peasants of the plain had worked on it, aroused from their millennial torpor by a sudden and foolish hope. And in one night it had collapsed like a house of cards, spectacularly, in one single night, succumbing to the elemental and implacable onslaught of the Pacific Ocean! Who, having omitted to study the origin of such a foolish hope, would not have been tempted to explain everything—from the unvarying misery of the plain to Ma's epileptic seizures—by the events of that fatal night? A natural calamity had been the cause of everything! It was a summary but captivating explanation, to which anyone might blamelessly cling.

Joseph always had to force Suzanne to go into the water. He wanted her to learn to swim well enough to go into the sea with him, at Ram. But Suzanne had her own ideas on the subject. Sometimes, especially in the rainy season, in one night the forest would be inundated, the drowned bodies of squirrels, muskrats, or young peacocks would float downstream—and these encounters filled her with disgust.

As Ma did not stop her screaming, Joseph decided to leave the river, and Suzanne, abandoning her lookout for motorcars, followed him.

"To hell with everything," said Joseph, "tomorrow we'll go to Ram!"

He raised his head in Ma's direction.

"We're coming!" he called. "Stop yelling!"

He no longer thought about his horse for he was now thinking about Ma, as he hurried to join her. She was red in the face and tearful, as she always was since she had fallen ill. She continued to lament.

"You'd better take your pills," said Suzanne, "instead of yammering."

"What sins did I commit before God in Heaven," screamed Ma, "to have such brats for children!"

Joseph walked past her, went up into the bungalow and came back with a glass of water and some pills. As always,

Ma began by refusing to take her medicine. As always, she ended up by taking it. Each evening, after their swim, they had to give her a pill to calm her down. For the one thing she could not tolerate in the depths of her heart was to see her children amuse themselves and thus forget, for a time, the existence they endured on the plain.

"She's getting vicious," Suzanne said, and Joseph could not contradict her.

Suzanne went to rinse off in the shower room, with jars of water, then she dressed herself. Joseph did not rinse himself, he stayed in his bathing suit night and day. When Suzanne came out of the shower room, the phonograph was already going on the verandah where Joseph, stretched out on a chaise longue, was no longer thinking of his mother but again of his horse, which he was looking at disgustedly.

"A piece of bad luck," he said.

"If you sold the phono, you could buy a good horse and make the trip three times a day instead of only once."

"If I sold the phono, I'd run away from home, and quick!"

The phonograph was a big thing in Joseph's life. He had five records and he played them every evening, regularly, after his swim. Sometimes, when he was fed up with life, he played them one after the other, without stopping, over and over throughout a long part of the night, until Ma got up two or three times and came to threaten him that she would throw the phonograph into the river.

Suzanne took an armchair and came to sit beside her brother.

"If you sold the phono and bought a horse, in two weeks you could buy a brand-new phono."

"Two weeks without a phono and I'd get the hell out of here."

Suzanne gave up.

Ma was getting dinner in the dining room. She had already lit the acetylene lamp.

Night fell very, very quickly in this country. The minute

the sun disappeared behind the mountain the peasants lit their fires of green wood to protect themselves from wild beasts and, cheeping like birds, the children returned home to their cabins. However, the tigers were much less hungry than the children, of whom they killed very few. What the children died of in the marshy region of Kam, bordered on one side by the China Sea—which Ma obstinately called the Pacific Ocean, since "China Sea" seemed to her somewhat trifling and provincial and because, when she was young, it was of the Pacific Ocean that she dreamed and not of any of those little seas which unnecessarily complicate things—and walled in towards the East by the long, long chain of mountains which ranged the coast from very far up in the Asiatic continent, following a descending curve to the Gulf of Siam where it submerged and reappeared again in a multitude of islands ever smaller and smaller, but all equally swollen with the same somber tropical forests— what the children died of was not tigers, but hunger, the maladies caused by hunger and the hazards of hunger.

The highway cut straight across the plain, lengthwise. In principle, it had been constructed to drain off the future riches of the plain to Ram, but the plain was so miserable that it had no riches other than its infants with their pink mouths always open upon their hunger. Thus, the road was useful, in fact, only to the hunters, who simply passed through it, and to the children, who assembled there in famished and playful packs. Hunger did not keep the children from playing.

"I'm going hunting tonight," declared Joseph suddenly.

Ma left off her work at the stove and came to plant herself in front of him.

"You shan't go. I tell you, you shan't go!"

"I'm going," said Joseph. "There's nothing to do about it, I'm going."

When Joseph stayed too long there on the verandah, looking at the forest, he could not resist the desire to go hunting.

"Take me," said Suzanne, "take me, Joseph."

Ma began to whimper.

"I'll not take a woman out hunting at night," said Joseph. "And you, if you go on yammering, I'll make tracks and quick!"

With which, he went to shut himself in his room to get his Mauser and cartridges ready. Whimpering, Ma returned to the dining room and went on getting the meal. Suzanne had not budged from the verandah. The evenings when Joseph went hunting, she went to bed late. Ma, on those occasions, usually worked on her "accounts" or pretended to. One wondered what the accounts could be. During those nights, in any case, she did not sleep. From time to time she would leave her accounts, go to the verandah and listen to the sounds of the forest, trying to glimpse the halo of light thrown by Joseph's lamp. Then she would get back to her accounts—"those crackpot accounts," as Joseph said.

"Dinner's ready!" said Ma.

Again, as usual, those stewed stilt-birds with rice! The Corporal's wife also brought up a few grilled fish.

"Another night without sleep," said Ma.

In the phosphorescent light, she looked almost pale. The pills were beginning to work. She yawned.

"Don't worry, Mamma, I'll come back soon," said Joseph gently.

"It's for you that I'm afraid, when I'm afraid of having an attack."

She rose, went to the sideboard and took from it a can of salted butter and a can of condensed milk which she placed before her children. Suzanne poured out a lavish amount of the milk on her rice. Ma buttered some slices of bread for herself and dipped them in a cup of black coffee. Joseph ate the bird. It had a fine, black and bloody flesh.

"It stinks of fish," said Joseph, "but it's good for you."

"That's right," said Ma. "You'll be careful, won't you, Joseph!"

When it came to feeding them, she was always gentle. "Don't you worry, I'll be careful."

"So it's not tonight that we're going to Ram," said Suzanne.

"We'll go tomorrow," said Joseph, "and it's not at Ram you'll find what you're looking for. They're all married, except Agosti."

"Never would I give her to Agosti," said Ma, "not even if he came and begged for her!"

"He'll not ask you for anything," said Suzanne, "and it's not here I'll find what I'm looking for."

"He wouldn't ask better," said Ma. "I know what I'm saying. But he can go on hankering!"

"He never even thinks about her," said Joseph. "It's going to be hard. Some girls manage to marry without money, but they have to be awful pretty and even then it's a rare thing."

"While we're about it," said Suzanne, "what I have to say for Ram isn't just about that, there's always something happening in Ram the day the mail-packet arrives. And there's electricity and a wonderful phonograph in the canteen."

"Stop blathering about Ram," said Joseph.

Ma put in front of them the rice-bread that came by bus every three days from Kam. Then she began undoing her braid. Her hair, in her work-worn fingers, made a rasping sound, like dried grass. She had finished eating and was looking at her children. While they ate, she sat before them, following all their movements with her eyes. She could have wished that Suzanne would grow a little more, and Joseph too. She believed it was still possible. This, in spite of the fact that Joseph was twenty and was already taller than she.

"Take some of the stilt-bird," she said to Suzanne. "That condensed milk isn't nourishing."

"And it rots your teeth, too," said Joseph. "It's rotted all my back teeth. They'll just have to go on rotting, though."

"When we have some money, we'll have some other teeth put in," said Ma. "Take some of the stilt-bird, Suzanne."

Suzanne took a small piece of the bird. It turned her stomach and she ate it by little mouthfuls.

Joseph had finished and was already getting his hunter's lamp ready. While going on braiding her hair, Ma heated up a cup of coffee for him. When he had finished with his lamp, Joseph lit it and fastened it to his cap, which he put on. After which, he went out on the verandah to verify its angle of visibility. For the first time that evening he had forgotten his horse. But it was at this moment that he once more saw the beast, by the light of the acetylene lamp.

"Goddam it!" said Joseph. "This time, he's dead!"

Ma and Suzanne ran out to Joseph. There, in the field of light, they also could see the horse. He had at last lain down full length. His head extended above the bank and his nostrils, buried in the young rice-shoots, were at the level of the gray water.

"It's terrible," said Ma.

She put her hand to her forehead, overwhelmed, and stood stock-still at Joseph's side.

"You ought to go and see if he is really dead," she said at last.

Joseph slowly went down the steps and turned towards the bank, preceded by the light which shone from his cap. Before he had reached the horse, Suzanne had gone back into the bungalow, sat down at the table, and tried to finish her piece of stilt-bird. But the little appetite she had had was now gone. She gave up trying to eat and went into the sitting room. There she doubled up in a rattan armchair and turned her back towards the horse.

"Poor beast," whimpered Ma, "and to think, only today he made the trip from Bante."

Suzanne heard her whimpering, without looking. She must be on the verandah watching Joseph. The week before, a child in the hamlet beyond the verandah had died. Ma had stayed up all night with it and when it died, in the morning, she had whimpered in the same way.

"What a tragedy!" cried Ma. "Well, Joseph?"

"He's still breathing."

Ma came back into the dining room.

"What can we do? Suzanne, go get the old checked blanket from the auto."

Suzanne went down under the bungalow, avoiding looking in the direction of the horse. She took the blanket from the back seat of the B-12, went up and handed it to Ma, who took it to Joseph. A few minutes afterwards, Ma and Joseph came in.

"It's terrible," said Ma, "he looked at us."

"Enough! Stop talking about the horse, tomorrow we'll go to Ram."

"What?" said Ma.

"Joseph's the one that said so," said Suzanne.

Joseph put on his tennis shoes and went off in a temper. Ma began to clear away the table and then she sat down to work on her accounts. On those "crackpot accounts," as Joseph said.

2

WHEN THEY WENT TO RAM, MA PUT UP HER HAIR AND WORE shoes. But she always wore the same old dark red cotton dress—in fact, she never took it off except to go to bed. When she had to wash it, she went to bed to sleep while it was drying. Suzanne also wore shoes when they went to Ram. She had only one pair, they were black-satin dancing slippers which she and Ma had found at a sale in town. But Suzanne changed her clothes for the occasion, putting aside her Malay pantaloons and wearing a dress. As for Joseph, he dressed as usual. More often than not he did not even bother to put on shoes. However, when it was the day for the mail-packet from Siam to arrive he put on his tennis shoes, in order to be able to dance with the ladies among the boat passengers.

On their arrival at the Ram canteen, they saw, parked in the courtyard, a magnificent seven-seater black limousine. Sitting inside it, a liveried chauffeur was patiently waiting. None of them had ever seen the car before. It could not belong to any of the big-game hunters, for they usually rode in convertible cars. Joseph jumped out of the B-12 and slowly drew near, walking round the big car. Then, standing in front of the engine, he examined it for a long time, much to the astonishment of the chauffeur.

"It's a Talbot or a Léon Bollée," said Joseph, not being able to make out the name. At last he tore himself away and decided to go into the bar of the canteen with Suzanne and Ma.

Seated at the tables were three employees of the Post Office, some naval officers with some women passengers, young Agosti, who never missed a mail-packet, and, alone at a table, the presumable owner of the limousine. He was unexpectedly young.

Pa Bart, the proprietor of the canteen, slowly heaved himself away from the cash register and came towards Ma. For twenty years he had managed the canteen of Ram. He had never left it but had grown old and fat there. Now in his fifties, he was apoplectic and obese, soaked in Pernod. A few years earlier Pa Bart had adopted one of the native children of the plain, who attended to all the work of the canteen, and who, in his spare moments, fanned his employer and foster-father, a veritable Buddha, sitting motionless behind the counter, under the drowsy influence of his Pernod. At no matter what hour of the day, Pa Bart was drenched with sweat, and always, within reach, there was a glass of Pernod, which he sipped from time to time. He never moved except to greet a customer. He did nothing else, and when he displaced himself it was with the slowness of a marine monster removed from its native element, almost without lifting his feet from the floor, so weighty was his unforgettable paunch, that barrel of absinth. He drank nothing but that, and scarcely did anything else. He lived, and had become rich, by selling it illegally. People came to him from great distances, as far off as the plantations of the North. He had no child, no family, yet he hung on to his money hard, refusing to lend, or rather asking such exorbitant interest that no one on the plain had ever been smart enough or foolish enough to come to terms with him. That suited him, for he was convinced that money lent to the plainspeople was money lost. Yet he was the only white man on the plain who could

be said to have an affection for it. True, he had found the
means of making a living there and at the same time had
found a reason for living: Pernod. People praised him as a
good man, because he had adopted a child. And what if he
did make that boy fan him? Surely, it was better for the
boy to do that than to herd buffalo on the plain in the hot
sunshine. His generous action in adopting that son had
given him such a good reputation that he was allowed to
pursue his contraband activities in relative peace. That
action and that reputation had doubtless counted for much
in the eyes of the Governor General, who had procured
for him the Legion of Honor, the award being made for his
having kept open for twenty years, to the glory and honor
of France, the canteen of Ram, "a distant post."

"Everything all right with you these days?" Pa Bart asked
Ma, shaking her hand.

"Pretty well, pretty well," said Ma, without much emphasis.

"You've got some swell customers today," said Joseph.
"Cripes, that big limousine . . ."

"One of the rubber planters from the North. A little better
off, those fellows, than you find here."

"You've got nothing to complain of," said Ma, "three mail-
packets a week, that's a godsend to you. Not to mention the
Pernod."

"Not an easy game. Dangerous. Every week now they
clap down on me, it's risky, it's a regular run-around every
week."

"Show us the planter from the North," said Ma.

"He's the fellow next to Agosti, in the corner. Just back
from Paris."

They had already noticed him, near Agosti. He was alone
at his table: a young man, about twenty-five years old,
dressed in a beige suit of tussore silk. On the table in front
of him he had put his felt hat which was the same color,

beige. When he lifted his glass of Pernod, they could see a magnificent diamond on one of his fingers. Ma gazed in silence, open-mouthed.

"Cripes, what a cattle-truck," said Joseph. Then he added: "But that's about all he's got. He looks like an ape."

The diamond was enormous, the silk suit was well tailored. Never had Joseph worn a silk suit. The soft hat looked like something in the movies. It was the sort of hat you put carelessly on your head before getting into a forty-horsepower car to dash to Longchamp to gamble away the half of your fortune because you have the blues on account of a woman. It was true, his face was certainly not handsome, nor was his figure. His shoulders were narrow, his arms were short, he must be much shorter than the average man. His small hands were well cared for, thin, rather good-looking. And that diamond gave to his hand a royal, almost an ethereal quality. He was alone, he was a planter, he was young, and he was looking at Suzanne.

Ma noticed the direction of his gaze and she, too, looked at her daughter. In the electric light Suzanne's freckles were not as visible as they were out-of-doors. Yes, surely, she was a pretty girl. Her eyes were shining, proud, and she was young, in the very flower of adolescence, and she was not shy.

"Why do you look as if you were at a funeral?" said Ma. "Can't you look pleasant for once?"

Suzanne smiled at the planter from the North. Two long records were being played: first a foxtrot, then a tango. At the third foxtrot, the planter from the North rose and came over to ask Suzanne to dance. When he stood up, his ugliness became apparent. But as he came towards them, they all looked at his diamond: Pa Bart, Agosti, Ma, and Suzanne. The boat passengers did not, for they had seen diamonds before. Nor did Joseph look at it; he had eyes only for motorcars. But all the people of the plain looked at it. That diamond there, worn so negligently by its ignorant owner, was worth, you might say, about what all the concessions on the plain were worth.

"Will you allow me, Madame?" asked the planter from the North, bowing before Ma.

Ma said, "Of course, certainly," and flushed. Already there were some officers on the dance floor, dancing with women passengers. Young Agosti was dancing with the Customs officer's wife.

The planter from the North did not dance too badly. He danced slowly, carefully, academically, trying to impress Suzanne, perhaps, with his good manners and consideration.

"Will you present me to your mother?" he asked politely.

"Sure," said Suzanne.

"You live in this part of the country?"

"Yes, we're from here. Is that your car outside?"

"You will introduce me as Monsieur Jo," he said.

"Where did you get it? It's marvelous."

"You like cars so much?" asked Monsieur Jo, smiling.

His voice was not like those of the planters or the big-game hunters. It came from somewhere else, it was soft and distinguished.

"Very much," said Suzanne. "Here, there aren't any cars like it. Mostly, here, there are convertibles."

"A pretty girl like you must find life boring on the plain," said Monsieur Jo, close to Suzanne's ear.

One night, two months before, young Agosti had taken her out of the canteen where the radio-phonograph was playing "Ramona" and, down by the port, he had said that she was a pretty girl. Then he had kissed her. Another time, a month later, one of the mail-packet officers had invited her to visit the boat and at the very beginning of the visit had taken her into a first-class cabin where he had kissed her. This was, therefore, the third time in her life that someone had called her pretty.

"What kind of car is it?" asked Suzanne.

"A Maurice Léon Bollée. My favorite car. If you like, we could go for a ride in it. Don't forget to present me to your mother."

"What horsepower is it?"

"I believe twenty-four," said Monsieur Jo.

"How much does a Maurice Léon Bollée cost?"

"It's a special model, custom-built in Paris. It cost me 50,000 francs."

The B-12 had cost something like 4,000 francs and Ma had taken four years to pay for it.

"Oh my, that's dear," said Suzanne.

Monsieur Jo was looking at Suzanne's hair, getting closer and closer, and from time to time he looked with lowered eyes at her mouth, which was just beneath his eyes.

"If we had a car like that, we'd come every night to Ram. That would give us a change! To Ram, or no matter where."

"Riches do not make happiness," said Monsieur Jo, nostalgically. "Although you seem to think so."

"Money's the only thing necessary for happiness," said Ma loudly. "It's only imbeciles that can't be happy with money." She added: "Naturally, when you're rich it's up to you to be intelligent."

More peremptorily than Ma, Joseph affirmed that money brought happiness, no doubt of it. Monsieur Jo's car alone would have made Joseph happy.

"I don't know," said Suzanne. "But I have a feeling we'd manage things so that money would make us happy."

"You are so young," said Monsieur Jo, softly. "Too young to know!"

"It's not because I'm young," said Suzanne. "It's because you are too rich."

Monsieur Jo now held her very close. When the foxtrot had ended, he was regretful.

"I could go on dancing with you . . ."

He followed Suzanne to her table.

"Let me introduce Monsieur Jo," said Suzanne to Ma.

Ma stood up to say How-do-you-do, and she smiled at him. For that very reason, Joseph did not stand up and did not smile.

"Sit down here at our table," said Ma, "and take something with us."

He sat down beside Joseph.

"No, the drinks are on me," he said. And, turning to Pa Bart: "Champagne, well chilled. Since I came back from Paris I haven't managed to find any good champagne."

"You'll find it here," said Pa Bart. "There's good champagne here every night the mail-packet puts in."

Monsieur Jo showed all his teeth—quite handsome ones —in a smile. Joseph noticed them and began to forget all else about Monsieur Jo. He looked a little jealous, for his own teeth were decayed and he could not afford to go to the dentist. Before his teeth went, there had been so many other things to spend money on. Sometimes it looked as though they never would get round to attending to his teeth.

"You're just back from Paris?" asked Ma.

"Just landed. I shall be in Ram for three days. I came down to supervise the loading of some latex."

Ma flushed, smiled, and drank in Monsieur Jo's words. He noticed her attitude and seemed very satisfied. It was rarely that people listened to him with such astonished attention. He bestowed upon Ma all his glances and took care, still, not to pay too much attention to what chiefly interested him: Suzanne. Thus far he had paid no attention whatsoever to Joseph, remarking only that Suzanne, for her part, had eyes only for her brother, who did nothing but stare alternately at Monsieur Jo's teeth and at the road outside, with a gloomily furious look.

"His car," said Suzanne, "is a Maurice Léon Bollée."

She always felt very close to Joseph when a third person was present, and particularly when he was visibly upset as he was this evening. Joseph seemed to wake up. He asked in a surly voice:

"What horsepower is a truck like yours?"

"Twenty-four," said Monsieur Jo, carelessly.

"Jesus! Twenty-four horsepower! Four speed gears, of course?"

"Yes, four."

"You can start off in second easy as not?"

"Yes, if you like, but it's hard on the gears."

"And she keeps to the road?"

"At eighty kilometers an hour, she rides like an armchair. But I'm not very fond of this car. I have a two-seater roadster, and I can make a hundred in that car without any trouble."

"How many liters per hundred?"

"Fifteen on the road. Eighteen in town. What's your car?"

Joseph looked at Suzanne, flabbergasted. Then he guffawed.

"It's not worth talking about . . ."

"It's a Citroen," said Ma. "A good old Citroen that has been a godsend to us. It's good enough for the road."

"Easy to see you don't often drive it," said Joseph.

The music had started up again. Monsieur Jo discreetly marked time, tapping on the table with his bediamonded finger. His replies were followed by long and heavy silences on the part of Joseph. But doubtless Monsieur Jo did not dare to change the subject of conversation. While replying to Joseph, he did not take his eyes off Suzanne. He could easily have done so, for Suzanne was so attentive to Joseph's reactions that she no longer looked at anyone else.

"And the roadster?" asked Joseph.

"What?"

"What about its consumption of gasoline? How many liters per hundred kilometers does it make?"

"More," said Monsieur Jo. "Eighteen on the road. It's a thirty horsepower."

"Cripes!" said Joseph.

"Citroens use less, I believe?"

Joseph laughed loudly. He finished his glass of champagne and poured himself another. He looked ready, now, to burst with laughter.

"Twenty-four," said he.

"My goodness!" said Monsieur Jo.

"But I can explain that," said Joseph.

"It's a lot."

"A lot more than twelve," said Joseph. "But wait till I tell you . . . The carburetor's a sieve."

Joseph was laughing uncontrollably and it was contagious. He was choking with laughter, like a child, still his laughter came out with such heartiness that it was irresistible. Ma became red in the face, tried to hold in, but couldn't make it.

"If that was all," said Joseph, "it wouldn't be anything."

Ma guffawed.

"That's so," she said, "if there was only the carburetor . . ."

Suzanne, too, was laughing uncontrollably. She hadn't the same laugh as Joseph, hers was sharper, a little whistling. It had happened in a few seconds. Monsieur Jo looked mortified. He began to feel unsure of his success and wondered how to get back on safe ground.

"And the radiator!" said Suzanne.

"Beats anything you ever saw," said Joseph.

"Tell how much, Joseph, tell him . . ."

"Before I fixed a tire, it used up to fifty liters the hundred."

"Haw, haw!" roared Ma, "if that was all, it wouldn't be anything!"

"Yes," said Joseph, "if that was all, if there wasn't anything wrong but the carburetor and the radiator . . ."

"That's so," said Ma, "if that was all—why, it wouldn't be anything!"

Monsieur Jo tried to laugh. He managed to laugh a little. They were forgetting him. They all looked a little beside themselves.

"And our tires!" said Joseph, "our tires . . . They . . .
They . . ."

Joseph was choking, he could not speak. The same invincible and mysterious laughter shook Ma and Suzanne.

"Guess what kind of tubes we use in our tires?" said
Joseph. "Guess!"

"Yes, go on, just guess!" said Suzanne.

."He couldn't, ever," said Joseph.

Pa Bart's foster son had brought them a second bottle of
champagne at Monsieur Jo's order. Agosti, who was listening to them, laughed heartily. The officers and the boat passengers, who did not understand what it was all about began laughing, too, but not loudly.

"Guess," said Suzanne, "go on, guess! But mind you, it's
not always, luckily . . ."

"Well, I don't know," said Monsieur Jo, as if he had suddenly found out how to dance this number, "but I suppose
they are inflated rubber inner tubes . . ."

"No, not at all! You're wrong," said Suzanne.

"Banana leaves," gasped Joseph. "We stuff our tires with
banana leaves—"

Monsieur Jo laughed frankly for the first time. But not as
loudly as they did. It was perhaps a question of temperament. Joseph had reached such a degree of hilarity that he
was breathless and his stifled laughter brought him to the
verge of paroxysm. Monsieur Jo had given up asking
Suzanne to' dance. Patiently he waited for all this to die
down.

"How original! Very funny! Screaming, as we say."

They did not listen to him.

"We, when we go out for a ride," said Joseph, "we fasten
the Corporal to the mudguard with a watering can beside
him—"

He hiccuped between the words.

"And in the place of a headlight—he's the headlight, too
—the Corporal is our radiator and our headlight," said
Suzanne.

"Ow! Shut up! I'm choking to death, shut up," said Ma.

"And the car doors!" said Joseph. "The car doors are fastened with wires . . ."

"I forget, I can't remember now," said Ma, "what the handles of the doors were like . . ."

"Ho!" said Joseph. "We don't need handles! We jump in, and hop! away we go—if we remember to get in on the side with a running board. Question of habit!"

"And we've got the habit," said Suzanne.

"Shut up," said Ma, "I'm going to have an attack."

She was very red. She was old, she had had so much misfortune and so little occasion to laugh about it that the laughter, in truth, took hold of her, shook her dangerously. The strength of her laughter did not seem to come from her but from outside. It was worrying, it made her look slightly insane.

"And we," said Joseph, "we don't need headlights. Any old lantern will do—"

Monsieur Jo looked at them as though he were wondering if this would ever come to an end. But he listened patiently.

"How nice it is," he said, "to meet people as gay as you are."

He was doubtless trying to get them off the inexhaustible subject of the B-12, to get out of this labyrinth.

"As gay as we are?" said Ma, astounded.

"What did he say? That we're gay?" added Suzanne.

"Ah, if he only knew! Hell, if he only knew," said Joseph.

Joseph, that one, clearly had a grudge against Monsieur Jo.

"And oh, if that was all," said Joseph. "If there was only the tank and the headlights—if that was all!"

Ma and Suzanne looked intently at Joseph. What was going to pop out of him now? They hadn't an idea, yet, but the laughter that had begun to die down began to shake them again.

"The wires," Joseph went on, "the banana skins—if that was all—"

"That's so. If that was all—?" said Suzanne, interrogatively.

"If there wasn't anything else but the car," said Joseph.

"It wouldn't be anything at all," completed Ma.

Eagerly, ahead of them, Joseph's laugh caught them up once more.

"But the car's not the only thing! Remember the sea walls —the sea walls——"

Ma and Suzanne whooped wild cries of intense satisfaction. In his turn, Agosti guffawed. And a faint gurgling sound by the cash register indicated that Pa Bart was getting in on this, too.

"Oh, yes!" exclaimed Ma. "The crabs . . . the crabs . . ."

"The crabs ate up the sea walls!" said Joseph.

"Even the crabs," said Suzanne, "they had to butt in!"

"That's so," said Ma, "even the crabs are against us . . ."

Some of the people in the canteen had begun once more to dance. Agosti continued to kill himself laughing, because he knew their whole story as well as his own. It could have been his own story, the story of all the land-holders on the plain. The dikes built by Ma in the plain, her "barriers against the Ocean," the whole thing was either a huge misfortune or a huge joke, depending upon the way you looked at it. It was a huge joke and a huge misfortune. It was terrible and it was screamingly funny. It depended on which side you took: the side of the Ocean which had knocked down everything, every stick and stone of the sea wall, at one blow, one single blow; the side of the crabs, which had made sieves of them; or, on the contrary, the side of the people who had taken six months to build that sea wall, in total forgetfulness of the certain damage that would be wrought by the crabs and the Ocean. What was amazing about it all was that there had been two hundred people who forgot all that when they set to work.

All the men of the neighboring villages of the concession to which Ma had sent the Corporal to speak for her, all had come. And after assembling them near the bungalow, Ma had explained to them what she wanted them to do.

"If you like, we can reclaim hundreds of hectares for growing rice, and that without any help from the agents, those swine! We are going to build a barrier against the Ocean. Two kinds of barriers: some parallel to the sea, others . . ."

The peasants had been a little astonished. To begin with, the sea had invaded the plain for thousands of years. They were used to it and had never imagined it could be held back. Then, their misery had accustomed them to passivity, their one and only defense against the spectacle of their children dying of starvation, their crops being destroyed by salt. They returned, however, every day for three days, always in greater number. Ma explained to them how the dikes could be built. According to her, the thing to do was to lay down a buttress of mangrove tree trunks. She knew where to get some. There were stocks of such logs just outside Kam, left over from the construction of the highway. Some contractors had offered to sell them to her cheap. She would assume the entire cost of these.

A hundred peasants adopted Ma's idea right from the first, but subsequently, when these had begun to go out in their boats, which left the bridge and stood out towards the points decided upon for the construction of the sea wall, others joined them in great number. At the end of a week almost all the peasants were at work on the building of Ma's "barriers." The least thing had sufficed to draw them out of their lethargy. An old woman without means, who had told them she had decided to fight, had made them decide to fight—as if they had waited only for that signal from the beginning of time.

And yet Ma had not consulted with any technician to find out if the construction of the sea walls would be effective. She had faith. She was sure. Always she acted like that, obeying evidence and a logic which she allowed no one to share. The fact that the peasants had believed what she told them strengthened her still more in the certitude that she had found exactly what was needed to change the life of the plain. Hundreds of hectares of rice-growing country would be salvaged from the tides. All would be rich, or almost. The children would no longer die of hunger. They would have doctors. They would build a long roadway which would follow the line of her barriers and open up the freed lands.

At last the mangrove logs had been purchased. Then three months elapsed, during which they had had to wait for the sea to recede and the land to be dry enough to begin the work of digging and embankment.

It was during this waiting period that Ma had lived the great hope of her life. She had spent the nights drawing up and improving the outline of her plan for the future participation of the peasants in the exploitation of the five hundred hectares which would soon be put under cultivation. But her eagerness was such that it was not enough to make mere plans while waiting for the moment to come. With what remained of her money, once the logs were paid for, without waiting, she had three cabins built at the mouth of the *rac*, three cabins which she called a "lookout village." The peasants who believed in her plan were so numerous that she herself now believed in it without a shadow of doubt. Not for one minute did she suspect that perhaps they had believed in her so firmly simply because she herself had shown such faith. Yet she had spoken to them with such certitude that even a cadastral agent himself would have been convinced. Once the "village" had been built, Ma settled three families there, gave them rice and boats and enough to live on until the prospective harvest of the reclaimed land.

The auspicious moment for the building of the sea walls

came at last. First, the men transported the logs from the road to the sea, then they set to work digging. Ma went down with them at dawn every day and returned with them at night. Suzanne and Joseph had hunted constantly during the period and they, too, had had hope. They believed in Ma's undertaking. They were sure that, as soon as the first harvest should have been made, they would make a long journey to the city and within three years they would definitely be able to leave the plain.

Sometimes in the evenings Ma distributed quinine and tobacco to the peasants, and on these occasions she spoke to them of the imminent changes in their existence. They laughed with her, in advance, at the faces the cadastral agents would pull when they would see the fabulous harvests soon to be made on the salvaged land. Point by point she recounted her story to them, at long length she described the organization of the trading activities that would be arranged for the concessions of the plain. The better to maintain their hopes, she explained to them how the expropriations, of which many had been victims to the profit of the Chinese pepper-planters, could also be attributed to the agents of Kam and their dastardly dealings. She spoke with enthusiasm, not being able to resist sharing with them her recent initiation into their peculation, the techniques by which the Kam agents crushed them. She freed herself at last from a whole past of illusions and ignorance, and it was as though she had discovered a new language, a new culture. She could not finish talking about it. The agents were dastardly swine, she said, swine! And the Ocean-barriers would be a revenge against them. The peasants laughed delightedly.

During the building of the sea walls, no agent passed that way. Ma was sometimes a little surprised at this. They could not be oblivious to the importance of the operation. They must be a little disquieted. However, she herself had not dared to write to them, for fear of arousing them and being forbidden to pursue an initiative which was, in spite of everything, still not officially recognized. She dared not write until the sea walls were finished. Then she announced to them that a great quadrangle of five hundred hectares, which embraced the entire concession, would soon be put under cultivation. The agents did not reply.

The rainy season came. Ma had sowed a vast seed bank near the bungalow. The same men who had constructed the sea walls came to take the seedlings and replant them in the big rice field which was surrounded by the sections of the dikes.

Two months passed. Ma often went to see the greening young plants. They always began to grow just before the great tides of July.

Then, in July, the sea had risen as usual, in an assault on the plain. The sea walls had not been strong enough. The logs had been eaten through by the dwarf crabs of the paddies. In one single night the sea walls had collapsed.

The families that Ma had settled in her lookout village had vanished with the Chinese junks and the provisions she had given them, going toward another part of the coast. The peasants of the outlying villages of the concession had returned to their homes. The children had continued to die of hunger. But no one had felt unkindly towards Ma or been resentful.

The following year, the small portions of the sea walls which had held collapsed in their turn . . .

"The whole story of our sea walls," said Joseph, "is enough to make you die laughing."

And, with two fingers, he tapped on the table, imitating the backward advance of the crabs upon the sea walls—in Monsieur Jo's direction. Still as patient as ever, Monsieur Jo disregarded the march of the crabs and stared at Suzanne who, her head thrown back, was laughing till she cried.

"You are droll," said Monsieur Jo, "you are formidably droll!"

He kept time to the foxtrot then playing, perhaps to incite Suzanne to dance.

"There's no other story like it," said Joseph, "there's nothing like our affair of the sea walls. We'd thought of everything—but we'd forgotten the crabs!"

"They'd been cut off from their route," said Suzanne.

"But that didn't bother them," Joseph went on, "they were ready for us! And with two bites—plok! plok!—the sea walls were finished!"

"Quite small crabs, the color of mud," said Suzanne, "created just for us!"

"What was needed," said Ma, "was some concrete. But where would we have got that?"

Joseph silenced her. The laughter died down.

"You see," said Suzanne, "it's not land that we bought—"

"It's a flood!" said Joseph.

"It's the sea, the Pacific Ocean," said Suzanne.

"It's crud!" said Joseph.

"An idea no one else could have had—" said Suzanne.

Ma stopped laughing and suddenly became very serious. "Shut up," she said to Suzanne, "or I'll box your ears!"

Monsieur Jo was shocked, but no one else was.

"It's crud, absolutely," said Joseph. "Crud or flood, take your choice. And there we are, waiting like damn fools for the crud to subside."

"It will surely happen one day," said Suzanne.

"In five hundred years," said Joseph. "But we have the time, we can wait."

"If it was crud," said Agosti from the bar, "it would be much better—"

"Rice grown in it," said Joseph laughing again, "would be better than no rice at all . . ."

He lit a cigarette. Monsieur Jo took out a package of English cigarettes and offered it to Suzanne and Ma. Ma, not laughing now, was listening to Joseph with passionate interest.

"When we bought the concession, we believed we'd be millionaires in a year," Joseph went on. "We built the bungalow while waiting for the rice to grow."

"It always begins to grow," said Suzanne.

"Then came the crud," said Joseph. "So we made the sea walls. That's the story. And now we're waiting like damn fools, we don't even know what for."

"We're waiting in our house, that house . . ." said Suzanne.

"That house that's not even finished," said Joseph.

Ma tried to speak.

"Don't listen to them. It's a good house, solid and strong. If I sold it, I would make a good profit. I could get thirty thousand francs for it . . ."

"Where'd you find a buyer? Who'd buy it?" said Joseph. "You'd never find a buyer unless you found some people as crazy as we are."

He stopped suddenly. There was a short silence.

"That's so," said Suzanne, meditatively, "we must be a little crazy . . ."

Joseph smiled crazily at Suzanne.

"Completely crazy," he said.

And then the conversation all of a sudden died.

Suzanne turned her eyes on the dancers. Joseph stood up and went over to ask the Customs officer's wife for a dance. He had slept with her at one time, over a period of several months, but now he was tired of her. She was a skinny little brunette. Since Joseph, she had been having an affair with Agosti. Suzanne now joined the dancers with Monsieur Jo, who invited her to dance every time a new record was played. Ma was left alone at the table. She sat there, yawning.

Then the mail-packet officers and the passengers gave the signal for departure. Monsieur Jo had one more dance with Suzanne.

"Would you like to try my car?" he asked. "I could ac-

company you to your home and then return to Ram. It
would give me great pleasure."

He held her close. A neat, clean man. And ugly. But his
car was beautiful.

"Maybe you'd let Joseph drive it?"

"That's a bit difficult," said Monsieur Jo, hesitantly.

"Joseph can drive any car," said Suzanne.

"If you will allow me, we will postpone that for another
time," said Monsieur Jo, politely.

"We'll ask my mother," said Suzanne. "Joseph can go
on ahead and we'll follow."

"You . . . you want Madame your mother to accompany
us?"

Suzanne leaned away from Monsieur Jo and looked at
him. He was disappointed, and his expression did not improve his looks. Ma, alone at her table, did not stop yawning. She was very tired, because she had had many misfortunes and she was old and not used to laughing. It was that
laughing that had worn her out.

"I would like," said Suzanne, "my mother to try your
car."

"Will you let me see you again?"

"Whenever you like," said Suzanne.

"Thank you," he said, and hugged her still more tightly.

Really, he was polite. She looked at him with some compassion. Joseph might not be able to stand him if he came
often to the bungalow.

When the dance was over, Ma stood up, ready to go.
Monsieur Jo's offer to drive Ma and Suzanne home suited
everyone. Monsieur Jo paid Pa Bart and they went down
together to the courtyard. While Monsieur Jo's chauffeur
got out and held open the door, Joseph climbed into the
Léon Bollée, started the engine, and for five minutes tried
the gears. Then, swearing, he got out and without saying
goodby to Monsieur Jo he affixed his hunter's lamp to his
head, started the B-12 by cranking it, and went off alone.

With heavy hearts, Ma and Suzanne watched him go. Monsieur Jo seemed already used to his manners and was not surprised.

Ma and Suzanne got into the back of the limousine and Monsieur Jo sat up beside the chauffeur. They caught up with Joseph very soon. Suzanne would have preferred not to pass him, but she said nothing to Monsieur Jo because, naturally, he would not understand. By the powerful head-lights of the Léon Bollée, they could see Joseph as if in broad daylight. He had lowered what was left of the wind-shield and was speeding up the B-12 for all she was worth. He looked even more ill-humored than when he had started off, and did not cast one glance at the Léon Bollée when it shot past him.

A little before reaching the bungalow, Ma fell asleep. During a whole part of the trip, completely indifferent to the way the big car sped along, she must have been thinking of what a good piece of luck Monsieur Jo was for them. But thinking of that good luck had not got the better of her weariness, and she had fallen asleep. She could sleep any-where, even in the bus, even in the B-12, which had no top, no windshield, and no hood.

Once arrived at the bungalow, Monsieur Jo reiterated his request. Could he come to see these people with whom he had spent such a delightful evening? Ma, half awake, cere-moniously told Monsieur Jo that the house was open to him and that he could come back whenever he liked. A little after Monsieur Jo had left, Joseph came along. He banged the door of the sitting room and did not open his mouth to say a word but went at once to his room, where he shut him-self in as he always did when he was sick of life. There he cleaned and greased his guns until well into the night.

This, then, was the acquaintance they had made in Ram. Monsieur Jo was the only son of a very rich speculator whose fortune was typical of those made in the Colony. He had begun by speculating in land adjacent to the largest city of the Colony, the growth of which had been so rapid that, in five years' time, he had realized sufficient profits to invest in new enterprises. Instead of speculating in more land, he developed what he had, constructing cheap houses called "native apartment buildings," which had been the first of the kind in the Colony. The apartments were in reality rows of double houses opening out on one side upon small courts and on the other side upon the street. They cost little to build and they met the needs of a whole class of native shopkeepers. They became the rage, and at the end of ten years such buildings existed in great number. Very soon they proved to be particularly favorable to the propagation of plague and cholera. The fact had been exposed in a survey made by the Colonial government. But since only the proprietors were advised of this, there were always people waiting to rent the "apartments," and always in greater number.

Then, Monsieur Jo's father became interested in rubber plantations in the North. The growth of that industry was such that many people with no competence for the work had become planters overnight. These plantations, mismanaged, were in jeopardy, and Monsieur Jo's father watched them closely, buying them up at the right moment. As they were in poor condition, he paid very little for them. Then he put managers in charge and set the plantations going once more. In rubber you made money, but not enough to suit him. One or two years later, he resold the plantations at a huge price to new arrivals, whom he particularly chose for their inexperience. In most cases, he was able to buy them back again within two years.

Monsieur Jo was the ridiculously incompetent son of this ingenious man, whose big fortune had but one heir and that heir without a trace of imagination. He represented the one failure in his father's life. For you cannot speculate on your offspring. You may think you are hatching out an eaglet, and what comes out from under the desk is a canary. What can be done when such things happen? What recourse is there against such injustice?

He had sent his son to Europe to study subjects for which he was unfitted. Stupidity has its clear-sightedness, all the same: Monsieur Jo had avoided studying. When his father had learned of this, he had sent for him and tried to interest him in business. Monsieur Jo honestly tried to repair the injustice of which his father had been the victim. But it sometimes happens that a person is not suited to anything particularly, not even to a life of scarcely mitigated idleness. However, he honestly tried. For honest he was and good intentions he had. That, however, was not the question. And maybe he would not have become as stupid as even his father had resigned himself to consider him had he not been brought up all wrong. Alone, without a father, without the handicap of that crushing fortune, he might perhaps have compensated more successfully for the nature with which he had been endowed. But his father had never thought that Monsieur Jo might be the victim of an injustice. He had never seen any injustice except that which had struck him in this son. And this fatality was inherent and irremediable. He could do nothing but mourn over it. Of the other injustice—the one of which his son was the victim —he had never discovered the cause. Yet he could have remedied that one. All he would have had to do would have been to disinherit Monsieur Jo. And Monsieur Jo would have escaped that heritage which was too heavy for him. But Monsieur Jo's father had not thought of this, although he was an intelligent man. Intelligence can be a routine way of thinking which may blind us to our own circumstances.

So this was the suitor allotted by fate to Suzanne, one night in Ram. You might also say that he was likewise allotted to Joseph and Ma.

3

THE ENCOUNTER WITH MONSIEUR JO WAS A TURNING POINT IN
their lives. Each of them in a specific way pinned faith in
Monsieur Jo. From the first days, from the time it became
evident that he would return regularly to the bungalow, Ma
made it clear to him that she expected him to ask her for the
hand of Suzanne in marriage. Monsieur Jo did not decline
Ma's solicitations, but he kept her on tenterhooks with
promises and, more particularly, with various gifts to Suzanne. At the same time he tried to profit by a relaxation of
vigilance as reward for the, as he thought, flattering rôle he
played in their lives.

The first thing of importance which he gave, one month
after their meeting, was a phonograph. He made a show of
giving it casually, as one offers a cigarette. In reality, he
had not neglected the occasion of securing a favor from
Suzanne in exchange for it. This had been when he became
convinced that Suzanne would never take an interest in
him for his own sake. After that, he tried to stake his fortune
for what it was worth. It seemed to him that the first thing
he could do with it was to open an acoustical breach in
their prison wall by giving them a new phonograph. Apart
from the choice he made later on in regard to the diamond,
this was the only flash of lucidity he had during the entire
period of their acquaintance.

She was not the one who had first talked or even thought about the phonograph; he, Monsieur Jo, was the one.

They were alone in the bungalow as usual when he talked to her about it. Every day they were left together for three hours, while Joseph and Ma busied themselves with this and that out of doors, waiting for the hour when they would all go to Ram in the Léon Bollée. Arriving after the siesta, Monsieur Jo would take off his hat and sit down listlessly in an armchair, after which, for three hours on end, he would wait and wait for some sign of hope from Suzanne, some encouragement, no matter how slight, which would allow him to feel that he had made some progress over the previous day.

These hours spent by the two together delighted Ma. The longer they lasted the higher her hopes rose. And if she demanded that they leave the bungalow door open, it was in order to give Monsieur Jo no alternative but marriage to satisfy his strong craving to sleep with her daughter. It was for that reason that the door stood wide open. Rigged out as usual in her straw hat and followed by her Corporal armed with a hoe, she passed and repassed in front of the bungalow, between the lines of banana trees bordering the road. From time to time she looked at the sitting-room door with a satisfied air: the work being carried out beyond that door was more serious than the work she pretended to be doing with the banana trees.

As for Joseph, he never entered the bungalow while Monsieur Jo was there. Ever since his horse had died, he busied himself interminably with the B-12, washing it when nothing was wrong with it which required repair. He never looked towards the bungalow. When he tired of the B-12, he went off in the countryside to look, he said, for another horse. When he was not looking for another horse, he went to Ram for no reason except the better to flee the bungalow.

Thus, Suzanne and Monsieur Jo were alone the greater part of every afternoon, until it was time to go to Ram. Occasionally, in compliance with her mother's instructions and—without too much conviction—in order to keep him on the right track regarding their relations, Suzanne asked Monsieur Jo for a few supplementary and precise details regarding their marriage. It was all you could ask of Monsieur Jo. He asked nothing. He was satisfied just to gaze at Suzanne with troubled eyes, to go on gazing, to enhance his view with another supplementary look, as is usual when one is devoured with passion. And when it happened that Suzanne became overcome with drowsiness from the fatigue and boredom of being stared at like that, she would wake up to find him still there, with his eyes upon her, more eagerly insistent than ever. And it just never finished. And if in the beginning it had been not too displeasing to arouse such emotions in Monsieur Jo, she soon found it, alas, an old story.

Still, she was not the one who had spoken about the phonograph. Unexpected as it might seem to be, it had been Monsieur Jo who had spoken about it. That day, moreover, he had arrived wearing a strange expression, an unaccustomed liveliness was in his eyes, a significant gleam indicating that, for once in a way, Monsieur Jo might have an idea in his head.

"What's that thing over there?" he asked, indicating Joseph's old phonograph.

"You see very well what it is," said Suzanne. "It's a phono. It's Joseph's."

Suzanne and Joseph had always known that phonograph. It had been bought by their father a year before his death and Ma had never separated herself from it. Before leaving for the concession, she had sold her old records and had told Joseph to buy some new ones. Of these, there remained only five which Joseph kept jealously in his room. He reserved the use of the phonograph to himself alone and no one other than he had the right to make it go or even to touch his records. Suzanne would never have dared to do such a thing to Joseph but, all the same, he was mistrustful and every night, after having played them, he took the records back to his room and put them in their place.

"Funny how much he likes that phonograph," said Ma. Sometimes she regretted having brought it to the concession, for music, above all things, made Joseph want to throw up the sponge and leave home. Suzanne disagreed. She did not believe that the phonograph was bad for Joseph. And when he had played all his records and then, invariably, declared: "I'd like to know what we're doing in this Hellhole," she fully agreed with him, even when Ma bawled him out for saying it.

"Ramona" was the most disturbing record. Inevitably, when it was played, their hopes revived. The cars that would carry them far away could not be much longer in coming. "And," said Joseph of this phonograph, "without a woman, without movies, without anything at all, life's still not so tough when you have a phonograph." Ma told him he lied, when it came to the woman part. In fact, he had slept with all the white women in Ram that were old enough and had slept with all the prettiest native women on the plain between Ram and Kam. Sometimes, when he was running his carrying trade, he made love to his women passengers in the carriage. "I can't help myself," Joseph said. "I believe I could sleep with all the women in the world." But all the same, the women of the plain, no matter how pretty they had been, were not the ones who could bring him to renounce the phonograph.

"It's old," said Monsieur Jo. "It's a very old model. I have some knowledge of phonographs. At home, I have an electric one that I brought back from Paris. You may not know it, but I adore music."

"So do we. But your electric machine is all right where there's electricity. We don't have electricity. So you can have your old machine!"

"There are other kinds of phonographs," said Monsieur

Jo, with an air of hinting at something. "Plenty of them are not electric but are just as good."

He had an enraptured look. He had already given Suzanne a dress, a powder compact, some nail enamel, some lipstick, some fine soap, and a beauty lotion. But usually he brought her things spontaneously without announcing them in advance. He would blow in, take out a little parcel from his pocket and hold it out to Suzanne. "Guess what I've brought you," he would say slyly. Suzanne would take it and open it. "What a funny idea," she would say. That is how it usually happened. But not this time. His behavior that day was something new.

Something new, indeed! After this conversation, Monsieur Jo asked Suzanne to open the door of the shower room so he could see her entirely naked, promising that if she did this he would give her a Victrola of the latest manufacture, with records in addition, the newest out in Paris. So it was done. While Suzanne took a shower, as she did every evening before going to Ram, he knocked softly on the door of the little room.

"Open the door," said Monsieur Jo, very softly. "I won't touch you, I won't come near, I will just look at you. Please open."

Suzanne stood stock-still in the dimness of the shower room, staring at the door beyond which was Monsieur Jo. No man had ever seen her really naked, except Joseph who sometimes came up to wash his feet while she was taking her shower. But that had always happened, ever since they were very young, so it did not count. Suzanne surveyed herself from head to foot: this was what Monsieur Jo wanted to have a look at, in his turn. Surprised, she began to smile, but did not reply.

"I beg of you; let me have just a glimpse," sighed Monsieur Jo. "Joseph and your mother are on the other side of the house."

"I don't want to," said Suzanne weakly.

"Why not? Why not, my little one? I want so much to see you. Being with you all day long makes me want to see you. Only a second."

Quite still, Suzanne waited to think out what she must do. Her refusal had been mechanical. She had said "No." First, imperiously. But Monsieur Jo again begged while that "No" slowly reversed itself and Suzanne, inert, walled in, allowed herself to drift. He had a great desire to see her. After all, it was the natural desire of a man. And there she was, worth seeing. There was only that door to open. And no man in the world had yet seen this body of hers that was hidden by that door. It was not made to be hidden but, on the contrary, to be seen and to make its way in the world, that world to which belonged, after all, this Monsieur Jo. She was on the point of opening the door and letting light in upon this darkness, letting Monsieur Jo's eyes look upon this mystery. Then, at that very moment, Monsieur Jo talked about the phonograph.

"Tomorrow you shall have your phonograph," said Monsieur Jo. "Tomorrow. A magnificent Victrola. Dear little Suzanne, open the door for only a second and you shall have your phonograph."

So then, it was just when she was going to open the door to let the world see her that the world prostituted her. With her hand on the latch of the door, she hesitated.

"You're a beast," she said weakly. "Joseph's right. You're a dirty swine."

And she thought: "I'll spit in his face." But when she opened the door the spittle dried up in her mouth. It wasn't worth while. This was just a misfortune, this Monsieur Jo, another misfortune like the broken sea walls, the horse that died. He was not a person: he was only a misfortune.

"There!" she said. "Take a look! I spit at you with my naked body!"

Joseph was always saying: "Me and my B-12—we spit at
you!" every time he passed close to the Léon Bollée, and
then he would give it a good kick in the tires.

Monsieur Jo, holding on to the doorjamb, looked at her.
He was red in the face and breathed hard, as if he had been
knocked on the head and was about to fall. Suzanne closed
the door again. He stayed there for a good minute, silent,
in front of the closed door. Then she heard him going back
to the sitting room. She put on her dress very quickly, as
she would do each time, afterwards, when she had vainly
let herself be seen by Monsieur Jo, who did not have the
look in his eyes that he should have had.

Next day, with that punctuality which Monsieur Jo considered one of the surest forms of dignity, he brought the
Victrola, as if to say: "I don't just talk, I act."

She saw him arrive with it—rather, she saw it arrive, held
under his arm, that enormous cardboard box. She knew it
was the Victrola and sat there in her chair, transfixed with
a secret and almost divine pleasure. She was witnessing an
event which she had brought about and she was even witnessing the astonishment caused by it. For she was not the
only one that had seen the big parcel. Ma and Joseph had
also seen it. And while it came up the driveway, carried by
Monsieur Jo, they had looked fixedly at it and they continued to look fixedly at the door through which it had passed,
as if waiting for some sign which would enable them to
discover the contents. But Suzanne knew that neither of
them, especially not Joseph, would make a move to know
what it was, even had it been as big as a house. To show the
least curiosity about anything given or brought or even
shown by Monsieur Jo—no, neither of them would ever give
way to such a weakness. Up to now, it is true, the parcels
that Monsieur Jo brought to Suzanne had been, for the
most part, small. They could be put in his pocket or held in
his hand. But this one, Joseph must logically size it up, see-

ing its dimensions, as containing without a doubt some object of more general interest than those that had preceded it. None of them recalled having seen a parcel of that size and destined for them arrive by no matter what means at the bungalow. Aside from the mangrove logs, the few letters from the cadastral agents or from the bank, and the occasional visit of Agosti, no one and nothing unexpected or new had ever arrived there for six years. That this should have been brought by Monsieur Jo did not obviate the fact that it doubtless came from beyond him, from a town, a shop, and that it was something new and destined for their use, their exclusive use. However, neither Joseph nor Ma deigned to show their curiosity by coming up to the bungalow. And the unusual behavior of Monsieur Jo, who had called out his greetings in an assured voice and had come up the drive bareheaded, forgetting his fear of sunstroke, had not sufficed to banish their usual reserve in regard to him.

Monsieur Jo arrived breathless before Suzanne, putting the parcel down on the sitting-room table and heaving a sigh of relief. That must be heavy. Suzanne did not budge from her chair, but looked at the parcel and at him, gloating over the mystery that it represented to the two outside, who were looking in the direction of the bungalow.

"It's heavy," said Monsieur Jo. "It's the Victrola. That's the way I am, I keep my promises. I hope you will learn to know I'm like that," he added, to settle his victory and just in case Suzanne herself might not make this reflection.

So there the phonograph was on the table, in the bungalow. And there, outside, framed in the open door, were Ma and Joseph, dying of curiosity like prisoners behind bars. And it was thanks to her, Suzanne, that it was now there on the table. And it was entirely good and perfectly beautiful. She felt she had earned that phonograph, deserved the happiness of being able to give it to Joseph. For, naturally, things like phonographs went to Joseph. As for herself, it was enough that, by her sole efforts, she had extracted it from Monsieur Jo.

Trembling and triumphant, Monsieur Jo went towards the parcel. Suzanne sprang towards him to prevent him from approaching it. Astounded, he let his arms fall to his side and looked at her in bewilderment.

"We must wait," said Suzanne.

The parcel must not be opened except in front of Joseph. The phonograph must not appear, must not be disclosed except in Joseph's presence. But it was as impossible to explain this to Monsieur Jo as to explain to him who Joseph was.

Monsieur Jo sat down and reflected deeply. His forehead wrinkled with the effort, his eyes widened. He clicked his tongue.

"I don't have any luck," he said.

Monsieur Jo was easily disheartened.

"It's like spitting into water," he went on. "Nothing I do affects you, not even my best intentions. I'm not your type. The kind of man you like is . . ."

Oh, the surprised look Joseph would have when he saw that phonograph! Surely they would come in soon! Monsieur Jo had come later than usual, doubtless because of the phonograph, and now, soon, they could not help but learn about it. As for Monsieur Jo, the minute he had given the phonograph he had ceased to that extent to exist. And really, deprived of his limousine, his tussore silk suit, his chauffeur, maybe he would become completely insubstantial, as empty of interest as an empty showcase.

"What kind of man do I like?"

"A man like Agosti . . . and like Joseph," said Monsieur Jo timidly.

Suzanne smiled openly at Monsieur Jo who, thanks to the phonograph, was able to sustain her smile.

"Oh, yes!" he said courageously. "I'm right. Joseph's the type of man you like."

"You could give me ten phonographs and it would make no difference to me."

Monsieur Jo, stricken, lowered his head.

"I'm unlucky! Even on account of the phonograph you say mean things to me."

Joseph and Ma were coming back to the bungalow, walking up the drive. Monsieur Jo, who maintained with dignity an offended silence, did not see them coming.

"They're coming," said Suzanne, getting up and going towards Monsieur Jo. "Don't pull such a long face."

It took very little to encourage Monsieur Jo. He stood up, drew Suzanne towards him and hugged her hard.

"I'm crazy about you," he declared gloomily. "I don't understand what's happened to me. I never felt like this before about any girl."

"Don't tell them anything," said Suzanne, automatically disengaging herself from his arms and smiling towards Joseph, towards the future that loomed ahead.

"Because I saw you naked yesterday, I couldn't sleep last night."

"When they ask what it is, I will tell them."

"I'm nothing to you, less than nothing," said Monsieur Jo, again depressed. "Every day I realize that, more and more."

Joseph and Ma climbed the steps of the bungalow and, Joseph in the vanguard, they burst into the room. They were dusty and sweaty, their feet were caked with mud.

"How do you do?" said Ma. "How are you?"

"How do you do, Madame?" said Monsieur Jo. "I'm very well, thank you. And you?"

Monsieur Jo was very good at standing up and bowing at Ma, whom he detested.

"As for us, things have got to be all right," said Ma, "now that I've taken it into my head to plant those banana trees. They'll keep me going a little longer."

Monsieur Jo took a couple of steps in Joseph's direction, then gave it up. He had tried before, it was useless to be

polite with him. Joseph never even said hello to Monsieur
Jo.

They could not help but have seen the big parcel on the
table, it was impossible for them not to have seen it. However, in no way did they show that they had seen it except
by their elaborate disregard of it, the way they gave the
table a wide berth, pretending to see nothing. But also, Ma
had a kind of smile on her face that evening and she didn't
scold, didn't complain of being tired, she even seemed to be
in good spirits.

Joseph crossed the room to go towards the shower. Ma lit
the alcohol lamp and called the Corporal. She had to yell
for him, although even that was useless, as she well knew.
It was to his wife she should have called to get him to come.
Wherever the Corporal's wife happened to be, she always
ran at once to her husband and gave him a slap on the back
to secure his attention. At this hour, squatting on the earth
terrace, the Corporal was enjoying a momentary rest and
waiting religiously for the second passing of the bus along
the road. He stared at the highway during all the leisure he
had, sometimes for an hour at a time, when Ma and Joseph
and Suzanne went to Ram. He didn't take his eyes off the
road until he saw them appear noiselessly out of the forest,
coming home at sixty kilometers an hour.

"He's harder and harder of hearing," said Ma, "harder
and harder of hearing."

She went to the store cupboard, came back to the dining
room, still with averted eyes. This, although the parcel was
more visible than the whole bungalow put together.

"It always surprised me that you hired a deaf man," said
Monsieur Jo, in a conversational tone. "For there are plenty
of servants in the plain."

Usually, when they decided not to go to Ram, he went off
shortly after Ma and Joseph came back to the house. But tonight he waited, standing with his back against the door.

Obviously he was waiting for his hour of triumph, the hour when the phonograph would be discussed.

"That's so, there are plenty of workers on the plain," said Ma. "But that one has had such hard luck. Whenever I look at his thin legs, I say to myself, well, he'll be on my hands for the rest of my life."

If they were not quickly told about the contents of that parcel, things might take a bad turn. Joseph, wild with curiosity, might give the rattan table a kick and go off alone to Ram in the B-12. But Suzanne, who certainly knew Joseph's moods, still kept quiet, sitting motionless in her chair. The Corporal came in, saw the parcel, looked at it a long time, then put down the rice and began to set the table. When he had finished, Ma looked at Monsieur Jo as if to say What-the-hell's-he-still-doing-here! It was long past their usual time to go to Ram, and he surely must be aware of it.

"You can stay to dinner if you like," Ma said to him. She was not usually that amiable. Her invitation was issued, no doubt, in order to prolong Joseph's and Suzanne's torment. She still had some youthful fire in her, could still occasionally enjoy a bit of fun.

"I thank you," said Monsieur Jo, "nothing would please me more."

"There's nothing to eat," said Suzanne, "I warn you. There's nothing but the stilt-bird garbage."

"Oh, you don't know me," said Monsieur Jo, not without malice aforethought, this time. "I have very simple tastes."

Joseph came back from his shower and looked at Monsieur Jo as if he were thinking, What-the-Hell's-he-still-doing-here! Then, seeing that four places were laid and that he was going to have to endure it, he sat down, determined to feed himself no matter what.

The Corporal again came up and lit the acetylene lamp. From then on, they were surrounded by the night, shut up in the bungalow with the parcel.

"I'm starving," said Joseph. "We got to eat this garbage again?"

"Sit down," said Ma to Monsieur Jo.

Joseph was already seated, alone at the table. Monsieur Jo, as usual agitated in Joseph's presence, was feverishly smoking a cigarette. He was unreasonably afraid of Joseph and instinctively he now sat down at the table opposite him, as far away as possible. Ma gave him a piece of the stilt-bird and said to Joseph, gently, as if to mollify him:

"I sometimes wonder what we'd eat if you weren't here to shoot game for us. This bird smells a little of fish, but it's good for you," she added, addressing Monsieur Jo.

"It may be good for us," said Suzanne, "but it's garbage."

When her children were feeding, Ma was always patient and indulgent.

"It's always the same thing every night," she said, "they're never satisfied."

They talked about the stilt-bird as if those birds signified something until then unknown, had some secret connection with the parcel that still stood there on the rattan table, enormous, untouched, like a bomb not yet exploded. Joseph ate quickly, gobbling his food in a way more revolting than usual, swallowing his wrath at the same time.

"Every night it's the same thing," Suzanne went on, "because we eat stilt-birds every night. There's never anything else."

Then it was that Ma saw a way out.

"That's so," she said, with a charming smile of suppressed malice, "it's a rare thing that anything new happens on the plain, from every point of view."

Suzanne smiled. Joseph still pretended to be in the dark.

"But something new sometimes does happen," said Suzanne.

Delighted to comprehend, Monsieur Jo began to eat the stilt-bird with appetite, contrary to his usual Parisian habit of barely tasting at the beginning things unfamiliar to him.

"It's a phonograph," said Suzanne.

Joseph stopped eating. His eyes flashed beneath his half-lowered lids. All three of them looked at it, as did even Monsieur Jo.

"We already got one," said Joseph. "We got a phono."

"I believe," said Monsieur Jo, "that this one is—how shall we say?—more modern."

Suzanne left the table and went towards the parcel. She tore off the bands of glued paper and opened the cardboard box. Then she took out the phonograph carefully and deposited it on the dining table. It was black, covered with marbled leather, and it had chrome handles.

Joseph had stopped eating and was smoking, while looking at it in fascination. Ma was a little disappointed. Phonographs, like Joseph's night hunting, were calamities which Joseph imposed upon her. Suzanne lifted the lid and the inside appeared: a green cloth disk, a chrome arm, dazzling. Inside the lid was a small metal label on which was a picture of a fox terrier, seated in front of a kennel three times his size. Printed above him were the words: HIS MASTER'S VOICE. Joseph raised his eyes, looked at the label with the false expression of a connoisseur and tried to work the arm of the machine. Then, having looked at it and touched the phonograph with his hands, he completely forgot Suzanne and Monsieur Jo, forgot that the phonograph came from Monsieur Jo, forgot that they were all three there, watching him and his joy, forgot his resolve not to show any surprise at the phonograph. He wound it up as if in a dream, set the needle in the arm of the machine and made it go. Then he stopped it and made it go again.

Suzanne went back to the parcel, took out an envelope full of records and brought it to him. They were all English records except for one called "Un soir à Singapour." Joseph looked at them one after the other.

"They're all trash," he said in a low voice, "but that don't matter."

"I picked the latest records, just out in Paris," said Monsieur Jo timidly, a little put out of countenance by Joseph's outburst and the total indifference with which he was being treated. But Joseph, without insisting, grabbed the phonograph, put it on the sitting-room table, and sat down beside it. Then he took a record, put it on the green cloth disk, set it in motion, and placed the needle on it.

A voice rose, new, strange, indiscreet, almost outrageous in the midst of the general silence:

> *"Un soir, à Singapour,*
> *Un soir*
> *d'amour.*
> *Un soir, sous les palmiers,*
> *Un soir*
> *d'été."*

At the end of the record the ice had melted. Joseph was having a wonderful time, Suzanne was having a wonderful time. Even Ma, too, was enjoying herself, for she said: "That's beautiful."

Monsieur Jo was bursting with joy. Maybe his case would be reconsidered . . . He looked from one to the other, hoping at last to be accepted as the benefactor of the family. But in vain. To none of these people around him was there any connection between the phonograph and its donor.

After "Un soir à Singapour," Joseph played the other new records, one after the other, listening indifferently to them —for the very good reason that he did not understand the words, which were in English. Anyway, that night you could not tell whether it was music that interested him or merely the working of the phonograph and its mechanical perfection.

At last Monsieur Jo went. Once he had gone, Ma asked Suzanne if she knew how much the phonograph cost. Suzanne had forgotten to ask Monsieur Jo. Ma, a little put out, asked Joseph to stop playing it. But that night, you might as well have asked him to stop breathing. Ma did not insist, but went off and shut herself in her room. When she had gone, Joseph said: "Now we'll play 'Ramona,' and he went to get his old records, of which "Ramona" was the most precious.

The French version was what they had, in which Ramona's lover tells her of his "wonderful dream," that they had gone away together, "far from jealous eyes," and that "never had lovers known sweeter nights."

> "Ramona, j'ai fait un rêve merveilleux,
> Ramona, nous étions partis tous les deux,
> Nous allions
> Lentement
> Loin de tous les regards jaloux
> Et jamais deux amants
> N'avaient connu de soirs plus doux."

Neither Joseph nor Suzanne had ever sung the words, but they hummed the tune. For them, it was the most beautiful thing they had ever heard, the most eloquent. The tune poured out sweet as honey.

Monsieur Jo always said they did not sing "Ramona" any more in Paris, had not for years, but this did not bother them. When Joseph played that record, everything became brighter, truer. Ma, who did not like that record, seemed to be older and they felt their youth knocking at their temples like a caged bird. Sometimes, when Ma did not scream too much and they could return from their swim without hurrying, Joseph whistled the tune. When they would leave all this, they would whistle that tune, thought Suzanne. It was the hymn of the future, of departures on journeys, of the end of long waiting. What they hoped for was to find again that tune, born of the giddy cities for which it was made,

where it was sung, tumultuous cities, cities full of love. It
filled Joseph with the desire for a woman of the city, one
who would be radically different from those of the plain,
where she would be unimaginably out of place. In Ram, Pa
Bart had "Ramona" also among his records, and it was not
as worn out as Joseph's. It was after having danced to that
tune one night that Agosti had taken her suddenly out of
the canteen and down to the port. He had said that she had
become a very pretty girl, and he had kissed her. "I don't
know why, but suddenly I want to kiss you," he had said.
When they returned together to the canteen, Joseph had
looked at her with a queer expression, then had smiled at
her, a sad smile of understanding. Since that time, Agosti
had perhaps forgotten and Suzanne never really thought of
it, but it was linked with the tune of "Ramona." And every
time Joseph played it, the memory of Jean Agosti's kiss was
in that tune.

When the record ended, Suzanne asked: "What do you
think about this phono?"

"Great. You almost don't have to wind it." Then, after a
few minutes of reflection, he added: "Did you ask him for
it?"

"I didn't ask him for anything at all."

"He just gave it to you, like that?"

Suzanne hesitated a little. "Yes," she said, "he just gave it
to me, like that."

Joseph laughed silently.

"He's a bastard. But the phono—it's great."

4

IT WAS SHORTLY AFTER MONSIEUR JO HAD GIVEN THEM THE
phonograph that Joseph, one evening in Ram, took it upon
himself to have a talk with him.

Monsieur Jo had decided to prolong his sojourn on the
plain, under the pretext of having to supervise the shipping
of some pepper and latex. He had taken a room at the Ram
canteen, and another room in Kam, spending the nights now
in one place, now the other, doubtless to elude the vigilance
of his father. Sometimes he went to spend a day or two in
the city, but soon came back, and spent every afternoon
visiting at the bungalow. After having built his hopes on
the effect of his wealth upon Suzanne, he began to despair
and, perhaps because of this very despair and doubt, began
really to fall in love. Ma's and Joseph's watchful waiting
also doubtless exasperated him still more, for soon he was
quite beside himself with what he now considered to be a
great passion.

At first, the over-simple motive for his visits had been to
take them to Ram to dance and amuse themselves.

"I'll take you for a breath of air," he would announce,
breezily.

"We got plenty of air here," said Joseph, "that's one thing
we don't lack."

But soon this habit of driving to Ram late each afternoon

became so natural to them that Monsieur Jo occasionally neglected to invite them. Moreover, it was usually Suzanne who announced the time for going to Ram. Despite his reluctance, Joseph accompanied them. First, because the trip could be made in a half hour by the Léon Bollée, rather than the hour required by the B-12, and that performance alone was enough to decide him to go; then, it was not unpleasant to drink and sometimes to eat at Monsieur Jo's expense. This was when Joseph learned that you can enjoy drinking.

Nevertheless, the fact escaped no one that these excursions were proposed each time by Monsieur Jo only to evade what was expected of him—his gifts were also for the same purpose. Very soon, indeed, these excursions were carried out in an atmosphere of disgust and wrath that Monsieur Jo, for all his amiability and generosity, was unable to dispel. Things became tolerable only after they—especially Joseph—had drunk enough to be able to forget Monsieur Jo, even to be forgetful of his presence. Since none of them, with reason, was used to champagne, the desired effect was quickly produced. Even Ma drank, although she did not precisely enjoy drinking. She drank, she said, to drown her shame.

"After two glasses of champagne, I forget why I came to Ram and imagine it's me that's bamboozling him, not the other way about."

Monsieur Jo, for his part, drank little. He had drunk a great deal in the past, he said, and alcohol now had almost no effect upon him. It did have the effect of making him feel, in regard to Suzanne, still more fervent and still more melancholy, however. He looked at her, while dancing, in such a languishing way that sometimes, when the canteen had no other distractions, Joseph watched him with interest.

"He's doing his Rudolph Valentino act," said he, "but he looks more like a damfool calf. If that head of his doesn't look like a calf's head, I'd like to know what it does look like."

Ma laughed, delighted. Suzanne, on the dance floor, could imagine what made them laugh. Monsieur Jo hadn't any idea. Rather, he prudently abstained from trying to find the cause of their fits of hilarity.

"It's a fine thing, a calf's head," said Ma, encouragingly. Joseph's similes, that evening, were not in the best of taste, but it didn't bother Ma. She found them perfect. Overwhelmed with disgust, discarding all scruples, she raised her glass.

"Here's to our expectations . . ." she said.

"And how!" said Joseph, with a guffaw.

"They're drinking a toast to us," said Suzanne, on the dance floor.

"I doubt it," replied Monsieur Jo. "They certainly never do so when we're with them."

"They're shy," said Suzanne, smiling.

"Your smile is absolutely maddening," said Monsieur Jo in a low voice.

"And in the meantime," said Ma, "I've never in my life drunk so much champagne."

Joseph loved to see Ma in this state of vulgar and relaxed hilarity—he was the only one who could arouse it in her. Sometimes, when he was terribly fed up with life, he would keep up his pleasantries for the whole evening and, sometimes less directly, even in Monsieur Jo's presence. For instance, when Monsieur Jo did not dance, Joseph would hum a tune while looking at Suzanne, selecting songs of doubtful suitability: "Paris, I love you, I love you, I lo-o-o-ove you . . ." And he would imitate Monsieur Jo's calf's eyes. Which made everyone laugh and brought a painful smile to Monsieur Jo's lips.

Usually, though, Joseph danced, drank, and paid no attention whatsoever to Monsieur Jo. Sometimes he went to chat with Agosti, or he strolled out to the harbor to watch the loading of the mail-packet, or sometimes he even went down to the beach for a swim. When he went for a swim, he announced his intentions to Suzanne and Ma, who followed him, being themselves followed at a distance by Monsieur Jo.

When he had drunk too much, Joseph would threaten to swim to the nearest island, a distance of three kilometers. He never proposed such a thing when in his right senses, but on these evenings he felt more than able to accomplish it. In reality, he would have sunk long before reaching the island. But Ma would begin to wail and would order Monsieur Jo to start up the Léon Bollée. Only the sound of that motor could make Joseph forget his project. Monsieur Jo, who rather approved of seeing his tormentor take the risk, obeyed Ma with manifest regret.

It was during one of these evenings passed at the Ram canteen that Joseph spoke to Monsieur Jo on the subject of Suzanne and placed before him, once and for all, his point of view. After which, he never spoke a word to him again, except much later, treating him thenceforth with royal disdain.

Suzanne, as usual, danced with Monsieur Jo, and Ma, as usual, watched them sadly. Sometimes, especially when she had not drunk enough, champagne made her very sad when she looked at Monsieur Jo. There was a crowd in the canteen that night, and among them, some women passengers. But Joseph did not dance. Maybe he was tired of dancing every evening. Or maybe his resolve to speak out to Monsieur Jo deprived him of the desire to dance. In any case, he watched Monsieur Jo, who was dancing with Suzanne a little more unrestrainedly than usual.

"He's what you might call a botch," Joseph suddenly began, "a failure."

"That doesn't mean a thing," said Ma, not quite agreeing. "Me, too, I'm a failure, the most complete failure." She became still gloomier. "The proof of it is," she went on, "that the only way out for me is to marry my daughter off to that good-for-nothing."

"It's not the same thing," said Joseph. "You didn't have any luck. And yes, you're right, it doesn't mean a thing. What counts is to get him to decide. We've waited about long enough!"

"I've waited too much in my life," Ma wailed. "I waited for the concession, I waited for the dikes. And now, only to get that mortgage on the five hectares, I've been waiting two whole years."

Joseph looked at her, as if suddenly inspired.

"You're right, that's all we do: wait. But one thing we can do is to decide we're not going to wait any longer. I'm going to have a talk with him."

Monsieur Jo and Suzanne had stopped dancing and were returning to the table. As he crossed the floor, Ma said:

"Sometimes when I look at him it's as if I was looking at my whole life—and it's not a pretty sight."

As soon as Monsieur Jo had sat down, Joseph started.

"It's been a helluva long time," said Joseph.

Monsieur Jo was used to Joseph's rudeness.

"I'm sorry," he said. "I'll order another bottle of champagne."

"That's not what I mean," said Joseph. "I mean *you* have been a helluva long time, keeping us waiting."

Monsieur Jo flushed to the eyes.

"We were talking about you," said Ma, "and we decided we're tired of waiting for you to make up your mind. It's gone on a long time now, too long, and we begin to see through you. You can bring us and bring us to Ram every night, but it doesn't fool anyone."

"We said, besides, that it's not normal to go on for a month like this wanting to sleep with my sister. Me, I'd never be able to hold out that long."

Monsieur Jo lowered his eyes. Suzanne felt sure he would get up and go. But apparently he had so little imagination that he did not think of it. Joseph had not drunk so very much, he was talking like this in a gust of sadness and revulsion, held in until now to such an extent that you could not help being relieved to hear him finally speak out.

"I do not conceal," said Monsieur Jo in a very low voice, "that I have a very tender feeling for your sister."

He told Suzanne every day of the feelings he had for her. "As for me," she thought, "if I marry him, it will be without any feelings for him! I can do without such feelings." She was more strongly on Joseph's side than ever before.

"Tell that to the fence-post," said Ma, with sudden coarseness, adopting Joseph's tone.

"It's possible," said Joseph, "but it's no use to us. The only thing that counts is for you to make up your mind and marry her."

He pointed to Ma.

"For her sake, I mean. As for me, the better I know you, the less I like the idea."

Monsieur Jo had regained his composure a little. Obstinately he averted his eyes. Everyone looked at his closed face. He was as blind as the cadastral agents, as the bank, as the Pacific Ocean. They realized that they had as little power over his millions as over those blind and reasonless forces. Monsieur Jo knew very little, but he knew he could not marry Suzanne.

"One does not decide," he said in a timid voice, "to marry someone in a fortnight."

Joseph smiled. In general, that was true.

"In certain particular cases," he said, "it can be decided in a fortnight. This is one of them."

Monsieur Jo raised his eyes for a second. He did not understand. Joseph could have tried to explain himself, but it was hard to do so, he'd never manage it.

"If we were rich," said Ma, "it would be different. Rich people can wait two years."

"You're out of luck if you don't understand," said Joseph. "It's that or nothing."

He waited a little, then said slowly and emphatically: "She can sleep with whoever she likes. We don't stop her. But in your case, if you want to sleep with her, you've got to marry her. That's our way of saying to Hell with you!"

Monsieur Jo raised his head a second time. His stupefaction before so much scandalous frankness was such that he forgot to take offense. Anyway, Joseph's words only remotely concerned him. You might say Joseph was merely talking to hear himself talk, to put into words his new-found and final opinion on all the Monsieur Jos in the world.

"I've wanted to say this to you for a long time," Joseph added.

"You people are hard," said Monsieur Jo. "I'd never have believed it the first evening . . ."

He lied. For a week at least, they had all been waiting for this.

"We're not forcing you to marry her," said Ma, in a conciliatory way. "We're only warning you."

Monsieur Jo did not turn a hair. The simplicity of Monsieur Jo would doubtless have touched many people.

"Besides," said Joseph, laughing suddenly, "even if we accept everything—phonographs, champagne—it don't get you anywhere."

Ma gave Monsieur Jo a glance of vague pity.

"We are very unhappy people," she said, by way of explanation.

Monsieur Jo at last raised his eyes towards Ma and realized that, seeing the injustice being done to him, an explanation was in order.

"I have never been happy, either," he said. "They always forced me to do things I did not want to do. During the last two weeks I have been doing a little of what I like to do, and so now . . ."

Joseph was no longer paying any attention to him.

"Before we go, I would like to dance with you," he said to Suzanne.

Joseph asked Pa Bart to play "Ramona." Then he and Suzanne went off to dance. He did not make one remark to Suzanne on the conversation with Monsieur Jo, but talked to her about "Ramona."

"When I get a little more money," he said, "I'll buy a new 'Ramona' record."

Ma, at the table, watched them dance. Monsieur Jo, sitting facing her, played with his diamond, pulling it off and putting it on again.

"He may be rough sometimes, but it isn't his fault," said Ma. "He hadn't any education."

"She doesn't care for me at all," said Monsieur Jo in a low voice. "She didn't say a word."

"Oh, but since you are so rich," said Ma.

"That hasn't anything to do with it. On the contrary."

Maybe he was less a fool than he looked.

"I must defend myself," he declared.

Ma looked at what she herself had to defend. They were waltzing to the tune of "Ramona." They were fine children. All things considered, she had produced, at any rate, fine children. They seemed to be happy to dance together. She thought they looked alike. They had the same shoulders— her own shoulders—the same coloring, the same hair, a little reddish—inherited from her—and in their eyes there was the same happy insolence. Suzanne looked more and more like Joseph. Ma believed she understood Suzanne better than Joseph.

"She is young," said Monsieur Jo, in a grief-stricken voice.

"Not so young as all that," said Ma, smiling. "If I was in your place, I'd marry her."

The dance came to an end. Joseph did not condescend to sit down.

"We're clearing out," he said.

From that day on, he never addressed another word to Monsieur Jo. They became more and more distant with each other. And actually, in their treatment of Monsieur Jo, all three of them took greater liberties in words and manners than before.

5

STILL IN THE SITTING ROOM AND STILL UNDER THE BROODING
observation of Ma, Monsieur Jo was teaching Suzanne the
art of enameling her nails. Suzanne was sitting facing him.
She was wearing the beautiful blue silk dress that he had
brought her, among other things, after the phonograph. Set
out on the table were three bottles of different colored nail
polish, a jar of cold cream, and a bottle of perfume.

"When you cut the cuticle, that stung," grumbled
Suzanne.

Monsieur Jo was not in such a hurry to finish, doubtless
wanting to keep Suzanne's hand in his as long as possible.
He had already sampled three colors.

"This is the one that suits you best," he said finally, con-
templating his work like a connoisseur.

Suzanne lifted her hand the better to see it. The enamel
chosen by Monsieur Jo was an orange-red, which made her
skin look darker. She had no very definite opinion on the
subject, so she gave her hand to Monsieur Jo for the enamel
to be applied. He took it, kissing the palm.

"Must hurry," said Suzanne, "if we go to Ram, there's still
the other hand to do."

In the field framed by the open door, they could see
Joseph who, with the help of the Corporal, was trying to

prop up the little wooden bridge of the driveway. The sun was scorching hot. From time to time, Joseph shouted abusive remarks, manifestly destined for Monsieur Jo, but Monsieur Jo was now used to this kind of treatment, no doubt, so pretended not to understand.

"Sonofabitch, with his twenty-four horsepower, damn him!"

"It's true," said Suzanne, "you were the one to smash up the bridge. You must leave your car out on the road, from now on."

After her fingernails, Monsieur Jo enameled her toe-nails. He had almost finished. She had put up one foot on the table to let the enamel dry, and he was doing the other foot to match.

"That's enough," said Suzanne, forgetting that even had Monsieur Jo wished to do more, it was not in his power.

He sighed, abandoning Suzanne's foot and sinking back in the armchair. He had finished and he was perspiring slightly.

"Supposing we dance a little here, instead of going to Ram?" asked Monsieur Jo. "Supposing we dance to the Victrola?"

"Joseph won't let anyone touch it," said Suzanne. "Besides, I'm tired of dancing."

Monsieur Jo again sighed and put on an imploring look. "It's not my fault if I want to hold you in my arms . . ."

Suzanne looked at her feet and hands with satisfaction. "Me, I don't want to be in anybody's arms."

Monsieur Jo lowered his head.

"You make me suffer very much," he said, in a stricken tone.

"I'm going to dress to go to Ram. Stay here. If she doesn't see you, I'm the one she'll jaw at."

"Don't fear," said Monsieur Jo, smiling very sadly.

Suzanne went out on the verandah and called.

"Joseph, we're going to Ram."

"We'll go if I want to," yelled Ma. "It's only if I want to that we'll go!"

Suzanne went back to Monsieur Jo.

"That's what she says, but she's really dying to go."

Monsieur Jo was not interested in the argument. He was looking at Suzanne's legs which showed through the transparent silk of her dress.

"You're still naked under your dress," he said, "and I, I've no right to anything."

He seemed to be terribly despondent as he lit a cigarette.

"I don't know, now, what I must do to make you love me," he went on. "I believe if we married, I'd be horribly unhappy."

Instead of going to dress, Suzanne sat down in front of him and looked at him with a certain curiosity. But she began to think of other things almost at once, while continuing to look at him without seeing him, as if he had been transparent, and she was obliged to look through his face to perceive the dizzy promises of wealth.

"If we married, I'd lock you up," concluded Monsieur Jo, resignedly.

"What car would I have, if we married?"

It was perhaps the thirtieth time that she had asked that question. But this kind of question she never tired of asking. Monsieur Jo put on an indifferent look.

"Whatever kind you liked, I've already told you that."

"And Joseph?"

"I don't know that I would give a car to Joseph," said Monsieur Jo, precipitately. "That I cannot promise you. I've already told you so."

Suzanne's gaze did not cease exploring the fabulous regions of wealth just beyond this obstacle which prevented her from enjoying herself there. Then her smile was wiped out. Her expression changed so much that Monsieur Jo went on almost at once:

"It would depend upon you, you know very well. How you behaved with me . . ."

"You could offer *her* a car," said Suzanne, with persuasive gentleness. "It would amount to the same thing."

"There never was any question of offering a car to your mother," said Monsieur Jo, with an air of desperation. "I am not as rich as you think."

"As for her, I'll not stand out. But if Joseph hasn't a car, then you can keep all your cars, mine included, and you can marry whoever you like."

Monsieur Jo seized Suzanne's hand and held her, as if to prevent her from slipping into cruelty. He looked imploring, as if close to tears.

"You know very well that Joseph will have his car. You're making me be spiteful."

Suzanne again looked towards Joseph, who had finished repairing the little wooden bridge. Now he was bracing the posts with stones which he went to find on the road. He was still fuming.

"We'll make the bastards do their own repairs next time! And if they begin again, we'll chuck sand in their carburetor, sand, that's what we got plenty of!"

For some time, whenever Suzanne thought of Joseph it was with a pang at her heart, doubtless because Joseph still had no one to love him while she, at any rate, had Monsieur Jo.

"Only holding your hand," said the latter, in a shaken voice, "does something terrific to me."

She had left her hand in his. Sometimes she let him hold her hand for a while. For instance, when it was a question of the car he would give Joseph if they married.

He looked at her hand, he breathed it in, kissed it—and generally this kept him in a good humor.

"Even if I wasn't his sister, it would make me horribly happy to give a car to Joseph."

"My little dear, I'm glad to hear that, be sure."

"I think he'll go crazy if we give him a car," said Suzanne.

"He shall have one, my little Suzanne, he shall have one, my treasure."

Suzanne smiled. "I'll bring the car at night, when he's out hunting," she reflected. "I'll put it under the bungalow and I'll hang a card on the steering wheel. I'll write on it: FOR JOSEPH."

Monsieur Jo was capable of promising a car to the Corporal if it would keep Suzanne in this radiant state of oblivion, he had got as far as her arm, above the elbow . . . Suzanne suddenly realized it and pulled herself away.

"I'm going to dress," she said, and off she went to lock herself in the shower.

A minute afterwards, Monsieur Jo was knocking at the door. Since the phonograph he had formed the habit. She, too. It was like this every evening.

"Open the door, Suzanne. Open, please."

"I wish she'd come this minute, oh, how I wish she would . . ."

"Only a second. Just enough to see you . . ."

"Either Ma or Joseph. He's strong, Joseph. With one kick he can send a person into the river."

Monsieur Jo was not listening.

"Just a tiny bit, just a second."

Monsieur Jo was not unaware of the risk he was taking. But when he heard the sound of the water falling on Suzanne, even the fear of Joseph could not make him resist the temptation. With all his strength he pushed on the door.

"To think you're there naked, completely naked," he went on in a toneless voice.

"My goodness, what a fuss to make!" said Suzanne. "If you were the one in here, I'd not want to see you!"

Whenever she called up the image of Monsieur Jo without his diamond, his hat, and his limousine, strolling on the beach at Ram, for instance, in a bathing suit, Suzanne's anger mounted.

"Why don't you go in swimming at Ram?"

Monsieur Jo recovered himself and pushed less hard against the door.

"Sea bathing is forbidden me," he said with what firmness he could command.

Suzanne happily soaped herself. Ever since he had bought her some soap perfumed with lavender, she took two or three baths a day in order to perfume herself. The smell of the lavender reached Monsieur Jo and allowed him the better to follow the stages of Suzanne's bath, rendering his torment still more acute.

"Why is sea bathing forbidden you?"

"Because I have a weak constitution and sea bathing fatigues me. Open the door, dear little Suzanne . . . just a second . . ."

"It's not so. It's because you look like a scarecrow."

She could imagine him there, glued to the door, swallowing the insult because he was sure of winning out in the long run.

"A second . . . only a second . . ."

She remembered what Joseph had said to him at Ram. "It's not that we stop her from sleeping with whoever she likes, but you, if you want to sleep with her, you've got to marry her. That's our way of saying to Hell with you!"

"Joseph is right, when he says . . ."

Monsieur Jo pushed against the door with all his might. "I should worry about what Joseph says!"

"That's not so. You're afraid of Joseph, you're scared stiff!"

Again he grew quiet and detached himself a little from the door.

"I think," he said in a low voice, "that I never saw anyone as mean as you are."

Suzanne stopped rinsing herself. Ma said the same thing. Was it true? She looked at herself in the glass, hunting for, without finding, some sign which would enlighten her. Joseph, he always said No, she wasn't mean but that she was hard and proud. He tried to reassure Ma. But to hear it said, and even to hear Monsieur Jo say it, rather terrified her. When Monsieur Jo said that to her, she always opened the door. Therefore, he said it to her more and more often.

"Go see if they're still on the other side."

She heard him bound into the sitting room. He went to stand in the doorway and lit a cigarette, forcing himself to be calm. But his hands trembled. Joseph and the Corporal had not finished bolstering the posts of the bridge. It did not look as though they would come in at once. Ma had joined them and seemed very absorbed, as she always was when watching work being done by Joseph. Monsieur Jo came back towards the shower room.

"They're still down below, quick, Suzanne!"

Suzanne half opened the door. Monsieur Jo bounded towards her. Suzanne closed the door savagely in his face. Monsieur Jo remained outside.

"Now, go into the sitting room," said Suzanne.

Suzanne began to put on her clothes again. She dressed quickly, without looking at herself. The night before, he had told her that if she would take a little trip to the city with him, he would give her a diamond ring. She had asked what price diamond. He had not stated it, but he had said it would be worth the bungalow at least. She had not talked about it to Joseph. He had said that he already had the diamond, that he was merely waiting for her to make up her mind before giving it to her. Suzanne pulled on her dress. It wasn't enough, now, for her just to open the door of the shower room. It had been enough for the Victrola, but it wasn't enough for the diamond. The diamond was worth ten, maybe twenty Victrolas. Three days in the city, he had said, and I won't touch you, we will go to the movies. He had talked about it only one single time, the night before, while they were dancing at Ram, and he had barely whispered it. A diamond which, alone, was worth the whole bungalow!

She opened the door and went to put on her make-up in the light, on the verandah. Then she went to find Monsieur Jo in the sitting room. It was the only minute of the day when she wondered confusedly if he did not deserve, all the same, some sympathy: after the scene at the door of the shower room, you would have said he was crushed, absolutely overwhelmed at having in his weakness to bear such a weight, such a storm of desire. That he had been elected to endure such a test—it made him seem, somehow, human. But no matter how much Suzanne racked her brains, she could never find a way of saying this to him without misleading him. So she gave it up. Anyway, it was at this hour of the day, every evening, that the trip to Ram was decided upon, and this subject soon assumed more importance than any other. Joseph had finished repairing the bridge, but Ma kept on talking to him about something.

"You are beautiful," said Monsieur Jo, without raising his head.

The cries of the children playing in the *rac* could already be heard. Ma was not thinking about going to Ram. She was old, was Ma. She was mean, she was crackbrained. There were men who came to Ram, hunters, planters, but what were they to her? One day Suzanne would leave the plain and would leave, at the same time, Ma. Suzanne looked at Monsieur Jo. After all, maybe it would be with this one, because she was so poor and the plain was so far away from all the towns where men were.

"You are beautiful and desirable," said Monsieur Jo.

Suzanne smiled at Monsieur Jo.

"I'm only seventeen, when I'm older I'll be even prettier."

Monsieur Jo raised his head.

"When I take you away from here, you'll leave me, I'm sure."

Ma and Joseph came up the steps. They were very hot. Joseph wiped his forehead with a handkerchief. Ma had taken off her straw hat and a red line circled her temples.

"Just look at you," said Joseph to Suzanne. "You don't know how to use make-up, you look like a whore!"

"She looks like what she is," said Ma. Then, to Monsieur Jo: "Why did you bring her all that stuff?"

She collapsed into an armchair while Joseph went disgustedly towards his room.

"Are we going to Ram?" asked Suzanne.

"What kind of monkeyshines have you two been up to?" asked Ma of Monsieur Jo.

"Madame, I respect your daughter too much . . ."

"If I ever see anything out of the way, I'll make you marry her in a week's time."

Monsieur Jo got up and went to lean against the door. As always, in the presence of Ma or Joseph, he smoked without stopping and never stayed seated.

"We didn't do a thing," said Suzanne. "He didn't even touch me. Don't you worry, I'm not such a fool, I know how . . ."

"Shut up. You don't understand anything."

Monsieur Jo went out on the verandah. Suzanne no longer wondered if they would go to Ram. With Ma, you never could tell. And you could not count on Joseph, who felt such revulsion towards Monsieur Jo that he would not speak of going to Ram, in spite of his daily wish to go there. Ma pulled a chair forward and put up her feet. You could see the soles of her feet, they looked something like the feet of the Corporal, the skin was calloused and broken by the stones of the fields. From time to time, Ma sighed loudly and mopped her brow. She was red and congested looking.

"Give me some coffee . . ."

Suzanne stood up and went to get the pot of cold coffee on the sideboard. She poured it into a cup and brought it over. Ma whimpered softly as she took the cup from Suzanne's hands.

"I'm at the end of my string, give me my pills."

Suzanne went for the pills and brought them back to her.

She obeyed in silence. That was the best thing to do: obey in silence. Ma's bad temper would disappear all by itself. Monsieur Jo was still on the verandah. Joseph was taking his shower. You could hear the sound of the can knocking against the jar in the shower room. The sun had almost set. The children were already leaving the *rac* and running towards the cabins.

"Give me my glasses."

Suzanne went into the bedroom for the glasses and brought them back to Ma. She could still ask for a few more things: her account book, her handbag, and she must be obeyed. It delighted her to test the patience of her children, it was sweet to her. When she had her glasses, she put them on and began to examine Suzanne furtively, with great attention. Suzanne, seated facing the door, knew that Ma was looking at her. She also knew what would follow, and tried to avoid Ma's eyes. She no longer thought about Ram.

"Did you speak to him?" Ma asked at last.

"I do all the time. I think it's on account of his father that he can't make up his mind."

"You must ask him once and for all. If he doesn't decide within three days, I'll speak to him and give him one week to make up his mind."

"It's not that he doesn't want to, but it's his father. His father wants him to marry a rich girl."

"He'll have a hard time finding one, rich as he is. A rich girl, who could take her pick, wouldn't have him. People have to be in our condition for a mother to give her daughter to such a man."

"I'll speak to him. Don't you worry."

Ma grew silent, but continued to survey Suzanne.

"You've not done anything with him, is that so?"

"Nothing. First of all, because I don't want to."

Ma sighed, then, timidly, in a low voice, she asked:

"What will you do if it works out?"

Suzanne turned and looked at her mother, smiling. But

Ma did not smile, and the corners of her lips trembled. Maybe she was going to blubber again.

"Oh, I'll manage," said Suzanne, "you'll see, I'll manage."

"If you can't face it, I'd rather you just stayed here. It's all my fault . . ."

"Hush," said Suzanne. "Don't say such silly things. It's nobody's fault . . ."

"No, it's my fault, it's my fault."

"Hush," begged Suzanne. "Stop. Let's go to Ram."

"Yes, let's go. We can do that at any rate, if it gives you that much pleasure."

6

MA CHANGED HER MIND, DECIDED THAT THEY OUGHT NOT TO
remain alone together in the bungalow any more, not even
with the door open. Undoubtedly she now felt that this
was not enough to exacerbate Monsieur Jo's desires. Since
he was still waiting for Heaven only knew what, said she,
although she knew very well it was waiting to propose marriage, she decided upon a new policy.

So it was that, henceforth, Suzanne received Monsieur
Jo on the bank of the *rac*.

Everyone was waiting for him to make up his mind. Ma
had spoken to him and had given him a week to do it. Monsieur Jo had agreed to the delay. He admitted to Ma that
his father had other things in view for him and that
although there were few young girls in the Colony with a
fortune to match his, there were, all the same, enough of
them to make it very hard to persuade his father to give in.
However, he promised to do everything in his power to persuade him. But while the days passed during which he said
he was doing everything to convince his father, he spoke
more and more, but to Suzanne alone, about the diamond.
It was worth, all by itself, the entire bungalow. He would
give it to her only if she agreed to go away with him on a
little three-day trip to the city.

Suzanne sat with him at the spot where, a few weeks

earlier, she had waited and watched for the big-game hunters' cars.

"I have never before been treated like this," said Monsieur
Jo.

Suzanne laughed. She, too, preferred to meet Monsieur
Jo there, she was completely in accord with Ma. For now
she could take her bath in peace, while Monsieur Jo
waited for her under the bridge. Thus he became almost ir-
resistibly funny and she was able to stand him better.

"If I told this to my friends, they'd not believe me," Monsieur Jo went on.

The afternoon was still burning hot and the sun was high.
The smallest children were still taking their naps in the
shade of the mango trees. The larger children were watching
the water-buffaloes, some were perched on the animals'
backs. Other children were fishing in the *marigots*. They
were all singing, their childish voices raised shrilly in the
burning hot, motionless air.

Ma was pruning the banana trees. The Corporal, following behind her, banked them up and watered them.

"There are already too many banana trees on the plain,"
said Monsieur Jo, ironically. "Here, bananas are fed to pigs."

"We've got to let her do what she likes," said Suzanne.

Ma pretended to believe that her banana trees, exceptionally well cared for, would bear exceptionally fine fruit
which she would be able to sell. But above all she liked to
plant—to plant no matter what, even banana trees, with
which the plain was glutted. Ever since the failure of the
sea walls, there never passed a day without her planting
something, no matter what, anything that would grow and
would give wood or fruit or leaves or nothing—anything
that would simply grow. A few months before, she had
planted a *guau* tree. *Guau* trees take a hundred years to grow
to any size and are then used by cabinet-makers. She had
planted it on a day of sadness when, no doubt, she completely despaired of the future and also when she was short

of ideas. When she had planted it she had tearfully considered the *guau*, lamenting that she could not leave traces of her passage through life more useful than this, a *guau* tree of which she would not even see the first flowers. Next day she had looked for the tree in vain: Joseph had torn it up and thrown it into the river. Ma had flown into a temper.

"Fool things that take a hundred years to grow," Joseph had explained, "it makes me gag to have to look and look at them all the time!"

Ma had resigned herself and afterwards had fallen back on plants of rapid growth.

"You have enough reasons to groan and moan," Joseph said to her, "without looking for others." He had then told her: "Try banana trees." That is what she had done, she had gone in for planting banana trees, particularly.

When it was not her plants, it was the native children in which Ma took an interest.

There were many children in the plain. They were a kind of calamity. They were everywhere, perched in the trees, on the railings of the bridge, on the backs of the buffaloes. They daydreamed or, squatting on the banks of the *marigots*, they fished, or they wallowed in the mud, looking for the dwarf crabs of the rice fields. In the river, too, there were children wading, playing, swimming. And in the prows of the Chinese junks which went out towards the open sea, towards the green islands of the Pacific, there were also children, smiling, delighted, cooped up in great willow baskets with only their heads visible, smiling better than anyone in the world had ever smiled. And always, before reaching the villages at the foot of the mountain, even before having perceived the first mango trees, you met the first children of the forest villages, coated with saffron to protect them against the mosquitoes. They were always followed by packs of stray dogs. Wherever they went the children drew after them their stray companions, the dogs, gaunt, mangy, thieving, which the Malays chased away from their courtyards

with stones. The Malays never consented to eat these dogs
except in periods of great famine, so skinny and tough were
they. Only the children could stand their company. And the
dogs would have had no resort but to die, had they not followed the children, whose excrement was their main nourishment.

As soon as the sun went down the children disappeared
into the interior of their straw huts, where they slept on the
floors battened with bamboo, after having eaten their bowls
of rice. And from daybreak on, they invaded the plain anew,
always followed by the stray dogs that waited for them all
night, crouched between the wooden piles of the cabins, in
the hot and pestilential mud of the plain.

There were children as there were rains, fruits, floods.
They came each year, by periodical tides, or, if you like, by
crops or burgeonings. Every woman of the plain, as long
as she was young enough to be desired by her husband, had
her child each year. In the dry season, when the work in
the rice fields slowed down, the men thought especially of
love and the women were naturally taken at that season.
And during the following months the women's bellies grew
big. Thus, besides those who had already been born, there
were those who were still in the womb. This went on regularly, with the rhythm of plant-life, as if, in a deep, long inhalation, each year, the body of each woman took in and
swelled with child, expelled in an exhalation a child and
then, in a second inhalation, took in another.

Until the age of one year or thereabouts, the children
lived attached to their mothers, in a cotton bag tied at the
woman's waist and shoulders. Their heads were shaved
until the age of twelve, that is, until they were big enough
to delouse themselves, and they went naked also until about
that age. Then they covered themselves with a cotton loin-
cloth. At the age of one year, the mother cast them far from
her, entrusting them to the older children, not taking them
again except to feed them, to give them from her mouth the

rice which she had previously chewed. When, by chance, white people witnessed this, they turned away in disgust. The mothers laughed at this. What place had such squeamishness here on the plain? Children had been fed like that for a thousand years. It was one way of saving some of them from starvation. For they died in such numbers that the mud of the plain contained many more dead children than there were children who survived long enough to sing on the backs of the buffaloes. They died in such numbers that they were no longer mourned, and for many long years it had been the custom to bury them without ceremony. On coming back home from work, the father merely dug a little hole in front of the cabin and there laid his dead child. The children returned simply to the earth like wild mangoes falling from high branches or like the little dead monkeys found at the mouth of the *rac*. They died of cholera, which the green mango causes, but no one on the plain seemed to realize it. Every year, at the mango season, the children could be seen, perched in the branches or waiting hungrily under the trees, and in the following days they died in great number. And other children the next year took the place of these children on the same mango trees, and in the following days they died. For the eagerness of hungry children confronted with green mangoes is eternal. Some of the children drowned in the *rac*. Others, still, died of sunstroke or became blinded with the sun. Others filled themselves with the same worms that devoured the stray dogs and died, suffocated.

And it was very needful that they die, some of them. The plain was narrow and the sea would not recede for many centuries, contrary to what Ma always hoped. Each year the flood tides invaded the plain more or less, destroying each time a part of the crops and, the evil done, they retired. But whether the sea rose much or little, the children were always relentlessly born. It was very needful that some of them die. For if, during a few years only, the children of the plain had ceased to die, the plain would have been overrun with them to such an extent that, no doubt, for lack of the means to nourish them, it would have been necessary to give them to the dogs or perhaps to expose them at the edge of the forest. But even then, who knows, the tigers themselves might have ended up by not wanting to eat more of them! So they died, and they died in every way, while other children were always born. But the plain still did not produce what it could of rice, of fish, of mangoes, of forest, or what it could also have given of corn, of wild boars, of pepper. And the pink mouths of the children were always that many more mouths open with hunger.

Ma, during the first years of her sojourn on the plain, always kept one or two children under her care. But now she was sick and tired of such efforts. For with the children she had also been unlucky. The last one she had taken care of had been a little girl one year old that she had bought from a woman passing on the road.

The woman, who had a bad foot, had taken a week to walk from Ram. All along the road she had tried to give her child away. In the villages where she had stopped they had told her, "Go as far as Bante. A white woman lives there who takes an interest in children." The woman had managed to reach Ma's concession. She explained to Ma that her child was such a burden that she would be prevented by it from returning to her people in the North, that she would never be able to carry it that far. A terrible sore had eaten away her heel and a part of her foot. She said she loved her child so much that she had walked thirty-five kilometers on that ailing foot, to bring it to her. But she did not want any more of this. She wanted to find if possible a place on the top of a bus which would take her to the North. She had been doing porter's work in Ram for the past year.

Ma had kept the woman for a few days and had tried to cure the foot. For three days the woman had slept on a mat in the shade of the bungalow, waking only to eat and promptly going back to sleep, without even enquiring about her child. Then she had said goodby to Ma, who had given her a little money to take the bus a part of the way towards the North. Ma had wanted to give back the child to her but the woman was still young and pretty and wanted to live her life, so she had obstinately refused. Ma had kept the child, a little one-year-old girl who looked as though she were only three months old. It was obvious to Ma from the very first day that the child would not live long. However, for some strange reason, she had taken the notion of having a little cradle made for her, which she placed in her room, and she had also had clothes made for the child.

The little girl had lived three months. Then one morning, in effect, just when Ma was undressing her to wash her, Ma saw that her little feet were swollen. Ma did not wash the child that day but merely put her back into the cradle after caressing her tenderly. "It's the end," she said, "tomorrow it will be her legs and after that her heart." She had watched over the child for two days and the night preceding its death. The child breathed its last after vomiting worms—Ma had pulled some of them out of the child's throat, wrapping them around her finger.

Joseph had buried the dead child in a clearing on the mountain, using the cradle as coffin. Suzanne had refused to look at it. The death of that child had been worse than the death of the horse, worse than all else, worse than the broken sea wall, worse than Monsieur Jo, worse than all their bad luck put together. Ma, even though she had anticipated it, had wept for days and days, working herself into a rage, swearing she would never again do anything whatsoever for children.

Then, like everything else, she had begun all over again. However, she no longer took in children to live with her.

"Let her alone," said Suzanne, "no one can stop her from doing what she wants to do."

For the moment, Ma obliged Monsieur Jo and Suzanne to meet outdoors.

"No, really, I was never before treated like this," Monsieur Jo repeated.

And he stared at Ma with a look of hatred. Now, every day, he risked his life because of her. There was never any shade under the bridge and he felt he was in danger of sunstroke. When he acquainted Ma with this, she had replied: "One more reason for you to hurry up and marry her!"

"At present," he said to Suzanne, "the programs at the moving-picture houses are very good."

Suzanne, barefoot, was amusing herself trying to pick up sprigs of grass with her toes. On the bank, facing her, a buffalo browsed slowly and on its back there was a blackbird feasting on its lice. That was all the spectacle provided by the plain. That, and then the rice fields and more rice fields, spreading out and out, all alike, from Ram to Kam, under a gray sheet-metal sky.

"She'd never let us," said Suzanne.

Monsieur Jo snickered. In his own class, it was understood that girls kept their virginity until marriage. But he well knew that in other classes of society this was not the case. And he found that, considering the way these people lived, their strictness in regard to Suzanne was, to say the least, an affectation.

"The life you lead here is impossible," he said. "You haven't any youth. And she's forgotten hers."

Suzanne was certainly fed up with the plain, with those children forever dying, with that eternal and implacable sun, with these endless liquid spaces.

"That's not the question. She doesn't want me to sleep with you."

He did not reply.

"Would we go every evening to the movies?" Suzanne asked, after a pause.

"Every evening," Monsieur Jo assured her.

He had put a newspaper under himself so as not to soil his clothes. He perspired a great deal, but perhaps it was not so much because of the heat as from looking at the nape of Suzanne's neck, which showed pale beneath her hair. He had never touched it.

The others were watching them ferociously.

"Every evening to the movies?"

"Every evening," repeated Monsieur Jo.

For Suzanne, as for Joseph, to go every evening to the movies represented, along with motoring, one of the forms which human happiness could take. In sum, everything that carried you off, everything that bore you up—whether your soul or your body, whether along the roads or along the truer-than-life dream-paths of the silver screen, everything which could give the hope of living quickly the slow experience of adolescence—these things represented happiness. The two or three times they had gone to the city, they had spent almost their entire days at the movies, and they still recalled the pictures they had seen, talking of them with as much precision as if they were memories of real things they had experienced together.

"And after the movies?"

"We'd dance. Everyone would look at you. You would be the prettiest girl of all."

"That's not so sure. Then what?"

Never would Ma allow it. And even if she did, Joseph would never allow it.

"We would go to bed," said Monsieur Jo, "but I would not touch you."

"That's not so."

She no longer believed in that voyage. Anyway, she felt she had exhausted the surprises that Monsieur Jo could reserve for her, so it didn't matter. During the past few days she had again, mechanically, begun to watch for the cars that passed with the big-game hunters and she did so now, while talking to Monsieur Jo about the city, the movies, marriage.

"When are we going to marry?" she asked, no less automatically. "You don't have many more days left."

"I repeat," said Monsieur Jo, slowly, "that it will be when you have given me proof of your love. If you agree to take the trip with me, then when we return I shall make my proposal to your mother."

Suzanne laughed again and turned towards him. He lowered his eyes.

"That's not so," she said.

Monsieur Jo flushed.

"It's not yet time to speak of it," he went on. "It would be useless."

"Your father would cut you off, don't deny it."

Ma had coached Suzanne on this conversation with Monsieur Jo.

"Your father, he's a poor dope, and that's what Joseph says you are."

Monsieur Jo did not reply. He lit a cigarette with the air of waiting for the storm to pass. Suzanne yawned.

It was Ma who told her to put the question to him every day. Ma was in a hurry. Once Suzanne was married off, Monsieur Jo would give her the money needed to rebuild the sea walls, which, next time, would be twice as big as the others and would be reinforced with concrete. He would also give her the wherewithal to finish the bungalow, change the roof, buy another car, and have Joseph's teeth attended to. Now she held Suzanne responsible for the delay in all these projects. This marriage was necessary, she said. It was, moreover, their last chance to get out of the plain. If the marriage did not take place, it would be one more defeat, in a class with the sea walls.

Joseph always let Ma go on in this vein, then would conclude: "He'll never pop the question, and so much the better for her!" Suzanne knew that this marriage would never take place. She had nothing more to say to Monsieur Jo. A hundred times he had described his fortune and the cars she would have when they were married. Now, it was useless to talk about all this or about all the rest—that trip, that diamond.

She was suddenly terribly bored. She wished that Monsieur Jo would go away and that Joseph would come to ask her to swim with him in the *rac*. Ever since Monsieur Jo had come into their lives, she had scarcely ever been with her brother. First, because Joseph, as he said, "couldn't breathe" in Monsieur Jo's vicinity. Then, because he was in on Ma's plan to leave her and Monsieur Jo alone together as long as possible every day. Suzanne saw Joseph only at the Ram canteen where, sometimes, he invited her to dance and where, sometimes, they went for a swim in the sea. But since Monsieur Jo did not go sea bathing, Ma felt it unwise to inflict solitude upon him. She feared it might make him resentful. And, in truth, when they went into the sea at Ram, Monsieur Jo looked at Joseph with murderous eyes. But with a blow of the fist Joseph would be able to crush Monsieur Jo. It was so evident, when you saw them together, that Monsieur Jo himself must surely realize it. He was too weak, too light-weight for Joseph, and so he could just go on hating him in peace.

"I brought them," said Monsieur Jo calmly.

Suzanne started.

"What? The diamonds?"

"The diamonds. You can take your choice. You can always choose, there's no telling what may happen."

She looked skeptically at him. But already he had taken out of his pocket a small parcel wrapped in tissue paper and was undoing it slowly. Three pieces of tissue paper fell to the ground. Three rings were displayed in the palm of his hand. Suzanne had never seen diamonds except on the fin-

gers of others and even then, of all the people she had
seen wearing them, she had approached none except Monsieur Jo. The rings were there, empty rings, in the extended
hand of Monsieur Jo.

"They were my mother's," said Monsieur Jo, sentimen-
tally. "She was crazy about them."

No matter where they came from, Suzanne's fingers were
naked of rings. She held out her hand, took the ring which
had the largest stone, lifted it in the air and looked at it
gravely for a long time. She lowered her hand, spread it out,
and slipped the ring on her ring finger. Her eyes did not
leave the diamond. She smiled at it. When she had been a
little girl and her father was still alive, she had had two children's rings, one set with a tiny sapphire, the other with a
real pearl. They had been sold by Ma.

"How much is it worth?"

Monsieur Jo smiled. He had expected this.

"I don't know. Maybe twenty thousand francs."

Instinctively Suzanne glanced at Monsieur Jo's own ring.
The diamond in it was three times bigger than the one she
had. Why, then, it was impossible to imagine . . . It was
real, and it was a thing apart, this diamond. Its importance
lay not in its sparkle or in its beauty but in its price, in the
possibilities, unimaginable until then to her, of its value in
terms of money. It was an object, an intermediary between
the past and the future. It was a key which would open the
future and definitely seal the past. The diamond was limpid
water, through which showed the sparkling future. You entered it, a little blinded and dizzy. Ma owed 15,000 francs
at the bank. Before buying the concession she had given
lessons at 15 francs an hour, she had worked at the Eden
Cinema every night for ten years at 40 francs an evening.
At the end of ten years, with savings put aside from that,
she had managed to buy the concession. Suzanne knew all
these figures: the amount of the debts at the bank, the price
of gasoline, the price of each square meter of the sea walls,

the price of a piano lesson and of a pair of shoes. What she had not known till then was the price of a diamond. He had said, before showing it to her, that it alone was worth the entire bungalow. But this comparison had not been clear to her until this moment when she had slipped the ring upon her finger. She thought of all the prices she knew in comparison with this and, suddenly depressed, she lay back on the bank and closed her eyes upon this new knowledge. Monsieur Jo was amazed. But he must have acquired the habit by now of being amazed for he said nothing to her for a moment.

"Is that the one you like best?" he asked softly, at last.

"I don't know. It's the most expensive one that I want," said Suzanne.

"You only think of that," said Monsieur Jo, laughing a little cynically.

"It's the most expensive one I want," Suzanne repeated seriously.

"If you loved me," began Monsieur Jo, annoyed.

"Even if I loved you. It can't be helped, if ever you give it to me we will sell it."

Joseph was approaching from the distance, down the road. He had decided to find another horse and he had been running from village to village for a week. As soon as she perceived him, Suzanne sat up. Stridently and joyously she laughed, calling out to him and going towards him.

"Joseph! Come, look!"

Joseph approached her without hurrying. He was wearing a khaki shirt and shorts, his cap was on the back of his head as always, and he was barefoot. Ever since she had known Monsieur Jo, Suzanne thought that Joseph was handsomer than ever. When Joseph was very near, Suzanne held out her hand and Joseph saw the diamond above her extended fingers. He showed no surprise. A diamond was something perhaps too small. A car would surely have impressed him, but a diamond did not impress him in the least. Joseph did not yet know all these things about diamonds. Suzanne regretted the fact. He, too, would eventually learn.

After having looked absent-mindedly at the ring, Joseph spoke to her about his horse.

"Impossible to find any for less than five hundred francs. It's not a country for horses. Even horses can't live here, they've all died off."

Suzanne, standing close to him, showed her extended hand.

"Look!"

Joseph looked again.

"It's a ring," said Suzanne, "it's worth twenty thousand francs."

Again Joseph looked.

"Twenty thousand francs? I'll be damned!" said Joseph.

He began to smile. Then he reflected. Then, resolved to overcome his distaste, he went towards Monsieur Jo who was fifty yards away, under the bridge.

Suzanne followed him. He approached quite near Monsieur Jo, sat down beside him and began to look at him fixedly.

"Why did you give her that?" he asked at the end of a good minute.

Monsieur Jo, very pale, looked down at his feet. Suzanne interceded.

"He didn't give it to me," she said, looking at Monsieur Jo in her turn.

Joseph did not seem to understand.

"He lent it to me, like that, to try it on."

Joseph made a face and spat into the *rac*. Then again he stared at Monsieur Jo, who had begun to smoke. Having stared at him well, he spat again into the water. It went on. Joseph reflected, and punctuated his reflections by spitting into the water.

"If it's not going to be hers," he said at last, "then it's not worth talking about."

"There's no hurry," said Monsieur Jo, tonelessly.

"Give it back to him," said Joseph to Suzanne. Then, turning again towards Monsieur Jo: "You brought it here like that, just to show it to her?"

Monsieur Jo made an effort to say something but evidently could not find a word. Joseph, facing him, seemed to be holding back something. He had spoken quickly and roughly, but his voice had not been at all high-pitched. Monsieur Jo's face got whiter and whiter. Suzanne bounded up, faced Monsieur Jo and she, too, began to stare at him. If she didn't tell Joseph now and at once exactly what kind of person Monsieur Jo was, she felt she would never be able to say it. Anyway, it was already half done. Monsieur Jo would never be able to survive this blow. Well, she had had enough of it all. It had to finish one of these days.

"He will give it to me if I go away with him," said Suzanne.

Monsieur Jo lifted his hand as if to stop Suzanne. His face had grown still whiter.

"Go away where to?" asked Joseph.

"To the city."

"For good?"

"No, only for a week."

Monsieur Jo beat the air in a gesture of denial. He looked as though he were going to faint.

"Suzanne expresses herself badly . . ." said he, in a supplicating voice.

Joseph was no longer listening. He had turned towards the *rac*. From his expression, Suzanne knew that now it was certain she would never go away with Monsieur Jo, whether married or not.

"Give it back to him right off, or I'll chuck it into the river," said Joseph calmly.

Suzanne pulled the ring from her finger and held it out to Monsieur Jo behind Joseph's back. One couldn't let Joseph seize the ring and throw it into the river. On this

point, Suzanne felt she was on Monsieur Jo's side. The diamond must be saved. Monsieur Jo took the ring and thrust
it into his pocket. Turning, Joseph saw him do it. Without
a word, he stood up and went towards the bungalow.

"So that's the end of that," said Monsieur Jo after a minute's silence.

"Finished," said Suzanne. Then: "It's always like this."

"Why did you have to tell him?"

"I'd have told him sooner or later. I couldn't have kept
myself from telling him about the diamond."

They stayed there for a while without saying anything.
The night before, they had come home very late from Ram
and Suzanne now found that she was sleepy.

Monsieur Jo was in a state of almost complete collapse.
She looked at him and she looked at his car. It was standing
on the other side of the road, beyond the bridge. Truly, it
was a magnificent limousine. It would return to the North
from where it had come and Monsieur Jo would go with it.
But maybe he had not understood?

"I don't believe it's worth your while to come again,"
said Suzanne.

"It's terrible," affirmed Monsieur Jo. "Why did you have
to tell him?"

"I'd never seen a diamond, I couldn't help myself, you
oughtn't to have shown it to me. You can't understand."

"It's terrible," repeated Monsieur Jo.

In the sky some wild ducks and hungry crows were fly-
ing. Sometimes a duck dropped down and danced on the
troubled water of the *rac*. These are the things, thought
Suzanne, that I shall see for the next few months, this is all
I'll see of the world for months to come.

"Some day I'll surely find a big-game hunter, one that's
passing through," said Suzanne, "or maybe a planter from
nearby, or maybe a regular hunter who'll come to live in
Ram. Maybe Agosti will decide to come here."

"I cannot, it's impossible," groaned Monsieur Jo.

He seemed to be struggling against an insupportable idea. He was trembling violently.

"I cannot, I cannot," he repeated.

If only he'd get the dickens out of here, thought Suzanne, I'd go for a swim with Joseph.

"Suzanne!" cried Monsieur Jo, as loudly as if she had already gone.

He had stood up and he seemed to be delivered of some weight. Exultant, jovial, he had found a solution to the problem.

"I'll give it to you, all the same!" he cried. "Go tell Joseph."

Suzanne also got to her feet. He had taken out the ring and was holding it out to her. She looked at it once more. It was hers! She took it, did not put it on her finger but shut her hand over it and, without saying goodby to Monsieur Jo, she ran towards the bungalow.

SUZANNE HAD COME RUNNING INTO THE BUNGALOW. JOSEPH had not been there. But she had found Ma busy getting dinner, standing by the stove. She had brandished the ring at her.

"Look, a ring. Twenty thousand francs. And he gave it to me."

Ma had looked, staying at a slight distance. And she had not said a thing.

Monsieur Jo had waited under the bridge for Suzanne to come back, but when she did not return, he had gone off.

An hour afterwards, a little before they sat down to the table, Ma had gently asked Suzanne to hand the ring to her so she could have a better look. Joseph, who was in the sitting room at the time, had heard the request.

"Give it to me," she had said gently. "I barely looked at it."

Suzanne had held out the ring. Ma had taken it and had contemplated it for a long time in the hollow of her hand. Then, without a word, she had gone to her room and shut the door. By her most unmistakable expression of assumed wrath, as she left the dining room, Joseph and Suzanne had understood: she had gone to hide the ring. She hid everything: quinine, canned goods, tobacco, everything that could be bought or sold. She had hidden it in the supersti-

tious fear of seeing it slip away from the too youthful hands
of Suzanne. Now the ring must be somewhere between the
laths of the wall or in the bag of rice or in her mattress or
maybe attached by a string round her neck and hidden
under her dress.

There was no further mention of it until dinner. Suzanne
and Joseph sat down at the table. But Ma did not. She sat
at a distance from the table, against the wall, in an armchair.

"Come, eat," said Joseph.

"Leave me alone," said Ma. Her voice was mean.

She did not eat, not even a piece of bread and butter,
and she did not even ask for her usual coffee. Joseph
watched her in a worried way. She, for her part, did not
look at anything, but stared vacantly and wrathfully at the
floor. That she should sit apart like that, against the wall,
while they ate, Joseph could not endure, no matter what the
reason was, no matter what.

"Why are you making such a face?" asked Joseph.

Her face went red and she screamed:

"That fellow's disgusting, disgusting, and he'll never see
his ring again!"

"We're not talking about that," said Joseph, "we're asking
you to eat."

She stamped her foot and again, at the top of her voice,
yelled:

"Anyway, what's it all about? Anyone in our place would
keep it."

Then, once more, she grew silent. A moment passed.
Joseph began again:

"You got to drink your coffee! At least, drink your coffee."

"I'll not drink my coffee, because I'm old and I'm tired
and I'm fed up, fed up with having such children as I have!"

She hesitated. Again very red in the face, her eyes became blurred with tears.

"To have such a slut of a daughter as that one, there . . ." she said. Then she took up her new refrain: "There's nothing more disgusting than a jewel. It's worth nothing, nothing. And the people who wear them don't need them, they need them less than anyone!"

Again she was silent and remained so long thus that they could have believed she had calmed down, except for that rigidity of her whole body. Joseph did not urge her again to eat. It was the first time in her life that Ma had had in her hands a thing worth twenty thousand francs. "Give it to me," she had said gently. Suzanne had given it to her. She had looked at it for a long time and she had become intoxicated with it. Twenty thousand francs. Twice the amount of the mortgage on the bungalow! Joseph, while she had looked at it, had turned his eyes away. Without a word, she had gone to hide it in her room. And now, she could not eat.

"Give him back his ring—a degenerate like that? After all the nasty things he came here to do? It would be a shame and a disgrace!"

Neither Suzanne nor Joseph dared to look at her or answer her. She was sick at the thought of having taken the ring as she had taken it, and of having kept it. For it was already impossible for her to return it, of that she was sure. So she kept on like an idiot repeating the same things, staring at the floor, ashamed. It was hard to look at her. Oh, what had Suzanne done when she showed her that ring? What youthfulness, what old suppressed ardor, what recrudescence of what lusts until then unsuspected had suddenly been awakened in her at the sight of the ring? Already, she had decided to keep it.

The storm burst when Suzanne got up from the table. Then it was that Ma had stood, had flung herself at Suzanne, had hit her with her fists, using all the strength that remained in her. With all the strength of her convictions, and also of her misgivings. While beating Suzanne, she had talked about the sea walls, about the debts, her illness, the roof, the piano lessons, the cadastral agents, her old age, her fatigue, and her death.

Joseph had not protested and had let her beat Suzanne. It lasted a good two hours. She stood, she flung herself upon Suzanne, and then she collapsed in her chair, worn out, exhausted, calmed. Then again she stood and again she flung herself upon Suzanne.

"Tell me the truth, and I'll let you alone."

"I did not sleep with him. He gave it to me like that, I didn't even ask for it, he showed it to me and he gave it to me, like that, for nothing."

Ma showered blows upon her again, as if driven by an irresistible compulsion. Suzanne, at her feet, half naked in her torn dress, wept. When she tried to raise herself, Ma kicked her down and shouted:

"For God's sake, tell me, and I'll leave you alone."

What she could not endure, it seemed, was to see Suzanne try to rise. As soon as Suzanne made one movement, Ma hit her. Realizing this, Suzanne, her head in her arms, did nothing but protect herself, patiently. She forgot that this force came from her mother, she endured it as she would have endured the wind, the waves, or any impersonal force. It was when Ma fell back again in her chair that she was again frightened of her, because of that face dazed with effort.

"Tell me," Ma repeated, and sometimes she said the words almost calmly.

Suzanne no longer replied. Ma got tired and forgot. Sometimes she yawned, and at one go her eyelids closed and her head sank back. But at the least movement from Suzanne, or simply when she opened her eyes, wakened by the jerking of her own head, and when she saw Suzanne at her feet, Ma stood up and hit her again.

Joseph leafed through *Hollywood-Cinema*, the only book —and it was six years old—that had ever been in the family

and of which he never tired. When Ma hit Suzanne, he
stopped leafing through the album. Then, suddenly, he
said:

"God damn it, you know she didn't sleep with him! So
why do you go on?"

"And suppose I want to kill her? Suppose it would please
me to kill her?"

Joseph stayed, because he did not want to leave Suzanne
alone with Ma in that state. That was certain. Perhaps
even he himself was not quite sure. After he had shouted,
Ma had hit Suzanne again, but less hard, and every time
she had a go at beating Suzanne it was for a shorter period.
So then, Joseph, each time, had again bawled her out.

"And even if she did sleep with him, what the hell?"

Yes, she was now hitting with less assurance. It was quite
two years since she had beaten Joseph. Before that, she had
often beaten him, until that day when he had grabbed her
by the arm and gently immobilized her. Stupefied, at first,
she had ended up by laughing uproariously with him, fun-
damentally glad to see that he had grown so strong. Since
then, she had not beaten him, not entirely because she
feared him but because Joseph had told her he would not
tolerate it any more. Joseph thought you had to beat your
children, especially your daughters, but not too hard and
only as a final resort. But since the crumbling of the sea walls
and since she no longer beat Joseph, Ma beat Suzanne much
oftener than before. "When she won't have anyone else to
take a punch at," Joseph had once said, "she'll take a punch
at herself."

Joseph would stay as long as Ma did not go to bed, that
was certain, Suzanne was sure of it.

"And even if she did sleep with him for the ring," said
Joseph, "I'd say it was a good job!"

Suzanne heard this and suddenly felt satisfied and tranquil. Ma could do what she would: the ring was there, in
the house. There were twenty thousand francs in the house.

That was what counted. Ma must already know what she intended to do with it. She couldn't be questioned tonight, but from tomorrow on they would doubtless speak freely about it. To hand it back was already impossible. Usually Suzanne could almost not endure a beating, but tonight she felt it was better for Ma to beat her, better than for Ma to have taken the ring and then to have come back calmly to the table, as if nothing had happened.

"A ring. What's a ring? It's a duty, in some cases, to keep a ring."

"And how!" said Joseph.

Who could have any other opinion? Maybe they would go buy a new car and rebuild a part of the sea walls. And maybe, from this ring onward, they would become rich with a wealth that would even surpass Monsieur Jo's. Ma could scold all she liked.

That night was a big night. They'd been able to extract that ring from Monsieur Jo and now it was there, somewhere in the house, and already no force in the world could take it away from them. That night had been a long time in coming, but here it was, it had arrived at last! And none too soon, since for years all projects had failed, one after the other. It was their first success—not a piece of luck, but a success. They had earned that ring, if only by the long years they had waited for it. A long wait it had been, but now at last success—and the ring—were there, on their side, in their part of the world. They had the ring. And it had been simply to approach her, to continue to be near her in the shadow of the bridge that the other had released his hold on it. But that victory, ah, that one, which resisted all blows, she could not share it with anyone, not even Joseph.

"What's a ring?" Ma repeated. "Nothing. To refuse it, in my case, would be a crime."

Who could think otherwise? Who, in the world, could think otherwise? Not to want it when it was offered to you would be simply unimaginable. There were enough gems that remained useless in beautiful jewel cases, while people in the world needed them so much. The one they had was beginning its career, henceforth freed and fecund. And, for the first time since the bloody hands of a black man had extracted the gem from its stony bed in one of those nightmare rivers of the Congo, it was released, delivered at last from the inhuman and concupiscent hands of its jailers.

Ma had stopped striking Suzanne. Listlessly, deep in thought, she was doubtless reflecting as to what she would do with the ring.

"Maybe we could trade in the old car for a new one," said Suzanne softly.

Joseph abandoned *Hollywood-Cinema* and placed it on the table. He, too, was reflecting. But Ma shot a glance at her daughter and again began shrilly to scold her.

"We'll not get a new car. We'll pay the bank, maybe the *Crédit Foncier*, and we will put on a new roof. We'll do what I want to do."

Then it was not over with, as one would have imagined. It would be necessary to wait a little longer.

But why, just at the sight of her smile, why was Ma impelled to shower blows on Suzanne again? Getting up, she flung herself upon Suzanne and knocked her over. Then she sank back, exhausted.

"I'm worn out," she said. "I ought to be in bed . . ."

Suzanne raised her head and looked at Ma.

"All right. I slept with him," she said, "and for that he gave me the ring."

She is going to kill me, thought Suzanne, and even Joseph won't be able to stop her. But Ma stared at Suzanne, her arms uplifted, as if ready to fling herself once more upon her, then she let her arms fall and said calmly:

"That's not true. You're a liar."

Joseph got up and went over to Ma.

"If you touch her again," he said softly, "just one single

time more, I'll clear out of here and take her with me to
Ram. You're an old crackpot, now I'm sure of it."

Ma looked at Joseph. Maybe if he had laughed she would
have laughed with him. But he did not laugh. So she stayed
in her chair, dazed and bewildered, unrecognizable with
sorrow. Suzanne, stretched out on the floor beside Joseph's
chair, was crying. Why had Ma begun beating her again?
Maybe she was insane. Life was terrible and Ma was as
terrible as life. Joseph had sat down again and it was now
at Suzanne that he looked. The only sweetness in her life—
he, Joseph, was that. Having discovered that sweetness, so
reserved, so buried beneath so much harshness, Suzanne
realized at the same time all the blows and the patience that
had been needed and no doubt would still be needed for it
to be brought into the open. And so she wept.

Soon Ma was completely asleep. And suddenly, her head
sunk forward, her mouth open, she was drifting in the milk
of sleep, floating lightly in entire innocence. You could not
now hold a grudge against her. She had loved life beyond
measure and it was her indefatigable and incurable hope-
fulness that had made her become a desperate woman, desperate of hope itself. That hope had worn her down, destroyed her, stripped her naked to such an extent that even
her sleep, which gave her some rest from it, even death perhaps could never take her beyond it.

Suzanne crawled towards the door of Joseph's bedroom
and waited to see what he was going to do.

He sat for some time looking at Ma sleeping, his hands
clutching the arms of his chair, his forehead wrinkled. Then
he stood up and went over to her.

"Go to bed, you'll be better off in your bed."

Ma woke up with a start and looked round her.

"Where is she?"

"Go to bed . . . She did not sleep with him."

He kissed her on the forehead. Suzanne had never seen

him kiss her except in those comas that followed her attacks when he believed she was going to die.

"God help me," said Ma, weeping. "I know it. I well know it."

Holding her head in her hands, she wept.

"God help me! I'm an old madwoman."

Joseph raised her up and led her into her bedroom. Suzanne could see no more, then, so she went to sit on Joseph's bed and wait for him. He was putting Ma to bed, she supposed. At the end of a minute he came back into the dining room, took the lamp, and joined his sister. Putting the lamp down on the floor, he sat on a bag of rice at the foot of his bed.

"She's gone to bed," he said. "You go too."

Suzanne would have preferred to wait. It was not often that she entered Joseph's bedroom. The barest room in the bungalow, there was no furniture in it except for Joseph's bed. However, the walls were covered with guns and the pelts he himself tanned, pelts which, decaying slowly, gave forth a sickly and nauseating odor. On the other side, at the far end of the room towards the *rac*, was the store-cupboard which Ma had had built into a portion of the verandah. There, for six years, she had accumulated canned things, condensed milk, wine, quinine, and tobacco. She carried the key to the cupboard on her, night and day, on a string around her neck. Maybe the ring was already in there, hidden behind a can of condensed milk.

Suzanne no longer cried. She was thinking about Joseph. He was seated on a bag of rice in the midst of these things to which he was still attached more than to anything else: his pelts, his guns. Joseph was a hunter, and only that. He still made more mistakes in spelling than she did. Ma had always said he was not made for study, that he was intelligent only in such things as automobiles and hunting. Possibly she was right. But possibly she said it only to justify herself for not having made him go on with his studies. Ever since they had arrived on the plain, Joseph had hunted. At fourteen he had begun to hunt at night, constructing for himself lookouts and going off without a single guide, barefoot, slipping away from Ma. There was nothing in the world he liked to do so much as to wait for a black panther at the mouth of the *rac*. He could wait whole nights and days on end for panthers and tigers, all alone, in no matter what weather, lying flat in the slimy mud. Once he had waited three days and two nights and had come back with a two-year-old black panther. He had placed it in the prow of his boat and all the peasants had gathered on the banks of the *rac* to see him pass.

When he was meditating as now, this evening, with difficulty and with disgust, you could not help but think him very handsome, you could not help but love him very much.

"Go," said Joseph again, "and don't you cry."

He looked tired. He told her to go and then immediately afterwards he obviously forgot she was there.

"Fed up?" asked Suzanne.

He raised his eyes, saw her sitting there on the edge of his bed in her torn dress.

"It's nothing. Did she hurt you?"

"That's not it . . ."

"You fed up, too?"

"Oh, I don't know."

"What's bothering you?"

"Everything," said Suzanne. "I'm like you, I don't know."

"Hell," said Joseph, "we've got to think about her, too. She's old, we can't imagine, and she's more fed up than we are. And for her, it's finished . . ."

"What's finished?"

"Fun. Good times. She never had much fun and she'll never have any now, she's too old for it now, there's not much time left to her . . . Go, go to bed. I want to lie down."

Suzanne stood up. As she went out, Joseph asked her:

"Did you sleep with him or didn't you?"

"No, I didn't sleep with him."

"I believe you. It's not just the business of you going to bed with a man. But he's not the one to go to bed with, he's a swine. And tomorrow you've got to tell him not ever to come here again."

"Never again?"

"Never again."

"So then, what will happen?"

"I don't know," said Joseph. "We'll see."

8

NEXT DAY MONSIEUR JO CAME AS USUAL. SUZANNE WAITED
for him at the head of the bridge.

As soon as she heard the honking of the Léon Bollée horn,
Ma stopped work on her banana trees and looked up the
road. She still had hope that everything might be settled
satisfactorily. Joseph, who was washing the car in a *marigot*
on the other side of the bridge, stood up and, with his back
turned towards the road, fixed Ma with a significant stare,
to prevent her from going towards Monsieur Jo.

Suzanne, barefoot, was wearing one of Ma's old blue cotton dresses, made over. She had hidden the dress Monsieur
Jo had given her. Now she had only her red toenails and
fingernails as souvenirs of their encounter.

It was at the noon meal that Joseph had announced his
decision to finish with Monsieur Jo and his visits to Suzanne.

"He needn't come here any more," said Joseph. "Suzanne's got to tell him once and for all."

It had been hard. From the time she woke up that morning, Ma had been simmering with plans. She was the one,
she pretended, who had decided to go to the city to sell the
ring. Joseph had willingly allowed this. He had not mentioned, early in the morning, the proposed rupture with
Monsieur Jo. Alone with Suzanne, Ma had again asked the

117

price of the ring. Twenty thousand francs, Suzanne had replied. Then Ma had come to ask her if she believed that Monsieur Jo had many other rings to dispose of that easily. Suzanne had told her he had let her choose one of three rings, that the other two were just as beautiful although not as big as that one, but that he had not implied he could give her the other two. He had always mentioned giving her one ring only.

"With those three rings, we'd be saved. If you could explain to him, maybe he'd understand, and we'd be saved."

"What the dickens does he care whether we're saved or not?"

Ma couldn't bring herself to believe that.

"If you explained it rightly to him, giving him the figures, it's impossible he wouldn't understand. To him, the rings don't mean much, do they? He can't wear them all at once. But if we had them, we'd be saved."

Suzanne had forewarned Joseph, but he had persisted in his decision to break with Monsieur Jo. He had announced this to Ma at lunchtime.

"Finished?" Ma had asked. "What business is it of yours?"

Joseph had replied calmly.

"Finished. If she won't tell him then I'm the one that's going to tell him."

Ma had flushed very red and had left the table, after giving Suzanne a questioning look, as if wanting her to say something. But Suzanne had kept her eyes down and had gone on eating. Then Ma had realized that the two were in league against her and she had despaired. Standing between the two, undone at one blow, she had screamed at them. But she had screamed less violently than usual, with a kind of timidity.

"So then? What's going to happen to us?"

"We'll see," Joseph had said gently. "Always, the hunters land here without any women. On the altitude there are

loads of hunters, and in the North, too. We'll find someone.
Maybe we can go there. But no matter what, it's finished
with Monsieur Jo."

Ma had continued to stand out, although from Joseph's
tone it was clearly useless.

"Those hunters," she had said, "they're a famished lot.
But with him I'd have had some peace."

Joseph had argued with her, but gently. He had stood up
and drawn near her. Suzanne had kept her eyes down, not
daring to look at them.

"Listen," Joseph had said. "Didn't you ever look at the
guy? My sister's not going to sleep with him. Even if she
don't have anything, I don't want him to be the man she
sleeps with."

Ma had sat down again. She had tried to get round him.

"I don't think Suzanne ought to break with him at once.
Better wait a little. What do you think, Suzanne?"

Joseph had become firmer, but still had not spoken about
the ring.

"It's got to be now," he had said. "Don't ask her what she
thinks. She hasn't ever slept with a man. She can't know
what it would be like."

"She must say what she thinks."

"I'd rather have a hunter," Suzanne had said.

"Yes, always your hunters and their misery! We'll never
find a way out."

No one had replied. And afterwards they had not spoken
of it again.

Then, at the usual hour, Monsieur Jo came over the
bridge, seated in the back of his magnificent limousine. It
had rained in the night and the car was all splattered with
mud. But Monsieur Jo came, no matter what the weather
and at fifty kilometers an hour to see Suzanne.

As soon as he glimpsed her he had the car stop near the
bridge. Suzanne went towards the car door and Monsieur Jo

got out at once. He was dressed in his silk suit. Never had Joseph had a silk suit. All of Monsieur Jo's suits were silk. When they were ever so slightly used, Monsieur Jo gave them to his chauffeur. He said tussore silk was cooler than cotton and that he would never have been able to stand anything else because he had a tender skin. There were certainly great differences between them and Monsieur Jo.

"You were waiting for me!" said Monsieur Jo. "That's nice of you."

Suzanne stood there quite near him. He took her hand and kissed it. He had not yet seen Ma and Joseph who, motionless, were waiting. Usually they worked harder, so as not to have to acknowledge his presence. Suzanne withdrew her hand from Monsieur Jo's and remained standing.

"I came to meet you to tell you not to come again to see me."

Monsieur Jo's expression altered. He lifted his hat, then put it on again, staring at Suzanne in bewilderment.

"What's this?"

His voice was suddenly subdued. He sat down on the bank, without worrying about getting his clothes dirty, without taking his newspaper from his pocket and spreading it on the ground as he usually did. Suzanne, still standing close to him, waited for him to comprehend. At a distance, Ma and Joseph were also waiting. Monsieur Jo ended up by perceiving them. Ma doubtless still hoped that things would be satisfactorily arranged and that Monsieur Jo, with this threat to help him, would return, but with his pockets full of diamonds, the better to pay amends. Joseph, because of Ma, hoped that Monsieur Jo would very quickly understand.

"You must not come here again," said Suzanne. "You must never come back at all."

He seemed scarcely to hear. He had begun to perspire and he continued to take off and put on his felt hat as if, from then on, he would never find any other gesture to

make. He looked from Suzanne to Ma and from Ma to
Joseph, from Suzanne to Joseph, and so on without stopping. Lost in hypothetical explanations, he tried to comprehend. He had been told that he could never come back, on
the very day after he had given the diamond. So, he continued to take off his hat and put it on again. It was clear
he'd not stop doing that until he could understand.

"Who decided this?" he asked in a stronger voice.

"She did," said Suzanne.

"Your mother?" asked Monsieur Jo again, completely
skeptical.

"She did. And Joseph agrees with her."

Monsieur Jo again threw a look towards Ma. She was still
looking at him with eyes of love. It could not have been
Ma.

"What happened?"

If only he would go away from here, thought Suzanne,
I'd go over to Joseph. Today Monsieur Jo was like his car
and his car was like him—they were the same thing. Yesterday the car still meant something to her, she was not indifferent to it as long as it was not utterly impossible that one
day they would own it. But today the car seemed to have
no relation to her, they were far apart. No thread, however
fine, attached her now to that car. The car had become ugly
and cumbrous. She wanted it to go away.

"They don't like you. And then, it's on account of the
ring."

Monsieur Jo took off his hat and continued to reflect.

"But since I gave it to you, like that, for nothing . . ."

"It's hard to explain."

Monsieur Jo put on his hat again, without result. He did
not get the point. He did not look ready to go, though, but
still waited for the thing to be explained. He had time. She
hadn't. Ma, seeing him go on prolonging the interview,
must be strengthened from minute to minute in her hopes.

"It's terrible," said Monsieur Jo. "It's unjust."

He seemed to be suffering a great deal. But his suffering was like his car, it was bothersome and uglier than usual. And no thread, however fine, could now hold him to her.

"You must go," said Suzanne.

Cynical, of a sudden, he began to laugh a forced laugh.

"What about the ring?"

It was Suzanne's turn to laugh. If he tried to take back the ring, this was going to be hilariously funny. Monsieur Jo was a fool. Rich as he was, beside them, he was an innocent child. He thought they were capable of giving back the ring to him! Suzanne laughed a fresh and natural laugh.

"I'm the one that's got it," said Suzanne.

"Well, then, let's see," said Monsieur Jo, whose cynicism now held a certain malice, "tell me just what you intend to do with it?"

Suzanne laughed again. Monsieur Jo's millions did nothing to alter his native stupidity. Why, that ring was now as much theirs and as difficult to take back as if they had eaten it and absorbed it into their flesh.

"Tomorrow we're going to the city to sell it."

Monsieur Jo said, "Well, well," without stopping, as if everything could be cleared up with a snicker which was, just possibly, significant. Then he said:

"Supposing I take it back?"

"You can't do that. Now, you must go away."

He stopped laughing. After giving her a long look, he flushed fiery red. He had not understood a thing. He took off his hat and spoke in a changed, sad voice.

"You did not love me. All you wanted was the ring."

"I didn't want the ring specially. I'd never have thought of it. You were the one that talked about it. I wanted a lot more than that. But now that we have the ring, I'd almost do anything, I think I'd rather throw it into the *rac* than give it back to you."

He could not force himself to get up and go. He still reflected. Time passed. Suzanne had to call him back to his senses.

"You must go," she said.

"You are profoundly immoral," said Monsieur Jo in a tone of deep conviction.

"We're like that. You must go."

He got up painfully. As he grasped the handle of the car door he waited a moment, then emitted a threat.

"It won't finish this way. Tomorrow I'll be in the city, too."

"It's not worth your trouble, going there won't do you a bit of good."

He got into the car at last and said something to the chauffeur, who began to make an abrupt turn. The road was narrow and it took him some time to do this, and a great deal of effort. Usually the car turned at two goes, using the drive which led to the bungalow. Today, with great dignity, it avoided using that road. All the same, from the edge of the *marigot*, Joseph observed the manoeuvre. Ma, still motionless and as if crucified was watching the irremediable departure of Monsieur Jo. Before his car had completely turned, she went running into the bungalow.

Suzanne walked down towards Joseph. When the limousine passed her she caught a furtive glimpse of Monsieur Jo, who gave her an imploring look through the car window. She turned aside, crossing the rice field to reach Joseph more quickly.

He had finished washing the B-12. Now he was pumping up the tires.

"That's that," said Suzanne.

"And not any too soon . . ."

The tire Joseph was working on had three punctures. The inner tube was still good and Joseph had put pieces of an old tire between it and the tire, so as to reinforce it. He pumped it up well so that the pieces would not slip.

Suzanne sat down at the edge of the *marigot* and watched him pump.

"You going to be long?" she asked.

"About half an hour. Why?"

"Oh, nothing."

It was very hot. Suzanne stopped watching Joseph's work, turned round, raised her skirt, and dipped her legs into the water. Then, with her hands, she splashed her legs up to the thighs. It was delightful. She suddenly realized that she had been waiting a whole month to be able to lift her skirt with impunity and dip her legs in the water. Her movement wrinkled the surface of the stagnant pond, frightening the fish. She had a fleeting desire to go to the bungalow for a fishing rod but did not dare go in without Joseph.

When the first tire was pumped up, Joseph attacked the spare tire, which was punctured. He took out the inner tube. You could never help Joseph when he was working on the B-12. From time to time he swore.

"Hell, blast and damn this whore of an old jalopy!"

In the pool, the mountain was reflected in undulating lines against a gray-white sky. It was going to rain again to-night. From the direction of the sea big purple clouds were mounting. Tomorrow it would be cool after the night's storm. They would arrive in the city late in the evening, that is if they didn't have a blowout on the way. They would sell the ring next morning, the first thing. The city was full of men. "Who's that pretty girl there?" "She comes from the South, no one knows who she is." Say what she liked, Ma was wrong. Surely, a man would be found for Suzanne somewhere in the city. Maybe a hunter, maybe a planter, but surely there was one for her.

Joseph had finished pumping up the tire.

"Want to go to the mountain with me? We'll go look for some chickens to eat on the way tomorrow."

Suzanne rose and laughed up at Joseph.

"Yes, yes, let's go now, Joseph."

"I'll put the car under the bungalow first, then we'll go."

It had been a long time, too, since Joseph had been to the city, and at the idea of going there he was happy.

Joseph stored the car under the bungalow but avoided going up into the house. It was undoubtedly still too soon after Monsieur Jo's departure. So, for once, Joseph decided to go into the forest without his gun.

They traversed the part of the plain which separated the bungalow from the road and from the mountain. The terrain began to slope gradually upwards and the rice fields disappeared, being replaced by a tall, coarse grass called "tiger grass" which the wild beasts crossed in their descent from the mountain at night. It took them a half-hour to reach the forest.

"What did he say to you?" asked Joseph.

"He said he was going to the city, too."

Joseph began to laugh. He seemed to be happy.

The path narrowed, the slope became steeper, and the forest announced itself in a clearing where browsed some goats and pigs. They went through a village most miserably composed of a few cabins. Immediately afterwards, the forest began, perfectly delineated by the cleared land bordering it. The inhabitants of the plain had never broken new ground beyond that line. It was useless, for the lands where pepper plantations could thrive were much higher in the mountain and the people here did not need much grazing land for the few goats they had.

"And what about the ring?" asked Joseph again.

Suzanne hesitated a little.

"He didn't say anything to me."

As soon as they had penetrated the forest, the path became very narrow, no wider than a man's chest and like a tunnel, enclosed by the forest, dense and somber.

"He's a dope," said Joseph. "Not mean, but just an awful dope."

The snakelike liana and the orchids in a monstrous, un-
natural invasion, hemmed in the forest, making of it a compact mass as inviolable and suffocating as the depths of the
sea. Lianas several hundred meters long lashed the trees together, and in the treetops, in the freest blooming imagi-
nable, immense "basins" of orchids, in the full light of the
sky, ejected a sumptuous florescence of which only the
edges could sometimes be seen. The forest rested under a
vast ramification of these orchid basins, holding rainwater,
and in which could be found the same fish as those in the
marigots of the plain.

"He said we were immoral," said Suzanne.

Joseph laughed again.

"We sure are that!" he said.

From all the forest rose the tremendous hum of mosquitoes, mingled with the sharp and incessant cheeping of
birds. Joseph led the way and Suzanne followed two steps
behind. Halfway between the plain and the village of wood-
cutters to which they were going, Joseph slowed down. A
few months before, in this same spot, he had killed a male
panther. It was a small clearing in full sunlight. Clouds of
flies danced above the yellow grass of the clearing, in the
midst of which were piles of dried and stinking feathers.

"Maybe I ought to have explained it to him, myself," said
Joseph. "I'll bet he didn't understand anything at all."

"Explained what?"

"Why we don't want you to sleep with him. It's hard to
understand, when you have as much dough as he has."

A little beyond the *rac*, which flowed through the clearing, they began to smell the resinous odor of mango trees
and to hear the cries of children. There was no more sunlight in this part of the mountain. And already the perfume
of the world came forth from the earth, the odor of flowers
of every kind, of assassin tigers and their innocent prey
with their flesh mellowed by the sun, in a chaotic, creation-
of-the-world intermingling.

The children gave them some mangoes and they helped the children catch the chickens. Then, while the women cut the birds' throats, Joseph asked the men if hunting was good at the time. Everyone was happy to see them. The men knew Joseph well, for they had often hunted with him. They asked about Ma, for it was from these villagers that she had procured the wood for the bungalow. They were all wood-cutters. They had fled the plain to settle here in this part of the forest as yet unsurveyed by the whites, so as to avoid the payment of taxes and the risk of being expropriated.

The children accompanied Suzanne and Joseph as far as the *rac*. Completely naked and rubbed with saffron from head to foot, they had the color and smoothness of young mangoes. A little before they reached the mountain torrent, Joseph clapped his hands to shoo them away. So savage were they that they fled like frightened birds, and indeed their strident cries recalled those of certain birds of the paddies. So many children died in these malarial-infested villages that Ma had given up ever going there, had not been there for two years, now. And many of them died without ever having known the joys of the road, died before they had the strength to walk the two kilometers of forest which separated them from the road.

Ma, seated in the dining room, had not yet lit the acety-lene lamp. She remained in the shadow, near the stove on which a ragout of stilt-bird simmered. No doubt she had seen them go off towards the mountain and had remarked that Joseph did not have his gun. For an hour she had been on the lookout for them. That she had not lit the lamp was surely so she could see them at a distance and not be blinded by the light. But when Suzanne and Joseph came in, she did not address a word to them.

"We went to get some chickens for the trip," said Joseph.

She did not reply. Joseph lit the lamp and took the chick-ens down to the Corporal to cook them. He returned up the

steps, whistling "Ramona." Whereupon, Suzanne also began
to whistle the tune. Ma, dazzled by the light, squinted and
smiled at her children. Joseph smiled back at her. It was
clear that she was not in the least angry and that she was
simply dejected because the diamond that she had hidden
would be the only one in her life, now that the source of
such things was dried up.

"We went to get some chickens to feed us on the way,"
Joseph repeated.

"You know where? In the village beyond the *rac*," said
Suzanne, "the second after the clearing."

"It's a long time since I've gone up there," said Ma, "but
I know the village you mean."

"They asked about you," said Joseph.

"You went without a gun," said Ma. "A risky thing to do."

"We wanted to get there quick," said Joseph.

Joseph went into the sitting room and began to wind up
Monsieur Jo's Victrola. Suzanne followed him. Ma got up
and put two plates on the table. Her movements were slow,
as if her long waiting in the darkness had ossified her to
the very soul. She turned out the stove and put a big cup
of black coffee between the two plates. Suzanne and Joseph
watched her, hopefully, as they had watched the old horse.
You could almost believe she was smiling, but it was rather her lassitude which softened her features, lassitude and
renunciation.

"Come, eat. Dinner's ready."

She put the ragout of stilt-bird on the table and sat down
heavily in front of the cup of coffee. Then she yawned, long
and silently, as she always did at that time of the evening.
Joseph helped himself to the ragout, then served Suzanne.
Ma began to undo her braids and to braid them up again
for the night. She did not appear to be hungry. Everything
was so calm this evening that you could hear the dull cracking of the wooden planks of the walls as they warped and

buckled. The house was solid, you could not deny it, the house held up, but Ma had been in too great a hurry to build it and the wood had been worked while too green. Many of the boards had split and they were disjointed one from the other to such an extent that often now, from your bed, you could see the daybreak through the cracks and, at night, when the hunters came back from Ram, their head-lights swept the walls of the bedrooms. But Ma was the only one to complain about this inconvenience. Suzanne and Joseph liked these conditions. On the side towards the sea, the sky was kindled with great streaks of red lightning. It was going to rain. Joseph was eating ravenously.

"It's great," he said.

"It's good," said Suzanne. "It's wonderful."

Ma smiled. When they ate with appetite she was always happy.

"I put in a drop of white wine, that's why."

She had made the ragout while waiting for them to return from the mountain. She must have gone to the store-cupboard, uncorked a bottle of white wine, and poured some of it religiously into the ragout. Whenever she had been too harsh with Suzanne or even sometimes when she was more than usually depressed, or when she was fed up with things, she would make a tapioca pudding with con-densed milk or banana fritters or a ragout of stilt-bird. She always kept such pleasures in reserve for the bad days.

"If you like it, I'll make it again sometime."

They each took another helping. Then she relaxed completely.

"What did you say to him?"

Joseph did not turn a hair.

"I explained things to him," said Suzanne, without raising her eyes.

"He didn't say anything?"

"He understood."

Ma reflected.

"What about the ring?"

"He said I could have it. For him, a ring isn't anything at all."

Ma waited a little more.

"What do you think, Joseph?"

Joseph hesitated. Then he declared in an unexpectedly firm voice:

"She'll be able to get any man she likes. Before, I didn't think so, but now I'm sure. You needn't worry any more about her."

Suzanne considered Joseph with stupefaction. You could never know what he was thinking. Maybe he was talking only to reassure Ma.

"What's this crazy talk?" asked Suzanne.

Joseph did not raise his eyes towards his sister. It was not to her that he had addressed himself.

"She knows how to manage. She knows who she wants and when."

Ma looked at Joseph with almost painful intensity, then suddenly she began to laugh.

"Maybe it's so, what you've just said."

Suzanne stopped eating, leaned back in her chair and, in her turn, surveyed Joseph.

"She certainly had him," said Ma.

"She only needs to want something," said Joseph.

Suzanne stood up and laughed.

"And you needn't worry all the time about Joseph, either," she said.

Ma ruminated gravely.

"It's the truth," she said then. "I worry about these things all the time."

And immediately afterwards she was seized with a mild frenzy.

"Rich people," she cried, "think they own the world, but they do not! And we'll not let ourselves be fooled by the first rich man that comes along!"

"Hell, no," said Joseph. "I'll say they're not the only ones. There's plenty of other people in the world. There's us. And we're rich, too . . ."

Ma was fascinated.

"We rich? We rich?"

Joseph thumped the table.

"If we want it we can be as rich as the next one. Hell, all we got to do is want it, and we're rich."

They laughed. Joseph banged his fist upon the table. Ma let herself go. Joseph was as good as the movies.

"Maybe so," said Ma, "if we really want to, we'll be rich."

"Hell, yes," said Joseph. "And then we'll show the others! We'll run over them on the roads. No matter where we find them, we'll run them down, we'll flatten them out!"

Joseph sometimes worked himself up like this. And when it happened—rarely, it is true—it was almost better than the movies.

"Ho, as to that, yes," said Ma, "we'll run them down, we'll flatten them out, we'll tell them what we think, and then we'll flatten them out . . ."

"And we'll not give a damn if we flatten them out," said Suzanne. "And we'll show them what we have but we—we'll not give them one little thing, I'll say we won't!"

PART TWO

1

IT WAS A LARGE CITY OF ONE HUNDRED THOUSAND INHABIT-
ants, spread out on either side of a wide and beautiful river.
As in all Colonial cities, there were two towns within this
one: the white town—and the other. And in the white town
there were still other differences. The periphery of the white
town was known as the *Haut Quartier*—the upper district,
comprising villas and apartment buildings. It was the largest
and airiest part of the city and was where the secular and
official powers had their palaces. The more basic power—
the financial—had its palaces in the center of the white
town, where, crowded in from all sides by the mass of the
city, buildings sprang up, each year higher and higher. The
financiers were the true priests of this Mecca.
In that epoch—the early twenties—the white districts of
all the Colonial cities of the world were always of an impeccable cleanliness, as were the white inhabitants. As soon as
the whites arrived in the Colonies, they learned to take a
bath every day, learned to be clean as children do. They
also learned to wear the Colonial uniform, suits of spotless
white, the color of immunity and innocence. With the as-
sumption of this costume, the first step had been taken.
From then on, the distance augmented by that much, the
initial difference being multiplied, white on white, making
distinctions among themselves and between themselves and
the others who were not white. The others washed themselves in the rain from heaven and in the muddy water of

the streams and rivers. White is, in effect, a color very easily soiled.

Thus, the whites became ever whiter, taking their baths and their siestas in the cool gloom of their villas, behaving much as do great beasts of prey, beasts with sleek and fragile pelts.

In the upper section lived only the whites who had made a fortune. And, still further to mark the superhuman difference between white people and the others, the sidewalks in this fashionable district were immensely wide. An orgiastic space, quite uselessly wide, was provided for the heedless steps of the powerful-in-repose. And through the avenues glided their cushioned cars on cushioned wheels, as if suspended in an impressive semi-stillness.

All this was asphalted, wide, bordered with exotic trees and divided in two by lawns and flowerbeds, along which were parked the shining taxicabs. Sprinkled several times a day, green and flowering, these streets were as well kept as the paths of an immense zoological garden, where rare species of whites watched over themselves. The center of the Haut-Quartier was their true sanctuary. Here only, in the shade of the tamarind trees, were spread out the immense terraces of their cafés. It was on these terraces, in the evenings, that the inhabitants enjoyed themselves in their own congenial company. Only the café waiters were natives, and they were disguised as whites, having been put into dinner jackets. Similarly, the palm trees of the terraces had been put into earthenware pots. And, until late at night, seated in rattan armchairs behind the potted palms and the jacketed waiters, you could see the whites sipping Pernods, whisky and soda or brandy, acquiring a Colonial liver, in harmony with all the rest.

The gleaming of the cars, show-windows and watered asphalt, the dazzling whiteness of the clothes, the shimmering coolness of the flowerbeds, made of the upper district a magic brothel, where the white race could enjoy, in undiluted peace, the sacred spectacle of its own existence. Here, the shops displayed for sale only hats, perfumes, imported blond tobaccos—nothing of utilitarian value. Even money, here, must appear to serve no real purpose. The wealth of the whites must not weigh heavily upon them. In this district everything was noble and aristocratic.

It was the glittering age, the *grande époque*. Hundreds of thousands of native workers bled the trees of hundreds of thousands of hectares of red earth, bled themselves to open the trees that grew in an earth which, by chance, had been called red before being possessed by a few hundred white planters of colossal fortune. Latex flowed. Blood, too. But only the latex was collected as precious, only the latex paid a profit. Blood was wasted. In that epoch the idea was avoided that there might sometime come a day when a great number of people would demand payment for all that blood.

The circuit of the trolley cars scrupulously avoided the fashionable upper district. Indeed, trolleys would have been useless in that part of the city where everyone rode in his own car. Only the natives and the poor white trash of the lower districts used the trolleys. The trolley circuits, in fact, strictly delimited the Eden of the upper district from the rest of the city. They encircled it hygienically, following concentric lines, of which the stops were all at a distance of two kilometers at least from the center of the city.

And it was only from these crowded trolleys and beyond that you could have any idea of the other city, that one in which no white people lived. White with dust and under an implacable sky, they lumbered along with a moribund slowness and with a thunderous clanking of metal. Old cast-offs of the metropolis, built for a temperate climate, these trolleys had been patched up and put back into service by the mother-country for use in the Colonies. The native conductors started out each morning wearing a uniform, but towards ten o'clock they tore it off their bodies, placing it

beside them and finishing the day invariably half naked,
streaming with a sweat caused partly by the big cups of
green tea drunk at every stop. The tea caused perspiration
and this, with a draught of air, enabled the conductors to
cool off. They had ensured themselves of that current of air
by calmly breaking the glass partitions of their driver's section, a thing that had been done during the first days the
trolleys were put into service. The passengers likewise, in
order to survive, had been obliged to break the car win-
dows. Once these precautions had been taken, the trolley
cars functioned satisfactorily. Numerous, and always full to
bursting, these trolleys were the most evident symbol of
Colonial progress. The incredible success of Colonial management was demonstrated by the development of the native zone and its constantly receding line. Naturally, no
white person worthy of the name would ever have ventured
to use these trolley cars; to be seen in one would be to lose
face—Colonial face.

It was in the district situated between the Haut-Quartier
and the native suburbs that were to be found the whites
who had made no fortune—the Colonial natives, you might
call them. There the streets were without trees, the lawns
disappeared. There, the shops of the white people were replaced by "native apartment-houses," those buildings for
which Monsieur Jo's father had found the magic formula.
The streets in this district were watered once a week only.
They swarmed with playful and screaming children and
with street peddlers who, in the burning dust, stridently
shouted their wares.

The Hotel Central, where Ma, Suzanne, and Joseph put
up, was in this zone. It occupied the second floor of a cres-
cent-shaped building overlooking the river on one side, the
central trolley line on the other. The main floor of the building was given over to cheap restaurants, half native and
half white, opium dens, and Chinese grocery stores.

The people who stopped at that hotel were resident salesmen, two prostitutes in business for themselves, a dress-maker, and a large number of subordinate Post Office and Customs employees. The transient guests of the hotel were minor Civil Service employees about to return to the mother-country, hunters, planters, and, at the arrival of every mail-steamer, sea captains and other officers. But chiefly there were prostitutes of every nationality who had come to stay at the hotel for a more or less extended period before find-ing a place for themselves either in the brothels of the fashionable district or in the swarming brothels of the har-bor, into which poured, in tidal waves, all the crews of the Pacific steamship lines.

Madame Marthe, a sixty-five-year-old Colonial, descend-ant in a straight line from one of the harbor brothels, was the proprietress of the Hotel Central. She had a daughter, Carmen, of uncertain paternity. Wanting to preserve her from a fate similar to her own, Madame Marthe had put aside, during the twenty years of her career as prostitute, sufficient savings to buy enough stock in the Association of Colonial Hotels to obtain the management of this hotel.

Carmen was now thirty-five years old. She was called Mademoiselle Carmen by everyone except the regular guests of the hotel who called her merely Carmen. She was a good and devoted daughter, full of respect for her mother, from whom she now took over the entire tricky job of managing the Hotel Central. Rather tall, neat and trim, with eyes that were small but of a bright clear blue, Carmen would not have been bad-looking had it not been for the prominent lower jaw with which she had unfortunately been endowed at birth. However, this defect was partly compensated by particularly fine teeth, big and strong, so noticeable that she always seemed to be trying to show them off, which gave to her mouth a likably greedy and carnivorous look. But what made Carmen Carmen, what made her irreplaceable and gave irreplaceable charm to her hotel management, was her legs. For indeed, Carmen had extraordinarily beautiful legs. Had her face been correspondingly beautiful, she would long ago have become the mistress of some bank director or rich northern planter, would have had an apartment of her own in the Haut-Quartier, would have been covered with gold and the glory of scandal—especially that —and she would have known very well how to accommodate herself to these things and still remain herself. Instead of this, Carmen had only her legs. Therefore she would presumably go on managing the Hotel Central for the rest of her life.

Carmen spent the better part of her time moving up and down the long, long corridor of the hotel. One end of it opened into the dining room, the other upon the open terrace, and on either side of it were aligned the bedrooms. This corridor, or rather, this empty tube, lighted only at its two extremities, was naturally destined for the naked legs of Carmen, and those legs exhibited their outlines of magnificent shapeliness during the entire day. None of the hotel guests could completely ignore those legs, no matter how great the wish to do so, and a certain number of the residents lived with the tormenting image constantly before them. This was particularly so since Carmen, in a spirit of revenge against the rest of her person—and this in no way altered the sweetness of her character—wore her skirts so short that her knees were revealed in their entirety. Her knee was perfect: smooth and round, with the suppleness and delicacy of a driving-rod. Any man might wish to sleep with Carmen simply for those legs of hers, their beauty, their lively way of articulating, of bending and unbending, of posing and of functioning. And, indeed, thus it came to pass. Because of those legs and her persuasive way of using them, Carmen had lovers in sufficient number to place her above having to search for them in the upper district. Also, her sweet disposition, which derived in a way from her self-satisfaction at possessing those legs, was so constant and real that her lovers all became faithful clients, regularly returning to the Hotel Central after sometimes two years of voyaging in the Pacific.

Thus, the hotel prospered. Carmen had her philosophy of life and it was not bitter. She accepted her destiny, you might say, light-footedly. And fiercely she resisted any attachment that might have affected this good humor. She was a true whore's daughter, used to the incessant arrival and departure of her male companions, used to the toughness of earning a living, possessed of a terrific independence. All of which did not prevent her from having her preferences, her friendships and doubtless also her loves, while accepting gracefully all the hazards of her life.

Carmen felt not only friendship but also respect for Ma. Every time Ma came to the hotel, Carmen reserved for her a quiet room on the side towards the river, charging her only the price of a room on the noisy trolley side. And once —that had been two years ago—she had taken Joseph's virginity in a burst of magnanimity that doubtless was not entirely gratuitous. Following this event, at any rate, every time Joseph put up at the hotel she would spend several nights in succession with him. And she had the good taste not to charge him anything for his room—thus cloaking her generosity with the pleasure she had with him.

This time, Carmen was naturally entrusted by Ma with the task of helping to sell Monsieur Jo's diamond.

The very evening of her arrival, Ma asked Carmen if she thought she could sell the diamond to one of the hotel guests. Carmen was amazed to see a ring of that value in Ma's hands.

"A certain Monsieur Jo," said Ma proudly, "gave it to Suzanne. He wanted to marry her but she did not want to because Joseph did not approve of him."

Carmen immediately understood that their sole motive for this trip to the city was to sell the diamond. She comprehended the importance of Ma's step and wanted to help her. On the whole, the hotel guests did not seem to her to be very likely buyers of a ring of that value, she said, but all the same she would try to palm it off on someone. The very next day she spoke to certain guests about it. In addition, she pinned up the following sign in the hotel office, well in view above her table:

FOR SALE
MAGNIFICENT DIAMOND. EXCEPTIONAL BARGAIN.
APPLY TO OFFICE.

But during the following days no one at the hotel paid any attention to it. Carmen said she had expected this. Even so, she thought it as well to leave up the notice, since the marine officers who put into port might be capable of an extravagance. But Carmen advised Ma to try to sell the ring herself, either to a jeweler or a diamond merchant. Ma should have the ring during the day, but it should be returned to Carmen at night, so as not to lose what chance there might be of selling it at the hotel.

However, at the end of three days, none of this strategy had accomplished anything.

2

POSSESSED OF THE RING, WHICH SHE CARRIED IN HER HANDBAG
and which was still wrapped in the tissue paper provided by
Monsieur Jo, Ma began to go everywhere in the city to try
to sell it at the price Monsieur Jo had put on it: twenty thousand francs. But the first diamond merchant to whom she
offered it would give only ten thousand francs. He declared
that the diamond had a serious flaw, a carbon spark. This
flaw greatly diminished the diamond's value.

Ma did not believe in this defect at first, and she stood
out for twenty thousand francs. But when she had seen a
second diamond merchant and he also had talked about the
defect, she began to waver. She had never heard of cheap
carbon sparks getting lost in a diamond, even the purest
diamond—and for a good reason: she had never before had
a diamond, whether pure or defective. But when a fourth
diamond merchant had again talked about the flaw, she
began, typically, to find an obscure relation between the
defective gem and the person of Monsieur Jo. After three
days of this sort of thing, she was formulating her idea in a
more or less vague way.

"It doesn't surprise me," she said. "It's only to be expected."

Soon, the word-association went so deep that she sometimes, when speaking of Monsieur Jo, slipped up and used
the same word for him as for the diamond.

"From the very first I should have known what he was, that cheap spark, I should have been on my guard right from the first day I saw him in the Ram canteen."

That diamond with its deceptive glitter was exactly the diamond for a man whose millions might also be illusory. And her disgust was as strong as if Monsieur Jo had stolen his millions.

"They're both defectives," she said. "They're both cheap sparks and worth about the same."

Decidedly, now, the two, confused as one, were regarded with the same loathing.

However, she continued to stand out for twenty thousand francs and "not one centime less." She persevered. She had always persevered, in a curiously desperate eagerness which increased in proportion to her failures. The less they offered for the diamond, the more she stuck to her initial price: twenty thousand francs. For five whole days she ran from one diamond merchant to another. She began with the whites. Entering a shop in the most natural way possible, she would relate that she wanted to get rid of a family heirloom, a jewel that was now of no use to her. They asked to see it, she took out the ring, they examined it under the lens, and they discovered the flaw. They offered eight thousand francs. They offered eleven thousand francs, they offered six thousand francs, and so on. She put the ring back into her handbag, quickly left the shop and usually screamed at Suzanne who, with Joseph, would be waiting for her in the B-12. Of the three diamonds that Monsieur Jo had offered her, Suzanne had naturally taken the worst one, as if on purpose!

But she kept on, she persevered. Regardless of the diamond's quality, she wanted twenty thousand francs for it.

After having seen all the white diamond merchants and jewelers, she began to make the rounds of the others, those who were not white, the yellow people, the black people. They never offered her more than eight thousand francs.

Since these merchants were fewer than the others, she took less time to get around to them. Her disappointment grew, as did her anger and disgust, but nothing at all made her diminish her demands. No matter what happened, she was determined to have exactly twenty thousand francs.

When at last she had seen all the diamond merchants of the city, white or colored, she decided that perhaps she had not used the right tactics. So, one evening, she told Suzanne that the only solution would be to see Monsieur Jo again. She spoke of this project to Suzanne in private. Joseph, she said, intelligent as he was, had his stupid side and, since he couldn't understand everything then he needn't be told everything. They would have to be clever, they would have to see Monsieur Jo again without letting him suspect that they had looked for him and then they could resume their old relations with him. They could take their time. What must be done was to resume relations with him to the extent of fooling him and giving him a new desire to reward them somehow. The essential thing was to get him excited, to get him crazy about Suzanne again, to muddle him to the point that he would return and again reach a point of despair sufficient to give her the other two diamonds or maybe just one of them.

Suzanne promised to make it up with Monsieur Jo if ever she happened to meet him again, but she refused to look for him. Ma said she would attend to that part of the business.

But how to find Monsieur Jo in the city? Naturally, he had not given them his address. So, while still running to a few more diamond merchants that she had overlooked, Ma began to search for Monsieur Jo. She waited and watched at the doors of moving-picture houses, she explored the café terraces, the streets, the luxury shops, the hotels. And she did this with the ardor and passion of a lovesick girl.

3

AT FIRST, SUZANNE AND JOSEPH ACCOMPANIED MA ON HER IN-
terminable errands to the diamond merchants. But their zeal
did not withstand the business of the flaw. At the end of
two days, having pronounced these errands to be absolutely
fruitless, Joseph went off by himself, of course in the B-12.
Ma had to resign herself to this. She knew from experience
how bitterly Joseph would feel towards her were he unable
to take full advantage of his sojourn in the city. It would be
worse for her than to go alone, afoot, or on the trolley car,
to tackle the diamond merchants and their diabolical clair-
voyance. Anyway, as it turned out, when she decided to
look for Monsieur Jo, Joseph's defection became unexpectedly a godsend. It was only when, in her turn, she abandoned the hope of ever finding Monsieur Jo that, completely in despair, she went to bed and slept throughout the
day, as she had done after the crumbling of the sea walls.

For a few days, Joseph still came back every evening to
Carmen's, and Ma therefore continued to see him in the
mornings, if only for a moment. But soon—and that was
the most important thing that happened during their stay
in the city—Joseph stopped coming back at all. He disappeared completely with the B-12. He had succeeded in selling a few freshly tanned pelts to some transient guests at
the hotel. Supplied with this money only, he disappeared.

Carmen managed to hide the fact from Ma, at least while

Ma was so busy with her diamond merchants and then with her search for Monsieur Jo that she was not much worried at not seeing Joseph every morning. For a time, Ma could still believe Suzanne or Carmen when they told her they had seen Joseph in the afternoons while she was out.

From the day that Suzanne decided it was superfluous to be bawled out every time Ma left a jewelry store, she quite naturally became a prey to Carmen's well-meant attentions. No sooner had Carmen concluded that Joseph was not going to return just yet than she eagerly took charge of Suzanne, going so far as to share her room with the girl. She did this to draw Suzanne away from Ma's heartbreaking relentlessness. It really seemed that each of the three awoke in Carmen the same devotion. Thus, after having discovered Joseph, Carmen discovered Suzanne. And during this stay it was especially Suzanne that she tried, as she said, to "enlighten."

Carmen talked to Suzanne about Suzanne's own life, expatiating to her on her fate, which she deemed most unfortunate. And she tried, with bitter words, to convince her of it. She knew, she said, that Ma was set on marrying her daughter off as quickly as possible in order finally to be alone and free to die. Well, that was no solution. It certainly was not when you were still, as Suzanne was, at the stage of youthful imbecility. "For," said Carmen, "we're all imbeciles in the beginning." It could not be a solution unless Suzanne married a man both stupid enough and rich enough to give her the material conditions to free herself of him. Joseph had told her about Monsieur Jo and she was a little sorry that the affair with him had not succeeded, because he seemed to her to be the ideal type. "You could have been unfaithful to him at the end of three months, and afterwards everything would have gone just right." But Monsieur Jo, or rather Monsieur Jo's father, had been elusive. And Carmen explained to Suzanne how hard it would be to find a husband for her even here, in the city, especially a husband of the "ideal type"—Monsieur Jo's type. Marriage for love at seventeen was, at any rate, out of the question. A romantic marriage with, for instance, the Customs officer next door, would mean having three children in three years. No, Suzanne had shown, up to now, too much submissiveness to Ma.

And this was the important thing: above all else, Suzanne must free herself of Ma, who could not understand that in this life you could win your liberty and dignity with weapons other than those she, Ma, had believed good. Carmen knew Ma well, she knew the story of the sea walls, the concession, and so forth. Ma made her think of a ravaging monster, she said. Ma had played havoc with the peace of hundreds of peasants on the plain. She had even tried to conquer the Pacific Ocean. Joseph and Suzanne must be on their guard against her. She had had so much misfortune that she had become a monster exercising a mighty spell, her children ran the risk of being forever held captive to console her in her grief, and they might never be able to leave her, but would have to go on bending to her will, go on letting themselves, in their turn, be devoured by her.

There were no two ways for a girl to learn how to leave her mother.

It may have shocked Suzanne a little to hear this said about Ma, but in the end it was true. Especially since the sea walls, Ma was dangerous. As for the rest, there was certainly no question of marrying the Customs officer next door; and she did not need a Monsieur Jo, either. Carmen oversimplified.

Carmen combed Suzanne's hair, dressed her, and gave her money. She then advised her to go for some strolls in the city, telling her all the same not to fall a victim to the first man she met. And Suzanne accepted Carmen's dresses and Carmen's money.

4

THE FIRST TIME SUZANNE TOOK A WALK IN THE HAUT-
Quartier, therefore, was to a certain extent the result of
Carmen's advice.

She had never imagined that there would come a day
which would be as important to her life as this one, when
alone and for the first time, at the age of seventeen, she set
out to explore a great Colonial city. She did not know that a
rigid order reigned there and that the categories of the inhabitants were so differentiated that you were lost if you
could not manage to be classified in one of them.

Suzanne tried to walk in a natural way. It was five
o'clock. It was still hot, but already the torpor of the afternoon was over. The streets, little by little, were filling with
white people looking rested from their siestas and their evening shower baths. People looked at her. They turned to
look, they smiled. No young white girl of her age ever
walked alone in the streets of the fashionable district. The
young girls you met there passed in groups, dressed in
sports clothes. Some of them had tennis rackets under their
arms. They turned to look. They smiled. When they turned,
they smiled. "Where does that poor creature come from?
How did she happen to stray here?" Even women were
rarely encountered alone. They, too, walked in groups. Suzanne passed them. They were surrounded with the smell
of perfume and of expensive cigarettes, the fresh odors of

money. She thought all the women were beautiful, and their summery elegance seemed to flaunt itself at everything unlike them. Especially she was impressed by the way they walked. They walked like queens, and they talked, laughed, moved absolutely in accord with the general movement, which was that of an extraordinarily easy way of life.

Insensibly a feeling had come over her from the very moment she had entered the avenue which went in a direct line from the trolley tracks up to the center of the Haut-Quartier. It became more pronounced, augmenting until, by the time she had reached the center of the fashionable district, it was an unpardonable reality: she was ridiculous and everyone saw it. Carmen had been wrong. Not everyone could walk in these streets, on these sidewalks, among these lordlings and these children of kings. It was not for everyone to move about with the same ease. All these people seemed to be going to a specific place; they were in a familiar setting and among people like themselves. But she —she had no place to go, there was no one like her, nor had there ever been, not on this stage.

She tried to think of something else.

They still noticed her.

The more they looked at her the more she was convinced that she was something scandalous, an object of complete ugliness and stupidity. It had been enough for one person to notice her, the thing spread like wildfire. Everyone she passed, now, seemed to be forewarned, the entire city was forewarned and she could do nothing, nothing but continue to advance, completely hemmed in, condemned to go forward to meet those stares and always more stares, to meet that laughter which was growing, which passed her, splattering her and again splattering her from behind. She did not fall dead, but she walked on the edge of the pavement and wished she could fall dead and float away in the gutter. Her shame mounted steadily. She hated herself, hated everything. Panic-stricken, she would have liked to

run away from everything, strip herself of everything—of
the dress that Carmen had lent her, on which big blue flowers were scattered, this Hotel Central dress, too short and
tight—of that straw hat, the like of which no one had ever
seen—of this hair arranged as no other girl had ever arranged her hair. But these things were nothing. She herself, from head to foot, was contemptible. Her eyes—where
to look? These heavy and awful arms, this heart, fluttering
like an indecent caged beast, these legs that were too weak
to bear her along.

And there she was, dangling in her hand an old handbag
—Ma's—oh, the slut! It was Ma's handbag. She wished her
mother would die! She wanted to throw the handbag into
the gutter, where it belonged, for what it contained was
worthless. But one does not throw one's handbag into the
gutter. People would come running, they would surround
her . . . All right, let them! She would then succumb,
gently die, stretched out in the gutter, with her handbag
close beside her. Then, they would have to stop laughing!

Joseph. She thought of him. At that time of day he was
still in the habit of coming back to the hotel. The Haut-
Quartier was not so very big. And where would Joseph be,
if not here? Suzanne began to scan the crowd for him. Perspiration streamed down her face. She took off her hat and
held it with the bag. She did not find Joseph. But suddenly,
the entrance of a moving-picture theatre loomed ahead, a
moving-picture theatre, where she could hide. She went in.
The picture had not begun. Joseph was not in the theatre.
No one she knew was there, not even Monsieur Jo.

The piano began to play. The lights went out. From then
on Suzanne felt invisible, invincible, and she began to cry
in sheer relief. It was an oasis, this dark vast room in the
afternoon, it was the night of lonely people, an artificial
and democratic night, the great equalitarian night of the
cinema, truer than the real night, more delightful, more
consoling than any real night. It was the chosen night, open

to all, offered to all, more generous and charitable than all
the charitable institutions, than all the churches, it was a
night in which to console yourself for all your shames, in
which to lose all your despair, in which to wash youth clean
of all the frightful filth of adolescence . . .

She was young and beautiful. She was in court dress. You
could not imagine her in any other kind of dress. The men
were crazy about her, they fell in her wake like ninepins,
and she advanced in the midst of her victims who, in the
foreground, marked her passage while she existed far off,
free as a ship, more and more indifferent, but always bur-
dened with her immaculate attributes of beauty. And be-
hold, there comes a day of beauty when she no longer loves
anyone. Naturally she has a great deal of money. She trav-
els. It is at the carnival in Venice that love awaits her. He
is very handsome, the other. He has somber eyes, black
hair, a blonde wig, and he is very aristocratic. Before the
least thing has happened you know that this is it, that he is
The Man. That is what's amazing, everyone knows it before
she does, you feel like telling her. It happens like a storm,
when the whole sky darkens. After many delays, between
two marble columns, their shadows reflected in just the
right canal, by the light of a lantern which evidently has
the habit of lighting up such things, they embrace. He says
I love you. She says I love you too. The dark sky of waiting
becomes suddenly bright. From the lightning of that kiss.
Gigantic communion of the audience with the screen. You
would like to be in their place. Oh, how you would like it.
Their bodies entwined, their lips approach with nightmare
slowness. And when their two pairs of lips are close together, their bodies become cut off, and then you see their
decapitated heads, what would be impossible to see in real
life, you see their lips facing, half open, open still more,
and their jaws falling apart as if in death and then, suddenly, in a brusque and fatal release, their lips join and suck
like octopuses in a crushing kiss, as if trying with the deliri-

ous hunger of starvation to devour, to absorb each other
and bring about a total and reciprocal disappearance and
absorption. Impossible idea, absurd idea, to which quite
evidently the physical organs are not adapted. The spectators would not, however, have seen anything but the
attempt. The failure would remain ignored by them. For at
that point the screen lit up and assumed the whiteness of a
shroud . . .

It was early, still. Once out of the moving-picture theatre,
Suzanne walked up the principal avenue of the Haut-
Quartier. Night had come during the show and it was as if
it were the night in the theatre which went on, the amorous
night of the moving-picture. She felt calm and reassured.
She began to look for Joseph, but for reasons other than before. Now, no longer able to resign herself to go back to the
hotel, she looked for him. And also because never before
had she felt such a desire to be with Joseph.

A half-hour after leaving the moving-picture house was
when she met him, perceived the B-12 coming down the
avenue, going towards the docks. The car came very slowly.
Suzanne took up her stand on the sidewalk and waited until it was beside her to call out to him.

Crowded in beside him were two women. The one who
was next to him had her arms around him. Joseph had a
queer look on his face. He looked drunk and happy.

Just at the moment when the B-12 was going to pass her,
Suzanne sprang to the curb and shouted: "Joseph!"

Joseph did not hear. He was talking to the woman who
had her arms around him.

All the same, the street was crowded and Joseph was driving very slowly.

"Joseph!" Suzanne cried again. Several people stopped.
Suzanne ran the length of the street, trying to catch up with
the car. But Joseph did not hear and did not see her. Then,
after having called twice to him, she began shouting con-
tinuously.

"Joseph, Joseph, Joseph!"

If he does not hear me the next time, she thought, I'll throw myself in front of the car and make him stop.

Joseph stopped. Suzanne stood still and smiled at him. She was so astonished and happy to meet him. It was as if she had not seen him for a very long time—not since their childhood. Joseph drew up to the curb. The B-12 had not changed. There were the same doors fastened with wire and the naked and rusty framework of the top, that top which Joseph had stripped off one day in a fit of rage.

"What the hell you doing here?" asked Joseph.

"Taking a walk."

"Cripes, you're rigged out in a queer way."

"Carmen lent me the dress."

"What are you doing here?" Joseph asked again.

One of the women asked Joseph something and Joseph said: "My sister." The second woman asked the first: "Who is it?" "His kid sister," said the first one. They both smiled at Suzanne with a kind of shy complacency. They had on a great deal of make-up and they were wearing tight dresses, one green, the other blue. The girl that had her arms around Joseph was the younger. When she smiled you could see that a tooth was missing on one side. They must both be girls from a harbor brothel and Joseph must have picked them up somewhere, Heaven knew where, perhaps in the front rows of a moving-picture theatre.

Joseph stayed in the car, looking bothered. Suzanne waited for him to ask her to get in. But visibly Joseph had no such intention.

"Where's Mamma?" he asked, more for something to say. "Why are you alone?"

"I don't know," said Suzanne.

"And the sparkler?" Joseph asked.

"Not sold," said Suzanne.

She was leaning against the car, on Joseph's side. She did not dare get in. Joseph realized this and he looked more

and more embarrassed. The two women seemed not to realize what was happening.

"Well, so long," said Joseph at last.

Suzanne quickly took her arm from the door.

"So long."

Joseph looked at her, embarrassed. He hesitated.

"Where are you going, like that?"

"What does it matter where I'm going?" said Suzanne.
"I'll go wherever I want to go!"

Joseph still hesitated. Suzanne went off.

"Suzanne!" called Joseph, weakly.

Suzanne did not reply. Joseph started the car slowly, going away without calling a second time.

Suzanne went back up the avenue to the Cathedral
square. She hated Joseph. Now she no longer noticed the
stares that followed her; or perhaps it was that now, because of the darkness, people were staring less at her. If
only Ma could have passed! But useless to hope for it: Ma
never passed this way because it was a place for prome-
naders. She was running to and fro in the city with her defective diamond, her cheap sparkler. Then, she was looking
for Monsieur Jo, too, she was on the hunt for Monsieur Jo.
Ma was a kind of old whore without knowing it, lost in the
city. In other times she had haunted the banks, now she
was haunting the diamond merchants. They would devour
her. For a long time, now, when you saw her coming back
so exhausted that, most of the time, she went straight to bed
to weep, without eating, you would have expected her
surely to die, either because of the banks or because of the
diamond merchants. But all the same, she had always managed somehow, and always she had begun again to indulge
in her vice, which was to ask for the impossible, to demand
her "rights" as she put it.

Suzanne sat down on one of the benches that were placed
around the Cathedral square. She had no desire to go back
at once. Ma would wail and complain again, whether

against herself or Joseph. Soon it would be finished with Joseph, he would go away. They were experiencing now, a little, the end of Joseph, who would soon be lost in the crowd, lost to them in the monstrous vulgarity of love. No more Joseph. Say what he would, he was not going to take care of Ma much longer, and already he was preparing her assassination. He was a liar. There were many liars. Carmen, in particular.

5

IT WAS AT THE MOVIES THAT JOSEPH MET HER. SHE WAS
smoking one cigarette after another and, since she had no
match or lighter, Joseph had lit her cigarettes for her. So,
each time, she had offered Joseph a cigarette. They were
very good and very expensive cigarettes, no doubt the
famous "555" brand. The two had left the movies together
and since that time they had not separated. At least, this
was the brief account that Carmen gave of Joseph's affair.

"He had reached a point where cigarettes were enough,"
she added.

Carmen said she had met Joseph in the upper district
and that he himself had told her everything. But how was
it possible to know when Carmen was telling the truth? She
had her own sources of information, her own channels. She
must even know where Joseph was, but she was careful not
to disclose it. And for seven days and seven nights Joseph
did not reappear at the Hotel Central.

Ma had almost finished with the diamond merchants and
the jewelers. She now counted only on the hotel guests and
on Carmen. From time to time, she would spring to life
and again go to see a diamond merchant she had overlooked,
but she no longer spent the days running hither and yon in
the city. She no longer even looked for Monsieur Jo. She
had looked too long and she was tired of it, tired as if of a

lover. She said that as soon as Joseph came back she would go to one of the first diamond merchants she had seen, the one who had offered eleven thousand francs for the sparkler, as she now contemptuously called it. Then she would return to the plain . . .

She now spent the greater part of her time waiting for Joseph to return. She had paid for her room and board up to the time of Joseph's disappearance but from then on she decided not to pay. She told Carmen she had no more money. She guessed that Carmen knew perfectly well where Joseph was but would not tell; consequently, she would tacitly agree not to be paid during the period that it was up to her to let Joseph have his good time. However, Ma took only one meal a day—you could not tell whether it was because of scruples or merely in a naïve attempt to force Carmen to take pity and speak out. Suzanne, for her part, ate at the table with Carmen and slept in Carmen's room. She saw Ma only at the evening meal. All day long, in effect, Ma slept. She took her pills and slept. Always during the difficult periods of her life she had slept like that. When the sea walls had collapsed, two years before, she had slept forty-eight hours on end. Her children were used to these habits and did not worry overmuch.

After that first attempt at a promenade in the upper district, Suzanne did not follow Carmen's instructions to the letter. When she went out in the afternoons, now, it was to go directly to a movie. In the morning, generally, she stayed in the hotel office and sometimes it happened that she replaced Carmen there.

The Hotel Central had six bedrooms that were called "reserved." These rooms caused a great deal of work. They were rented by the hour, most of the time to marine officers and newly arrived prostitutes. Carmen had secured a special license to keep such rooms. By it she made her biggest profits. But she pretended that this was not her reason for asking for the license; she said it was a matter of personal taste. It would have bored her, she said, to run a respect-able hotel.

Sometimes the prostitutes stayed a month, waiting for their fate to be decided. They were well treated at the hotel. Occasionally some of them, usually the youngest, went away with hunters or planters they had casually met. But rarely did they accommodate themselves to the life of the bush or the high plateaus, and so they returned and once more en-tered the brothels. Apart from the new ones who came to the Colony direct from the capital, there arrived others from Shanghai, Singapore, Manila, and Hong-Kong. Those were the great adventuresses, the globe-trotters, the hottest lot of them all. They went from port to port in the Pacific, never remaining in any one port more than six months. They were the greatest opium smokers in the world, and they were the ones that taught the Pacific crews the delights of opium.

"They're old wrecks," said Carmen, "but they're the ones I like best."

She did not go into detail, but she said she really liked prostitutes, that she herself was a daughter of one but it was not for this reason. Rather, it was because being a pros-titute was still the most honest profession in this Colony which was nothing but a huge house of prostitution.

It goes without saying that Carmen suggested to all these women that they try to get some man to give them the dia-mond. In all the "reserved" rooms she had put up copies of the notice that was posted in the office. She went so far as to explain the whole thing to Ma.

"But of course," said Carmen bitterly, "men don't offer sparklers to girls like them."

Ma shared this bitterness. All the same, the hotel was the only place left where there was a chance of selling the dia-mond at the price Ma wanted. In the hotel there was no magnifying glass to reveal that flaw, said Carmen. With her, too, the sale of the diamond had become a constant preoccupation, though less obsessing than Ma's. Anyway,

Carmen never let herself become obsessed by anything. Her only real obsession was the constant need for a change of men. This alone could make her abandon everything at the hotel and go out on a hunt, as she periodically did, usually upon the arrival of a ship in port. After dinner she would dress herself up, paint her face, and slip off along the river towards the harbor. On coming back, at night, she went so far as to tell Suzanne, in a rush of affectionate exuberance:

"You'll see, it's out of doors that they're the best. You mustn't shut men up in a house. It's in the street that they're much better."

"But how . . . in the street?" said Suzanne, embarrassed.

Carmen laughed.

When she was not in Carmen's office, Suzanne was in the movies of the upper district. After lunch she left the hotel to go directly to a movie. Then she went to another. There were five in the town and the programs changed often. Carmen understood this liking for the movies and gave her money so she could see as many as she cared to see. Smilingly she said there was little difference between her own riverside jaunts and Suzanne's trips to the movies. The great value of the movies, according to her, was that they aroused desire in girls and boys, making them eager to leave home. And the first thing necessary was to leave home and get rid of one's family, if it was a real family. Suzanne evidently did not understand Carmen's teachings very well, but she was proud to have Carmen take an interest in her.

Every night when she came back she asked Carmen for news of Joseph and the diamond. Joseph did not return. The diamond did not get sold. Monsieur Jo did not reappear. But what especially counted was that Joseph did not return. The more time passed, the more Suzanne realized that she counted less and less in Joseph's life, perhaps she counted no more, at times, than if she had never existed. It was not impossible that he might never return. As Carmen said, Ma's fate no longer presented any real problems, it was clear. If Joseph came back, Ma would live. If he did not come back, Ma would die. Ma's fate was less important than what had happened to Joseph, than what had happened to Carmen so long ago but which, it seemed, had marked her forever, was less important than what would surely happen to Suzanne one day soon. Already, the event was brewing. At every corner of the street, each turn of the street, each hour of the day, each image of every moving-picture, each face of a man glimpsed by her, she could already say that these things were bringing her closer to Carmen and to Joseph.

Ma never asked about how she spent her time. There was only Carmen to take an interest in Suzanne. Carmen often asked her, for lack of other things to talk about, to tell her the stories of the movies she had seen. Then she would give Suzanne money for the next day. She was worried about Suzanne and the longer Joseph stayed away the more she worried. Sometimes she worried terribly. What was going to happen to Suzanne? It was absolutely necessary, she repeated, for Suzanne to find a way of leaving her mother, especially if Joseph did not come back.

"Her miseries, in the long run, are a kind of fascination," she kept repeating, "you must forget them, like you forget a fascination. I can't see what would make you forget her, except her death—or a man."

Suzanne thought that Carmen, in her persistence, was a little rudimentary. She concealed from Carmen that she no longer strolled in the Haut-Quartier. She had never told her about her first promenade. Not because she had resolved to keep silent, but because it seemed to her impossible to recount. In effect, no incident had marked it and Suzanne had no idea as yet that you could confide anything other than concrete events. The rest was shameful or too precious; in any case, impossible to tell. She let Carmen go on talking, Carmen, who still was unaware that the only humanity Suzanne dared face was that of the silver screen, prodigious, reassuring.

When Suzanne came back to the hotel, Carmen drew her into her room and questioned her.

Carmen's room was her weakness. She had resisted many things in life, but she could not resist the charm of artificial flowers, of divans buried under handpainted cushions, and, hung on the walls, souvenirs of dances long past. Suzanne felt a little stifled in that room. Still, she had rather sleep there than in Ma's room. Suzanne knew that it was in this room that Joseph had slept with Carmen. When Carmen undressed in front of her, she thought of it every time. And every time that made one more difference—not with Carmen, but with Joseph. Carmen was tall, she had a flat stomach, small breasts set rather low, and her legs were miraculously beautiful. Suzanne itemized her every evening, and every evening her difference from Joseph was accentuated. Suzanne had undressed in front of Carmen only once. Then, Carmen had taken her into her arms. "You are as white as a peeled almond," she had said, after which she silently wiped away a tear. It was that same evening that Carmen asked her to bring her the first man she picked up. Suzanne promised. But never again did she undress in front of Carmen.

When dinnertime came, Suzanne went to Ma's room to fetch her. It was always the same thing. Stretched out on her bed, Ma was waiting for Joseph. She was always in darkness, because she hadn't even the desire to light the lights. On the night-table, beside her, beneath an inverted glass, reposed the diamond. When she woke up she looked at it disgustedly. The "cheap sparkler," she said, made her want to die. It was a piece of bad luck, she said, that no one could even have imagined. Sometimes, when she had been taking too many pills and had wet the bed, Suzanne went over to the window so as not to see.

"Well?" asked Ma.

"I haven't seen him," said Suzanne.

Ma began crying. She asked for another pill. Suzanne gave her one and returned to the window. She repeated to her what Carmen said: "He'll come back sooner or later."

Ma said she knew that, but it was all the same terrible to lose Joseph so suddenly. She used the same tone to speak of Joseph, of the diamond, and, while she was still hunting for him, of Monsieur Jo. And sometimes, when she said: "If only he'd come back," it was impossible to know whether her words referred to Joseph or Monsieur Jo.

She rose, staggering under the effect of the pills. Suzanne had to wait while Ma dressed. It was a long wait. Suzanne sat there, leaning against the window. The noise of the trolley car came up, muffled, into the room. But all that Suzanne could see of the city from that window was its great river, half covered with a swarm of big Chinese junks that had arrived from the Pacific, and some harbor tugboats. Carmen was wrong to worry about her. Already, from having seen so many movies, seen so many people in love with each other, seen so many departures, embraces, definitive kisses, so many solutions and predestinations, so many desertions, cruel but inevitable and fatal, already what Suzanne could have wished for was to go away from Ma.

6

THE ONLY MAN SUZANNE HAD THE LUCK TO MEET WAS ONE
stopping at the Hotel Central: a salesman for a spinning
factory in Calcutta.

He was passing through the Colony and would be em-
barking for India within a week. His circuit took two years
and he passed but once each trip through the Colony in
question. On every trip he had tried to find a French girl
to marry, very young, a virgin if possible, but he had never
succeeded in finding her.

"There's a fellow that might be just the thing," Carmen
had said to Suzanne. "At any rate, it might mean a way out
for you if Joseph never comes back."

Burner was a forty-year-old specimen, tall; with graying
hair and tweed suits, who talked calmly, smiled little and
looked like the typical salesman for a big firm. It was not
with impunity that he had, for fifteen years, visited all the
big textile factories of the world, there to boast of the quality of his yarn. Moreover, he had gone round the world several times and had a rather peculiar mental vision of the
world's capacity to absorb, in kilometers, the cotton yarn
from the G.M.B. factory in Calcutta.

Carmen spoke to him about Suzanne, and that very day
he wanted to make her acquaintance. He was in a hurry.
The introductions were made in Carmen's room, late at
night after Ma had gone to bed. Suzanne gave in to Carmen's wishes, as she always did. After the introduction,

Burner talked about his business, about world-trade in cotton yarns, the unimaginable consumption of cotton yarns. Nothing else happened that evening. Next day, through Carmen, he invited Suzanne to go out with him in order, said he, to improve their acquaintance. Suzanne joined him after dinner.

They went to the movies in Burner's car, a very funny car, of which he was very proud. Once arrived in front of the moving-picture theatre, he planted himself before Suzanne and made a detailed demonstration of the extraordinary improvements he had added to that car. It was a red two-seater, and the rumble-seat had been transformed into a kind of big chest of drawers, in which Burner carried his samples. The drawers were yellow, blue, green, and so forth, corresponding exactly to the color of the yarns inside them. There were easily thirty drawers, which opened out completely, opening and closing automatically by a push-button inside the car. There were no two cars like his in the world, said Burner, and he was the one, he alone, who had had the idea of thus transforming it. He added that the car was still not as perfect as he wanted it to be; for instance, customers sometimes put back the yarns into the wrong drawers. That was an inconvenience he hoped to remedy. He had already worked out a method. He would affix bobbins to the bottom of the drawers in such a way that only he could take them out or put them back again. Always, he said, he was looking for ways to perfect these drawers; such things were not created all at once. Nothing happened all at once, things had to evolve, he said, with a meaning look. As he talked, twenty or so people had gathered round the car to benefit by his demonstration.

Seeing that car and hearing him talk, there was no possible shadow of doubt in Suzanne's mind. This was another piece of bad luck. The only thing she could hope to do with him was to palm off the sparkler on him. And she thought of Joseph with intensity.

After the movies, they went to dance at a combination dance hall and swimming-pool in the outskirts of the town. Burner went there without any hesitation and it was clear he must have spent much of his time there whenever he was in the Colony—no doubt each time accompanied by a new young-lady-candidate from the Hotel Central.

There was a green painted bungalow in the midst of a grove of trees. Because of the Chinese lanterns swinging in the treetops, it was almost as light as day there. Beside the bungalow was the famous swimming-pool which gave the dance hall its celebrity. It was a great natural rocky basin, fed by a stream which had been dammed up. The water being constantly renewed by a trickling stream in its depths, it remained very clear. Three projectors lit the pool from above, showing the bottom and sides of it, which had been left in their natural state, draped with long water weeds, through which appeared the bottom of orange and violet colored rocks and pebbles, flashing with the splendor of under-water flowers. So clear and calm was the water that these things showed up in their most precise details and gradations, as though they had been transfixed in crystal. In addition to the projectors, the pool was lit by Chinese lanterns which, multicolored and moving, swung in the green canopy of the grove.

Surrounding the pool were large, well kept lawns, where stood a row of bath-houses also painted green. Occasionally one of these cabins opened and the figure of a man or woman appeared, entirely naked, of a surprising whiteness and so radiant that the luminous shadow of the woods was as if dimmed by comparison. The naked figure crossed the lawns at a run, flung itself into the pool, causing a fountain of sparkling water to shoot up. Then the jet of water subsided and the body of the swimmer appeared within the water, bluish and fluid like milk. The dance music suddenly stopped and the lights went out while the naked man or woman swam there. Sometimes, the more audacious swimmers plunged into the depths, passing through the long water weeds, disturbing their solemn immobility, losing themselves there in under-water swimming strokes, slow and convulsive. Then the naked swimmer reappeared at the surface, in a glorious whirlpool of luminous bubbles.

Leaning on the balconies of the dance floor, men and women observed the scene in silence. Although these baths were open to everyone, few dared exhibit themselves. Once the swimmer had disappeared, the lights came on and the orchestra started up again.

"Amusements of millionaires," said Joseph Burner.

She was sitting across the table from him. Everywhere around them, dining or dancing, were all the vampires of the Colony, people who had made their fortunes in rice, rubber, and usury.

"I don't take alcohol," said Burner, "but perhaps you would like a glass of something?"

"I'd like some brandy," said Suzanne.

She wanted to shock him, but all the same she smiled at him. No doubt she would have liked to be there with someone else, at whom she would not have had to take the pains of smiling. Now that Joseph had gone away and Ma wanted so much to die, truly, each day the need of that someone was felt more and more.

"Is Madame your mother in bad health?" asked Burner, for something to say.

"She's waiting for my brother," said Suzanne, "and it makes her sick."

Suzanne believed that Burner had been informed of everything by Carmen.

"We don't know where he is, but he must have met some woman or other," she added.

"Oh!" said Burner indignantly. "That's no excuse for him to stay away. Never would I leave my mother. But then, my mother is a saint."

The saintliness of his mother was something to shudder about.

"Mine's no saint," said Suzanne. "And if I was in my brother's place I'd do the same."

Suzanne collected her wits. Now was the time to strike.

"If you think your mother's a saint, why don't you prove it to her?"

"Prove it?" asked Burner in astonishment. "But I do prove it. I believe I may say I have never failed my mother."

"You ought to give her a fine present, once and for all, then afterwards you'd have peace."

"I do not understand," said Joseph Burner, still astonished. "I don't know what you mean by peace."

"If, say, you gave her a beautiful ring, then afterwards you'd never have to think of giving her anything else," said Suzanne.

"A ring? Why a ring?"

"I say, for example, a ring."

"My mother," said Joseph Burner, "does not like rings. She has very simple tastes. Every year I buy her a piece of land in southern England, and that's what gives her the most pleasure."

"Me, I prefer sparklers," said Suzanne. "More often than not, land is just muck."

"Oh!" said Burner. "Oh! What kind of language is this?"

"The word's in the dictionary," said Suzanne. "I'd like to dance."

Burner stood up and invited Suzanne to dance. He danced very correctly. Suzanne was much shorter than he and, while dancing, her eyes were on a level with his mouth.

"Frenchwomen are the best and the worst in the world," he began, as they danced.

But although his mouth was on a level with her eyes and hair, not once did he even touch the hair of this Frenchwoman with his lips.

"When you take them young you can make the most devoted companions out of them, the surest helpmates," he went on.

He was going away in a week's time and would be gone for two years. He was therefore in a hurry. What he wanted precisely was a young girl of eighteen that no man had yet approached, not because he had any prejudice in that regard (he supposed such things were necessary, he said) but because his experience had taught him that you could mold the inexperienced ones better and quicker.

"All my life I have searched for this young French girl of eighteen, this ideal girl. It is a wonderful age, eighteen. Girls of that age can be turned into lovely little things."

Joseph would say: "Lovely little things, my ass! You can have your young virgins!"

"As for me," said Suzanne, "I think I want to grow up to be like Carmen."

"Oh!" said Mr. Joseph Burner.

No doubt of it, he must have tried to sleep with Carmen, but Carmen wouldn't have a bird like this. All the same, she tried to palm him off on someone else!

"Like Carmen, only better," said Suzanne.

"You do not understand!" said Burner. "One doesn't marry a woman like Carmen."

He laughed pityingly at Suzanne's artlessness.

"Not everyone could marry her; it depends who," said Suzanne.

When they arrived back at the hotel, before they got out of the car, Burner said something he must have often said before to specimens such as Suzanne:

"Would you like to be that young girl that I have searched for, such a long time?"

"You must speak to my mother," said Suzanne. "But I warn you, I'm a Carmen type."

Nonetheless it was agreed that next day, after dinner, he should make Ma's acquaintance.

7

"I'M ONE OF THE TOP SALESMEN OF THAT FACTORY," SAID
Burner.

Ma looked at him with very mild curiosity.

"You're lucky to have succeeded," she said. "Not everyone can say as much. Well! So you sell yarn, do you?"

"It doesn't sound like much," said Burner, "but it's an
industry of considerable importance. You can't imagine the
amount of yarn consumed in the world, and you can't imagine the sums it sells for."

Ma maintained a skeptical attitude. Manifestly she had
never imagined it was possible to make a decent living in
such a business. Burner told her of the fortune he was beginning to make and which was beginning to be important,
he said. Every year he invested in a piece of land in southern England where he intended to settle when he retired.
Ma listened absent-mindedly. Not that she doubted Burner's word, but she did not see the sense of investing in land
in southern England. It was too far away. Still, at the word
"investment" her eyes lit up like the flashing diamond. But
it was a very fugitive light and did not revive her. She had a
tired and vague look. However, this thing was important:
after all, it was the first time anyone had asked for Suzanne's
hand in marriage. She made a visible effort to listen to
Burner, but in reality her thoughts were far away, with
Joseph.

"And you've been searching like this for a long time?" she asked.

"For years," said Burner. "I see Carmen has talked to you about me. All things come to him who waits, as I believe you also say in French."

"You speak French very well," said Ma.

That makes two fatheads, thought Suzanne. Bad luck and more bad luck, in this and everything.

"It must be very fatiguing," said Ma, musingly. "Waiting! I've spent years waiting, and it's done me no good. But I go on waiting. It's never over."

"I don't like to wait," said Suzanne. "As Joseph says, patience makes me puke."

Burner jumped slightly. Ma only heard the name Joseph.

"Maybe he's dead," she said in a low voice. "After all, why shouldn't he be dead?"

"From waiting like that all this time," said Suzanne, "I imagine you're not as hard to please as you once were."

"On the contrary, I am harder and harder to please," said Burner flatteringly.

"Under a trolley car," said Ma in a low voice. "Something tells me he is lying under a trolley car."

"Ha, ha," said Suzanne, "the one thing I'm sure of is that he's not under a trolley car."

Burner stopped talking about himself for a while. He did not take offense at their lack of interest. He guessed that they were talking about Joseph and his escapade. His smile showed that he had a certain experience with such adventures.

"Not only isn't he under a trolley," said Suzanne, "but I'll bet he's much happier than you are, so don't worry, he's a thousand times happier than you are."

Ma stared out at the concentric trolley lines in the Avenue de l'Ouest, as she often stared at them now, from her window, looking for the B-12 to come down that street.

"It's what you call the escapades of a young man," said

Burner at last, with emphasis, and he added with an insin-
uating smile, "it's well to pass through such things but it's
still better to have ended with them."

He was fiddling with his glass. His thin, well-cared-for
hands recalled Monsieur Jo's hands. He also wore a ring,
but without a diamond. The only ornament on it was his
initials, a J lovingly interlaced with a B.

"Joseph won't ever end with such things," Suzanne
affirmed.

"There you're right," said Ma.

"Life will steady him down," said Burner, not without
pride, as if he himself knew what life held in store for fellows like Joseph.

Suzanne recalled the hands of Monsieur Jo which had
tried to touch her breasts. Burner's hands on my breasts
would be the same thing, she thought. They're the same
kind of hands.

"Life won't do a thing to him," said Suzanne. "Joseph
isn't just anyone."

Burner did not lose countenance but followed her line of
thought.

"It's not that type of man that makes women happy, believe me," he said.

Ma remembered something.

"So then," she said, "you want to marry my daughter?"

She turned towards Suzanne and smiled at her in an ab-
sent-minded but gentle way. Burner flushed slightly.

"Quite right," said Burner. "It would make me very
happy."

Joseph, Joseph. If he were there he would say, "She shan't
sleep with him!" Carmen told me he's offered Ma thirty
thousand francs to take me away, ten thousand more than
the sparkler's worth. Joseph would say, "That's no reason."

"And you sell yarn?" asked Ma, much to Burner's astonishment, for it was the third time she had asked that.

"I wouldn't quite put it that way," he explained patiently. "I would say, rather, that I represent a textile firm in Calcutta. I take enormous orders throughout the world for my firm."

Ma reflected, still without ceasing to stare out at the concentric trolley lines.

"I don't know if I'll give her to you or not. Curious thing: I don't have an opinion on the subject."

"A queer business," whispered Suzanne to her.

"Most of the time," said Burner, who had overheard but who was broad-minded as to what he called Suzanne's mischievousness, "most of the time I am very free. I deal always with the directors of companies. You must understand that in the grade of business I conduct everything is concluded on paper. So I have a great deal of time to myself."

Which means, thought Suzanne, that I wouldn't even have the time to go off with someone else. Finished the idea of a way out, as Carmen puts it.

"You speak French very well," said Ma again, in a curious voice.

Burner smiled, flattered.

"And she would go everywhere with you?" pursued Ma.

"The G.M.B. pays the travelling expenses of its agents and their wives," said Burner, added pointedly, with all that remained to him of youthful daring: "and their children."

Really it was impossible to imagine what kind of company it was that Burner worked for. This must have been Ma's conclusion for, after a silence, she said brusquely:

"In the last count, I'm neither for nor against. That's the funny thing."

"It's often like that. When you least expect it, something happens," said Burner, who was easily encouraged.

"That's not what she meant to say," said Suzanne.

Ma yawned widely, with no restraint. She'd had enough

of trying to concentrate while her mind was wool-gathering.

"The best thing to do is for me to think it over tonight," she said.

When she and Suzanne were alone, Ma asked: "Do you have any opinion on him?"

"I'd rather have a hunter," said Suzanne.

Ma did not reply.

"It would mean going away forever," said Suzanne, "with this man."

"Forever?"

"For three years."

Ma reflected once more.

"All the same, if Joseph doesn't come back, it would be better for you. It's a queer business he's in. But supposing Joseph doesn't come back?"

Her eyes fixed, Ma stared, unseeing, at the square of black sky cut out by the open window. Suzanne knew what Ma's thoughts were. It was always the same thing: Suzanne's going to stay on my hands, it won't ever finish. She was not thinking about the thirty thousand francs. What she was thinking about was her death.

"Joseph will come back," cried Suzanne, "sooner or later, he'll come back."

"It's not sure," said Ma.

"Even so . . . I'd rather have a hunter."

Ma smiled, suddenly relaxed. She stroked her child's hair.

"Why do you always want a hunter?"

"I don't know."

"Don't you worry, you could always have a hunter. Tomorrow I'll speak to him, I'll tell him you don't want to leave me."

Then suddenly, in the tone of one who remembers that the essential thing has been forgotten, she asked: "What about the diamond?"

"I tried," said Suzanne, "and it's not worth while insisting with him."

"They're all alike," Ma concluded.

Next morning, for the first time since Joseph's departure, Ma rose early and immediately went to Burner's room. Suzanne never knew what she said to him. She saw him again in the office that afternoon, when she was replacing Carmen at the desk. He looked a little upset as he told her that her mother had talked with him.

"I must admit, I'm a little discouraged. For ten years now I've been searching. You seemed to be . . ."

"Don't regret anything," said Suzanne.

She smiled, but he did not.

"As for me being a virgin, that's finished with long ago."

"Oh!" said Burner. "Why did you conceal that?"

"It's not a thing you go shout from the housetops."

"It's horrible!" cried Burner.

"It's like that."

In despair, Burner raised his eyes and beheld Carmen's notice:

FOR SALE—MAGNIFICENT DIAMOND

"Is it . . . is it your diamond?" he asked in a weak voice.

"It certainly is," said Suzanne.

"Oh!" said Burner again, completely disconcerted by so much immorality.

"Well," said Suzanne, "you sell yarns, don't you?"

8

STILL, SUZANNE DID RUN ACROSS ANOTHER MAN—MONSIEUR
Jo.

One afternoon, as she left the Hotel Central, she found
his limousine stationed in front of the entrance. As soon as
he perceived Suzanne, Monsieur Jo went towards her with
an apparently tranquil step.

"Good-day!" said he triumphantly. "I have found you!"
He was perhaps better rigged out than usual, but he was
as ugly as ever.

"We came to sell the ring," said Suzanne. "But that's nothing to you."

"I don't give a damn about the ring," said Monsieur Jo,
posing as a good sport and forcing a laugh. "What's important is that I have found you at last!"

He must have been looking for some time. Maybe three
days, maybe longer. Here in the city, far from the watchful
eyes of Joseph and Ma, he seemed to be less intimidated
than at the bungalow.

"Where are you going like that?"

"I'm going to the movies. I go every day."

Monsieur Jo looked skeptically at her.

"Like that, all alone?" he said. "A pretty girl like you, all
alone at the movies?" he added, with his habitual perspi-
cacity.

"Pretty or not, in any case yes, it's like that."

Monsieur Jo lowered his eyes, remained silent for a good minute then declared, this time with real timidity: "And suppose you renounced going today? Why go so often to the movies? It's unhealthy, it gives you false ideas of life."

Suzanne looked at the perfectly polished limousine. The impeccable chauffeur, in white livery, seemed to be a part of the car which he drove. Perfectly impassive, his entire attention was given to appearing as inattentive as possible. But all the same, he must know everything that had transpired between her and Monsieur Jo. She essayed a smile at him, but he remained as impassive as if she had smiled at the automobile itself.

"As far as false ideas go," said Suzanne, "you can come again, as Joseph says. And as for the movies, I don't feel like renouncing them, as you say."

He still had his enormous diamond on his finger. That one was at least three times bigger than the other and doubtless had no flaw. You wondered what it was doing on his finger, as you might wonder what its owner was doing in the city or, for that matter, in the world.

"We might take a drive," said he, flushing. "I would like to talk with you about our last interview . . . You know, I suffered terribly."

"Maybe," said Suzanne. "But as for the movies, I want to go, all the same."

Monsieur Jo looked her up and down. For the first time since he had known her he was alone with her, without other witness than his chauffeur, and his expression was something like that he had had when she had showed herself to him in the shower. She had already been looked at like this by men she passed in the Haut-Quartier, when she went to the movies. Once or twice, as she returned to the Hotel Central, Colonial soldiers had accosted her. But it was, she imagined, because of the dresses Carmen lent her, for the Colonial troops usually accosted only prostitutes. However, she had seen some men she wouldn't have minded going off with, but those men never accosted her. Once in the movies, especially, she remembered a man she would willingly have gone off with. Often during the picture they had looked at each other in silence, their elbows touching on the arm of the seats. He was with another man, and when the picture ended they had left the theatre, disappearing in the crowd. Left alone, she had recalled the warmth that had come to her from that unknown man's arm, a consoling warmth with a kind of sadness in it, like Jean Agosti's kiss. After that, she was surer than ever that where you met them was in the palpitating gloom of the movies. It was at the movies that Joseph had met the woman he was looking for. It was there, too, about three years ago, that he had picked up the first woman, after Carmen, with whom he had ever slept. It was only there, in front of the screen, that everything became simple. To be with an unknown person in front of the same image gave you a desire for the unknown. The impossible became attainable, obstacles flattened out or became imaginary. There, at least, you felt an equality with the city, whereas in the streets it eluded you and you escaped it.

"If you go," said Monsieur Jo, "I will accompany you."

They drove to the movies in the Léon Bollée. The chauffeur waited for them in front of the entrance. During the entire picture, Monsieur Jo looked at Suzanne while she looked at the film. But that was no more bothersome than it had been in the plain: in a way, even, it was better to be with Monsieur Jo and his limousine than alone once more at the movies. From time to time he took her hand, squeezed it, bent his head and kissed it. And there in the darkness of the movies it was tolerable.

After the show, Monsieur Jo offered her a drink in a café of the fashionable district. He still had a happy look and seemed to be hatching some plans. He spoke of this and that, doubtless putting off until later what he really wanted to say. It was Suzanne who spoke to him about the ring.

"We sold it very dear," she said, "for much more than you'd think."

Monsieur Jo did not pay much attention. He had finished with all his mourning and sentimentality over the ring.

"And what about Joseph?" he asked.

It was now ten days since Joseph had disappeared.

"Oh, he's all right. He's probably at the movies. We're getting all we can out of the city before leaving. Never did we have as much money as this. And she—she has paid a part of her debts and is very satisfied."

What Monsieur Jo would have liked to know was whether Ma and Joseph had reconsidered their judgment against him.

"And even if she wanted to see you again," said Suzanne, "you shouldn't see her. She would absolutely ruin you. To tell the truth, what she'd like would be a ring a day! Now that she's acquired the taste . . ."

"I know," said Monsieur Jo, reddening, "but just to see you, what I wouldn't do!"

"A ring a day, all the same, you couldn't . . ."

Monsieur Jo evaded the question.

"What is going to happen to you?" he asked with profound compassion. "It's a hard life you have there on the plain."

"Don't you worry, it won't last long," said Suzanne, staring at Monsieur Jo, who again flushed violently.

"Do you have some—some plans?" he asked, put to the torture.

"Maybe," said Suzanne, laughing, "maybe I'll fix myself up with Carmen. But they'll have to pay very dear for me. Again, on account of Joseph."

"If you like, I will take you back to the hotel in my car, now," said Monsieur Jo, to put an end to this interview, of which he did not quite know what to make.

Suzanne accepted, and got into the car with Monsieur Jo. It was comfortable there. The car glided through the city, which was full of others like it, gleaming. When night fell, the car was still gliding through the city which suddenly became illuminated, a chaos of surfaces bright and dark, among which they penetrated with ease, the chaos each time dropping away at the car's approach, each time forming again in its rear. The car itself was a solution: things had meaning as you advanced into them. It was like the movies. Especially since the chauffeur drove without a goal, without an end, as is not usual in real life . . .

When night had come, Monsieur Jo had drawn near Suzanne and had put his arms around her. The car continued to roll through the chaotic brilliance and darkness of the city. And Monsieur Jo's hands trembled. Suzanne could not see his face. Almost without knowing it, he had pressed her close to him, and Suzanne allowed it. She was intoxicated with the city. The car drove onward, the only reality, a glorious reality. And in its wake all the city fell back, crumbled away, brilliant, swarmingly alive, endless. Sometimes Monsieur Jo's hands touched Suzanne's breasts. And once he said:

"Your breasts are beautiful."

The thing had been said very softly. But it had been said. For the first time. And while the naked hand was on the naked breast. And above the terrifying city, Suzanne saw her breasts, saw the erection of her breasts higher than anything that stood up in the city. Her breasts, then, would be justified. She smiled. Then, frenziedly, as if it were urgent that she know at once, she again took Monsieur Jo's hands in hers and placed them round her waist.

"And this?"

"What?" said Monsieur Jo, stupefied.

"What about this part of me?"

"It's very beautiful."

He looked at her closely. She, while looking at the city, was really only regarding herself. She was regarding in solitude her empire, over which reigned her waist, her legs, her breasts.

"I love you," said Monsieur Jo softly.

In the only novel she had ever read, as in the films that she had since seen, the words "I love you" were pronounced but once, in the course of a conversation between lovers which lasted barely a few minutes but which concluded months of waiting or ended a terrible separation, infinite griefs. Never yet had Suzanne heard the words addressed to her. For a long time she had believed that it was infinitely more serious to say them than to surrender to a man after having said them. She had believed that the words could be said but once in her whole life and that afterwards never, her whole life long, could they be said again, under pain of bringing upon herself an abominable dishonor. Now she knew that she had been mistaken. You could say the words spontaneously, in an outburst of desire, and you could say them even to prostitutes. It was a need that men felt sometimes, they had to pronounce them, if only to feel for the moment their exhausting force. And to hear them spoken was also sometimes necessary, for the same reason.

"I love you," Monsieur Jo repeated.

He leaned forward a little more over her face and suddenly, like a blow, she received his lips on hers. She pulled away from him with a cry. Monsieur Jo tried to hold her back in his arms, but she sprang towards the car door and opened it. Then Monsieur Jo moved away from her and told his chauffeur to drive back to the hotel.

During the journey they did not speak a word to each other. When they arrived at the hotel, Suzanne got out of the car without giving Monsieur Jo a look. Once outside, she said only:

"I can't. It's no use. With you, I never could."

He did not reply.

Thus it was that Monsieur Jo disappeared from Suzanne's life. But no one ever knew anything about it, not even Carmen. Except Ma—but that was very much later.

9

ONE AFTERNOON CARMEN DASHED INTO MA'S ROOM AND ASKED for the diamond.

"It's Joseph," cried Carmen. "It's Joseph who's managed to sell it!"

Ma sprang up and shouted that she wanted to see Joseph. Carmen told her that he had not come to the hotel but that he had telephoned asking her to meet him immediately in a café of the Haut-Quartier. It would be best for Ma not to go along. Joseph might believe that she came to urge him to take them back to the plain. And as to that, according to Carmen, it was clear Joseph had not yet decided.

Ma resigned herself and gave the diamond to Carmen, who ran to meet Joseph at an unknown place.

When Suzanne returned from the movies that same evening, she found Ma all dressed up, pacing the corridor in front of her bedroom. She was holding a wad of paper money—thousand-franc notes.

"It's Joseph," she announced triumphantly. And she added in a lower voice: "Twenty thousand francs. What I wanted for it."

Then at once she changed her tune and began to lament. She said she was tired of staying in bed and that she would have liked to go immediately to the banks to pay the interest on her debts but that she had received the money too late, now the banks were closed. It was just another piece

of her usual bad luck! As soon as she heard Ma talking to
Suzanne, Carmen came out of her room. She seemed very
satisfied and she kissed Suzanne. But there was no calming
down Ma. Carmen suggested that they dine quickly and
go out after dinner. Ma scarcely ate a bite. She talked without stopping about Joseph and his qualities, about her projects, and so forth. After dinner she went along with Suzanne
and Carmen to a café in the upper town, but she refused to
go to the movies, saying it would keep her up too late and
she wanted to reach the banks early next morning, when
they opened.

Carmen told Suzanne, when they were alone together,
that it was the woman Joseph had met who had bought the
diamond. Carmen had seen her for only a very short time.
Joseph had not asked about either Ma or Suzanne. He
seemed to be so happy that she had not told him about Ma's
impatience to be gone. Carmen was sure that anyone, no
matter who, would have done the same. No one could have
had the heart to disturb the overwhelming happiness of
Joseph. When they had parted, he had told her that
he would come to the hotel very soon to take Ma and
Suzanne back to the plain. He did not know exactly what
day. Carmen advised Suzanne not to speak about it to Ma.
She said that Joseph himself was not sure when he would
return.

Thus it was that Ma, for a few hours at least, had the sum
of twenty thousand francs in her hands.

The very next day she ran to the bank to pay a part of her
debts. Carmen had advised her not to do this, but she had
not listened to her. She said it was to regain their confidence
in her and to be able to borrow again, afterwards, the sums
necessary for the construction of new sea walls. At the bank,
the underlings with whom she spoke seemed very ready to
accept the money she wanted to reimburse but said they
could not take the initiative in approving her request for a

new loan. That settled, she secured an appointment to see
the bank manager, so as to ask him for new credit. Then,
the appointment made, she realized that it was so far off
that the slender amount of money that would remain to her
once the interest money had been paid would be used up
in the wait, so she tried to get her appointment moved up
to an earlier date.

Her efforts—particularly the latter—took a great deal of
time and, when she realized that her efforts here were completely useless, she addressed herself to a second bank,
again making two kinds of applications. And again, her efforts proved completely useless, because of the unshakable
solidarity reigning among the Colonial banks.

The interest on the debts was much higher than Ma had
expected. And the entire proceedings had taken a much
longer time than she had anticipated.

At the end of a few days, Ma had very little money left.
Then she went to bed, took her pills and slept the days
away. It was all she could do, while waiting for Joseph, she
said. Joseph, the cause of all her woes.

10

JOSEPH RETURNED. ONE MORNING, TOWARDS SIX O'CLOCK, HE knocked at Carmen's door and went in without waiting.

"We're off," he said to Suzanne. "Get up, quick."

With a bound, Suzanne and Carmen were out of bed. Suzanne dressed herself and followed Joseph. He went into Ma's room without knocking and stood in front of her bed.

"If you want to leave, now's the time," he said.

Ma sat up on her bed with a wild look. Then, without a word, she began to cry softly. Joseph did not cast a glance at her. He went to the window, opened it, leaned against the frame, and began to wait. As Ma did not budge, at the end of a few minutes he turned round and said:

"It's now or never. Get a move on."

Ma, still without replying, painfully left her bed. Half naked, she was wearing an old slip that was not very clean. She pulled on her dress, lifted her braids, still weeping, then she took two valises out from under the bed.

Joseph, still at the window, was smoking English cigarettes, one after the other. He had lost weight. Sitting on a chair in the middle of the room, Suzanne had eyes only for him. He looked as though he had not slept for several nights. His expression was something like that he had when he returned at daybreak from night hunting. His whole body was tense, with a restrained wrath which prevented him from giving up to fatigue. Certainly he alone had not been

185

the one to decide to come back for them. Someone must have said to him: "All the same, take them back home," or maybe, "You must take them home all the same, I know it's hard, but you can't drop them like this."

"Help me, Suzanne," said Ma.

"I'll only go if I want to," said Suzanne. "I like it here, never have I liked it so much anywhere. If I want to, I'll stay here."

Joseph did not turn. Ma rose up and awkwardly tried to box Suzanne's ears. Suzanne did not dodge, but grabbed Ma's hand and held it firmly. Ma, scarcely surprised, looked at her, then disengaged her hand and, without saying a word, began to stuff things pell-mell into the valises. Joseph had not seen anything, he was looking at nothing and at no one. He continued to chain-smoke his English cigarettes. Then, as she packed her valises, Ma began to tell the story of the salesman from Calcutta who had been willing to pay thirty thousand francs, to marry Suzanne.

"Just imagine," she said, "only three days ago someone proposed to Suzanne."

Joseph was not listening.

"If I want to, I'll stay here. Carmen will keep me," said Suzanne. "I don't need anyone to take me away. People who think they're indispensable make me puke, as they say so well themselves."

Ma did nothing, at this, but went on with her own train of thought.

"A yarn salesman," she said, "from Calcutta. A fine position."

"Me, too, I can do without everyone," said Suzanne.

"But I don't like that kind of business," said Ma. "You're independent without being independent. And it must be stupefying to sell yarns all the time and all the time."

"He doesn't give a hang about your story," said Suzanne. "You'd do better to get a move on."

Joseph still did not turn towards them. Once more, Ma

made a lunge in Suzanne's direction, then changed her mind and went back to her valises.

"Thirty thousand francs," she continued without a change of tone. "He offered me thirty thousand francs. What's thirty thousand francs? The ring alone was worth twenty thousand. And as if you could even compare such things! As if we would descend to that . . ."

Someone knocked at the door. It was Carmen, bringing a platter on which were three cups of coffee, some bread and butter, and also a package tied up with string.

"You must drink some coffee before you go," said Carmen. "I made you some sandwiches for the road."

Her hair was uncombed, she was in a dressing gown, she smiled. Ma stood up from her packing and she, too, smiled, her eyes still full of tears. Carmen bent, kissed her, and tip-toed out without another word.

Joseph heard nothing, seemed to see nothing. Suzanne took a cup of coffee and began very slowly to eat Carmen's bread and butter. Ma drank her coffee at one gulp, without eating anything. When she had finished, she took the third cup over to Joseph.

"Here's your coffee," she said gently.

Joseph took the cup without thanking her, drank his coffee with a grimace of disgust, as if the coffee itself had changed. Then he put down the empty cup on a chair and said:

"People who are down and out have no business going to town to show off and talk big. Try it and you're sunk. Some folks are made to drag a ball and chain, always the same ball and chain. They can't take a step without dragging a ball and chain . . ."

Suzanne did not quite recognize Joseph's language. Before, he had never spoken with such profundity, had rarely formulated judgments of a general kind. He was surely repeating something he had heard and which had struck him. But if he had come back, Suzanne felt sure it was because

the money from the sale of his pelts had run out, because he
had no more money in his pockets. It was not because he
had been advised to come, after all. And so, everything was
different from what you might have thought . . .

During the greater part of the journey, Joseph did not
utter a word. Ma, on the other hand, talked interminably
of her projects. She said she had secured from the banks
strong assurances of the possibility of a new loan at a lower
rate than the old.

"I did a good stroke of business," she said. "Instead of
five per cent I got two per cent for future interest. And I
have liquidated all past interests. So now I have a clean
slate."

Joseph pushed the B-12 to the limit. He looked like an
assassin fleeing the city where he has committed a crime.
From time to time he stopped, dipped water from a paddy
and emptied it from the bucket into the radiator, urinated,
spat with disgust at something—doubtless at having the
two of them there, once again. Then he got back into the
car without giving them a look.

"I've always liked to be square and open and that's how
I've always pulled out of tight places," said Ma once. Then:
"It's good to go back home. What I need to do now is to take
out a good mortgage. Not on the paddies, of course, but on
the five hectares of the upper land. As to the house, God
help me! that's settled long ago."

She was talking for Joseph's benefit. Moreover, for the
first time in her life, she was not reproaching him for anything. Not once did she allude to the week she had spent
waiting for him at the hotel. To hear her talk, her affairs
were running on greased wheels.

"To pay at one go the total of two years' interest, that
makes a good impression. After that, I need a good mortgage to pull me out. They should give me the five hectares
outright, I've earned them, since I've had them under culti-

vation every year. You can't ask for a mortgage on land
that's not yours, it's only normal."

Her tone was light, almost jovial. To hear her talk, you
would have thought she had just closed a most successful
deal.

"The cadastral agents will hear about it, of course. I know
it will go against their grain to give me the title deeds to
the house and the upper land, to cut the concession in half,
but against the grain or not, it's my right. What do you
think about it, Joseph?"

"Let him alone," said Suzanne, at the end of three hundred kilometers. "It may be your right but you'll not get it,
you think you have a right to everything, but you don't
have a right to anything, it's always the same."

Ma raised her hand to strike, but then thought better of
it. Useless to try to hit Suzanne now. She went on talking.

"You'd do well to keep quiet," she said. "You don't even
know what you're talking about. If it's my right, I'll have it.
What's awful about these mortgages is the way people mis-
use them. More than half the plain is mortgaged. People
are irresponsible. First they take out a mortgage with the
bank, then a mortgage with an individual. Then the bank
sells them up. It'll finish like that with the Agostis . . ."

She talked for a good part of the day, all alone, without
getting the least encouragement from either Suzanne or
Joseph. It was not until they reached the last village before
the highway that Joseph spoke his first words.

At this village he got out, examined the engine, went to
the wells and took in a supply of water. Then he re-oiled
and re-fuelled. It was necessary, since they would pass
through no more villages on their way to the plain but
would be driving straight through the forest for two hundred kilometers. After he had put the car in shape, having
nothing else to do, Joseph sat down on the running board
and ran his hands through his hair, slowly, forcefully, like
someone who is just waking up. His impatience suddenly

left him and he did not seem to be so eager now to go on. Suzanne and Ma looked at him but he did not see them. You felt he was in a new solitude, from which they had definitely lost their power to drag him. Or rather, it was that he was no longer alone: the other person did not have to be there for them to feel that he was with her. And Suzanne and her mother had no further rôles to play in his life except those of helpless witnesses, vaguely indiscreet, of his and the other's self-sufficiency. His thoughts were so far-off and at the same time so personal and precise that there, seated on the running board of the B-12, he had become as absent from them as if in sleep. "Only if I would die would he look at me now," thought Suzanne. Joseph had driven since morning. It was now six o'clock in the afternoon. Around his eyes were big rings of white dust which disguised him and made him still more foreign to them. He seemed to be attenuated with fatigue but steady and sure, as if he had reached a goal. Then it was that he passed his hands slowly through his hair, rubbed his eyes, yawned and stretched, still as if just awakening.

"I'm hungry," he said.

Ma quickly undid the package Carmen had given them and extracted three sandwiches. Joseph ate one, climbed back into the B-12, and while driving swallowed the second in a few mouthfuls. While her children ate, Ma, suddenly worn out, took a nap. Until that moment she may have doubted that she would ever again have to feed them. When she woke up, an hour later, it was night. Her thoughts had returned into their old and more normal channels.

"Maybe," she said, "I ought not to have paid up my interest as I did." And she added, as if speaking to herself, "They swindled me, all of them."

She had been warned by Carmen but had not paid any attention.

"It's honesty misplaced. Carmen was right. For them, what I paid is a drop in the bucket, less than a drop. But for me . . . for me . . . I thought that, afterwards, they would lend me fifty thousand francs or so, at least."

All at once, seeing that no one replied to her, she began to cry.

"I paid them up, paid everything. You're right. I'm an imbecile, an old crackpot."

"It's no good to say it," said Suzanne, "you should have thought about it before."

"I wasn't sure," lamented Ma, "but now I am sure, I am nothing but an old crackpot. When I remember that Joseph has such bad teeth . . ."

Joseph spoke for the second time.

"Don't you worry about my teeth. Go to sleep."

Ma drowsed again.

It must have been two o'clock in the morning when she woke up. Taking the blanket from under her, she spread it over her. She was cold. They were in the depths of the forest. The B-12 drove ahead at top speed. They must not be very far from Kam. In a tearful voice, Ma started up again.

"After all, if you want to that much, we could sell up everything and leave."

"Sell what?" asked Joseph. "Sleep. It's no good talking."

He began to hunt through all his pockets, still driving, found what he was looking for and held it out to Ma with one hand, the other still on the wheel. In the glimmer of the headlights, the thing showed up at first imprecisely, small and sparkling, then suddenly unmistakable: the diamond.

"Here," said Joseph, "take it back."

Ma let out a cry of terror.

"The same one! The sparkler!"

As if crushed, she looked at the diamond without taking it.

"You might explain yourself," said Suzanne in a neutral voice.

His hand still held out with the diamond, Joseph waited

for Ma to take it. He did not get impatient. Yes, it was the same diamond, only it was no longer wrapped in tissue paper.

"It was given back to me," he said at last in a tired voice, "after they had bought it from me. Try to understand that, if you can!"

Ma put out her hand, took the diamond and placed it in her handbag. Then, gently, she began again to cry, in silence.

"What are you squalling about now?" asked Suzanne.

"It's all going to begin again. I've got to begin it all over again."

"You've got nothing to complain about," said Suzanne.

"I'm not complaining. But I don't have the strength to begin all over again."

11

MA HAD HIRED THE CORPORAL IMMEDIATELY UPON HER arrival in the plain. It was now six years that he had been working for her. No one knew his age, the old Malay himself did not know it. He believed he was between forty and fifty, but he did not know exactly, for he had spent his life looking for work and this had so monopolized his energies that he had lost track of the passing years. All he knew was that he had come to the plain fifteen years before, to work on the construction of the highway, and that he had never left it.

He was a tall man with very thin legs planted in enormous feet like rackets, feet that had flattened and spread out from having soaked in the mud of the paddies, feet that you could hope he would one day take as far as the water, but as to that, alas, there was no question as far as the Corporal was concerned. His misery, when he came to Ma one morning to beg a bowl of rice, in exchange, he said, for a day's work of transporting logs from the forest to the bungalow, was complete and unsurpassable. Ever since the completion of the work on the road until that morning, the Corporal, with his wife and stepdaughter, had spent his time scouring the plain, looking for food in the garbage under the cabins and in the outskirts of the villages, trying to find something to sustain them. For years they had slept under the huts in Bante, the village upon which Ma's concession bordered. When she had been younger, the Corpo-

193

ral's wife had played the whore throughout the entire plain for a few sous or a little dried fish, to which occupation the Corporal had never made any objections. Moreover, during the fifteen years that he had roamed the plain, he had made no great objections to anything, except a too protracted and too urgent hunger.

The road had been the great thing in his life. He had come to the plain to work on it. They had said to him: "You who are deaf, you ought to go to work on the road that's being built to Ram." He had been hired from the very first days of the project. His work had consisted in clearing the ground, banking it up, paving it, and pounding it with wooden hand-pounders.

It would have been work like any other if at least eighty per cent of it had not been effected by convicts and supervised by native troops who, in ordinary times, were put in charge of the Colonial prisons. These convicts, these great "criminals" that, like so many mushrooms, had been discovered by the whites, were serving life sentences. Thus, they were made to work sixteen hours a day, chained together by fours, in close ranks. Each rank was supervised by a soldier dressed in the uniform of the "Native Militia for Natives," chartered by the whites. Besides these convicts there were a few recruited laborers, such as the Corporal. If in the beginning there was some distinction made between the convicts and the other hands, it gradually became attenuated except for the fact that the convicts were fed while the recruits were not. And finally the convicts had the advantage of being without their wives while the others had theirs with them, following in moving camps to the rear of the construction yards. These wives were eternally bearing children and were eternally starving. The militiamen saw to it that there were always some labor recruits, in order to have women available, even when isolated in the forest and at a distance of many kilometers from any hamlet. Moreover, the women as well as the men and children died of malaria at a regular rate so that they could be replaced sufficiently often by the militiamen who, themselves, had a ration of quinine to assure their own survival and the maintenance of their authority which daily became more assured and more fantastic. They could effect a change of women with enough frequency, since the death of an enlisted man's wife immediately lost that man his job.

Thus, it was largely on account of his wife that the Corporal had held on to the job, although he was very deaf. Another reason was that from the first days of his employment on the road, thanks to his ingrained craftiness, he had realized that it was to his interest to become fused with the convicts and to make the militia gradually forget his uncertain position as a recruit. At the end of a few months, they had got so used to him that they absent-mindedly chained him up with the convicts, flogging him as they flogged the convicts, and they would no more have thought of discharging him than they would have thought of discharging a criminal. During this time, as did all the wives of the recruits, the Corporal's wife gave birth to children, one after another, thanks to the virility of the militiamen. During all this time, too, there were the sixteen hours of road-pounding with heavy cudgels under a sun which deprived the recruits and the convicts alike of all power of initiative, even the most natural. One only of her children had survived, the others having died of malaria or starvation. It was a girl, and the Corporal had kept her with them. How many times in six years had the Corporal's wife borne a child in the midst of the forest, to the deafening sound of the road-pounders and the axes, the yells of the troops and the cracking of their whips? She could not now remember. What she did remember was that she had been kept constantly pregnant by the militiamen and that it was the Corporal who had got up at night to dig the little graves for the dead children.

The Corporal said he had been flogged as much as a man

could be without dying, but flogged or not, during the construction of the highway he had eaten every day. When the
road was finished, it had been quite another story. He had
worked at or tried to work at every kind of job: he had gathered pepper, unloaded ships at Ram, cut down trees, and
so forth. Because of his deafness, the only work he had
found of a lasting kind was work ordinarily reserved for
children. He had herded buffalo and, each year at harvest
time, he had acted as scarecrow in the rice fields. His feet
in the water, naked to the waist, his stomach empty, under
the torrid sun for years he had contemplated his pitiful image reflected, among the rice plants, in the clouded water
of the paddies, while he brooded over his long hunger. After
so much, so very much misery, he had still kept one of his
old ambitions, which was to become a conductor on the
buses that ran between Ram and Kam. But in spite
of many efforts he had never been hired, because of
his deafness. And not only had he never been hired, even
on trial, but he had never once even ridden on one of those
buses which, thanks to him as one of the road-builders,
now ran on the highway. All that he knew was that they
ran along and he watched them careening past, tooting
their horns, making a thunderous noise in the silence.

   After his employment in Ma's service, Joseph frequently
took him for long rides in the B-12, when he went to get a
reserve of water for the leaky radiator. Then he would tie
the Corporal to the mudguard, a watering-pot in his hand,
and the Corporal became the happiest man on the plain,
happier than he had ever thought he could be on earth.
Those rides were always unexpected, for they depended
upon Joseph's whims. But soon the Corporal found ways
to bring them about. When he saw Joseph take the car out
from under the bungalow, he would run to get the watering-
can, would climb up on the mudguard and stand where the
missing headlight should be, tying himself with a cord to
the hood. As the car sped along, he watched the road flicker
past at sixty kilometers an hour and always his amazement

was the same when he beheld this road which he had spent
six years to help build.

Ordinarily the wife and daughter of the Corporal worked
in the rice fields, cooked the meals, fished, and took care of
the yard. As for the Corporal, he helped Ma in whatever
she was doing. Besides taking charge of the replanting of
the seedlings and the harvesting of the five hectares of the
upper land, he did whatever Ma took it in her head to have
done—he paved, planted, transplanted, trimmed, dug out,
replanted all she liked. And at night, when she wrote to the
cadastral agents or to the bank, or when she worked on her
accounts, she required him always to be there, seated in
front of her at the dining-room table, sharing her occupa-
tions in approving silence. Often, exasperated at his deafness, she had felt like discharging him, but had never done
so—"on account of his legs," she always said. She could not
look at those legs and at the same time discharge him. The
Corporal had, indeed, been so beaten that the skin of his
legs was blue and thin as cheesecloth. Because of his legs,
no matter what he had done, no matter how deaf he got
with the passing years, she had kept him on.

The Corporal was the only servant Ma had. Upon their
return from the city, she told him she could no longer pay
him but that she would continue to feed him. He decided
to remain and his zeal did not diminish. He was conscious
of Ma's misery but he could never manage to find a common denominator for his and her poverty. At Ma's they ate
every day, no matter what happened, and they slept under
a roof. He knew her whole story and the story of the concession. Often, when he was hoeing around the banana
trees, Ma had told these things to him, yelling them at the
top of her lungs. But in spite of his efforts to find a relation
between her destiny and his, or between the things that had
happened to him and the distraints of the cadastral agents
on the plain, Ma had never been able to cure him of his
incurable incomprehension: he was poverty-stricken, he said,
because he was a deaf man and the son of a deaf man, and he

held nothing against anyone, except the Kam agents, and that only because of the wrongs they had inflicted upon Ma. After their return, the Corporal had almost nothing to do. Ma neglected the banana trees and did not plant anything more. She slept throughout most of the days. They had all become very lazy and sometimes slept until noon. The Corporal waited patiently for them to get up so he could bring them their rice and fish. Joseph practically never went hunting. However, sometimes by chance, and from the verandah, he managed to shoot a stilt-bird or heron that had strayed to the edge of the forest. Then the Corporal's hopes rose as he ran to get the dead bird for him. But Joseph no longer hunted at night and the Corporal, who was doubtless unaware that waiting for a woman could keep you from hunting, must have wondered what malady had struck Joseph. However, when Ma bought him a new horse with what money remained to her, Joseph sometimes in the afternoons ran a passenger service. He did this so as to earn money with which to buy the most expensive English cigarettes, those "555s." The rest of the time he spent playing Monsieur Jo's Victrola. He had changed his mind about the English records now and, aside from "Ramona," they were the only ones he liked. He slept a great deal, or chain-smoked, lying on his bed. He was waiting for that woman.

At night, the Corporal's hopes rose. For then, from long habit, Ma worked on her accounts and drew up plans. Before asking for the title deeds of the concession, she wanted to know if a new mortgage on the upper land would be enough to build some new sea walls, small ones this time, the kind only she would have thought of building. The Corporal stayed up late at night with her. That is to say, she made her calculations out loud and he always approved. "If he listens to me," said Ma, "though I'm sure he doesn't understand a thing, I've reached the stage where I'm happy enough just to have him."

It was during these nights that she wrote her last letter to the cadastral agents. She knew it was perfectly useless, she said, but she wanted to do it one last time. "It will calm me down to tell them off," she said. And for the first time she kept her word: that letter was the last one she ever wrote to the Kam agents. A new thing was that, after having sent the letter, she decided to sow only enough rice for the upper five hectares of land. Until then, despite her annual failures, she had always sown a part of the concession farthest from the sea, as a trial, she said. Even during the two years following the affair of her sea wall, she had continued doing so. This year, she gave up. It was definitely useless, she decided. Anyway, she had no more money, none at all.

So it was that, following their stay in the city, they had taken the stand of being more reasonable, and they seemed determined to face their situation squarely, without the usual resort to insane hopes. Ma's hope, the only one that she still had concerning the concession, had become minute and limited in time. Her only hope now was to receive some kind of reply from the cadastral agents, or, if that failed, to go to Kam to insult them one last time.

"If I go there," she said, "I will tell them off to such an extent that they'll give me the five hectares, at any rate."

Although she did not write to them again after her last letter had been sent, she made interminable notes every night on the subject, setting forth the arguments and reasonings that would justify her demand if one day she managed the trip to Kam. For a time, she vaguely hoped that Joseph would give her the receipts of his passenger service. She even asked for them. But Joseph refused, saying that if he hadn't enough money to buy his "555" cigarettes, he would leave home sooner than he intended to. She capitulated. Then, gradually, she began to look covetously at Monsieur Jo's Victrola.

"Why two phonographs? What do we, in our condition, need with two phonographs?"

But neither Suzanne nor Joseph suggested selling the phonograph. Suzanne could never have brought herself to do so. Only Joseph could do that. And it was hard to know whether Ma was suggesting selling the phonograph merely to assert her power over Joseph one last time by getting him into a temper, or whether she really wanted, with the money from the sale, to go to Kam for a week to badger the cadastral agents. Little by little she began to talk as though all three of them had decided to liquidate it, the only uncertainty being as to when they could agree to do without the phonograph.

"We never thought about it," said Ma, "but there we have two phonographs, while Joseph hasn't even one good pair of sandals."

And in three days' time she had formed the habit of basing the future on the sale of the Victrola, as she had done on the mortgage of the five hectares, as she had done on Monsieur Jo's ring and, more generally and over a longer period, on the sea walls.

"In our situation," she said, "one phonograph is already something. But two phonographs! Well, no one would believe that! The funniest thing is that we never thought about it before."

Soon, moreover, she no longer said precisely what she intended to do with the money from the sale of the Victrola. In the beginning, she said it was to go to Kam "to tell them off." But very soon she had gone beyond that. She said the machine was fine enough to bring in, alone, as much as the B-12, the half of the cost of a new roof, or the cost of two weeks' stay at the Hotel Central. A stay— but she did not say this—which would perhaps have enabled her to sell Monsieur Jo's diamond a second time.

As for Joseph, he had nothing to say on the subject of the Victrola or on anything else in this part of the world. He was neither for nor against its liquidation. However, one day, perhaps as a result of hearing Ma talk about it, or more likely because he was fed up and bored, he decided to go to Ram to sell it. During lunch, a little before leaving the table, he announced:

"I'm going to settle this business of the Victrola."

Ma did not reply, but she looked at him with horrified eyes. If he agreed to sell the phonograph it must be because he could do without it, which meant that his time of departure was irremediably approaching. It meant that he knew the date of his departure, that he had known it ever since his return to the Hotel Central.

Joseph took the Victrola, put it into a bag, put the bag in the one-horse carriage and went off in the direction of Ram without having given a word of explanation as to how he expected to sell it. Stupefied, the Corporal was the only one who watched the departure of that strange instrument of which he had never heard the least sound.

Thus it was that the phonograph left the bungalow without stirring up a word of regret on the part of anyone. Joseph came back that evening with the empty bag and, as he sat down to the table, he held out a piece of paper money to Ma.

"Here," said Joseph, "I sold it to that crook, Pa Bart. It was worth twice the amount but I couldn't manage to get more."

Ma took the note and went to put it in her room, then she returned to the dining room. After which she served the dinner and everything went off as usual, except that Ma did not eat anything. At the end of the meal she declared:

"I'll not go to Kam to see those cadastral agents, the swine, because it would be just like the banks all over again. I'll keep the money."

"That's the best thing to do," said Joseph very gently.

She made an effort to speak calmly. Her forehead was covered with sweat.

"It would be completely useless to go to Kam," she said. "I'm going to keep the money for myself."

And all at once she began to cry.

"For myself, all alone, just for a change. For myself, all alone."

Joseph rose and stood in front of her.

"God damn it to hell, you're going to begin again!" he said.

His voice was gentle and low, as if he were talking to himself. As if the unalterable certitude of his departure, of his happiness, had a hard and hidden side of which they knew nothing. Maybe he, too, was to be pitied. Ma seemed surprised at Joseph's gentle tone. She looked at him as he stood there looking down at her, and suddenly she was soothed.

"Why did you sell the phonograph, Joseph?" asked Ma.

"So that there'll be nothing left to sell. So that I can be sure there's nothing left to sell. If I could burn down the bungalow, hell, I'd do it, and how!"

"There will still be the B-12," said Suzanne.

"But who would drive the B-12?" asked Ma.

Joseph did not reply.

"And there will always be the sparkler to sell," Suzanne went on ruthlessly, "whether you mention it or not, there will always be that to sell."

It was the first time since their return from the city that the subject of the diamond had been broached. Ma stopped crying and pulled the diamond out of her bosom where, since their return, she had worn it, tied round her neck on the same string that held the store-cupboard key.

"I don't know why I keep the worthless thing," she said, hypocritically.

"Better ask why you wear a ring on a string around your neck," asked Joseph. "Can't you wear a ring on your finger like anyone else?"

"I'd be seeing it all the time and it would be too disgusting," said Ma.

"That's not so," said Suzanne.

Squatting in a corner of the dining room, the Corporal saw the diamond for the first time. Not understanding anything about it at all, he yawned widely. Not realizing that, along with the diamond, he was henceforth their only property.

12

"I WENT TO THE MOVIES," JOSEPH TOLD SUZANNE. "I'D SAID TO myself 'I'm going to the movies to pick up a woman.' I was sick and tired of Carmen, it was almost like sleeping with a sister when I slept with her, especially this time. For a long time I'd not liked the movies much. I realized that, shortly after we went to the big town. When I was in the movies I was all right, but when I had to decide to go to them, it wasn't like what it had been before. I always seemed to have something better to do. It was like losing my time, and I didn't have any time to lose, not like before. But when I tried to think what it was that I ought to be doing instead of going to the movies, I couldn't think what it was and so I always ended up by going. You must understand this. It happened when I didn't like the movies as much as I did before. And maybe in the end I'd have finished up by not caring so much for Ma, even. You must tell her all this.

"When I was in the movies, I always had hopes. Up to the last minute I always had hopes that I'd find out what I ought to have been doing instead of being there, and that I would find out before the picture had begun. But I never found out. And when the lights went off, when the screen lighted up and everyone got quiet, then I was like before, I wasn't waiting for anything, I felt comfortable. I'm telling you all this so you'll remember me and what I'm saying when I've gone. Even if Ma dies. I couldn't do anything else, now.

"I was wrong about the movies, for it was at the movies that I met her. She came late, when the lights had already dimmed. I don't want you to forget anything. I want to tell you everything, everything. But I don't know how to manage it.

"I didn't see her very well at first. 'Well, there's a woman next to me,' I thought, and that's all I said to myself. She wasn't alone. There was a man with her. He was on her right side and I was on her left. To the left of me there wasn't anybody. I was at the end of the row. I don't know now very well but it seems to me that while the newsreel was on and all through the beginning of the main picture, for maybe half an hour, I forgot her. I forgot there was a woman next to me. I remember the beginning of the film very well, and almost all of the second part of it. When I say I'd forgot, it's not the whole truth. At the movies I never have been able to forget when a woman is next to me. I mean, she didn't stop me from concentrating on the show. How long it was after the main picture began I don't know, maybe half an hour. Since I didn't know what was waiting for me, I didn't pay any attention to these points and I'm sorry, because ever since we came back to this hell-hole here, I've been trying to remember. But it's no use, I'll never manage it.

"So that's the way it began. All of a sudden I heard someone near breathing a heavy and regular breathing. I leaned over and turned round to see where it came from. It was the man who'd come in with her. He was asleep, his head was leaning back, his mouth was open. He was sleeping as though he was worn out. She saw I was looking and she turned to me and smiled. I saw her smile by the light from the screen. 'It's always like this,' she said, almost in a loud voice, loud enough to wake up the guy. But he didn't wake up. I asked: 'Always like this?' And she answered: 'Always.' When she smiled, I thought she was pretty, but her voice

was just terrific. All at once when I heard her say 'Always,'
I wanted to go to bed with her. She said that word like I've
never heard it said, it was as if I'd never understood what
that word meant before she said it. It was as if she had said
to me, it was exactly as if she had said: 'I've been waiting
for you always.'

"We went on looking at the picture. I'm the one that
began to talk to her again. I asked her: 'Why?' 'Oh,' she
said, 'I suppose because it doesn't interest him.' I didn't
know what else to say to her. For a while I tried so hard
to think of something that I couldn't follow the picture at
all. Then at last I was tired of thinking and I asked her right
out: 'Who is the guy?' So then she laughed more outright
and she turned completely in my direction. I saw her mouth,
her teeth, and I said to myself, 'When she goes out of the
theatre with the guy, I'll follow them.' She thought a while.
Maybe she wasn't sure what to say to me, but finally she
said: 'He's my husband.' I said: 'Cripes, he's your husband?'
It seemed horrible to me for her husband to go to sleep in
the movies beside her. Even Ma, who is old and has had
so many troubles, doesn't go to sleep in the movies.

"Instead of answering me, she took a package of cigarettes
out of her handbag. They were 555s, and she offered me one
and asked me for a light. I knew right away, I was sure she
had asked me for a light so she could see me better by the
light of the match. And she says she wanted right off to sleep
with me. Even before I saw her, I guessed she was a woman
a lot older than I am, a woman who wasn't ashamed of
wanting to sleep with a fellow like me. All at once she began
to talk, in a low voice, so as not to wake up the guy. 'Do you
have a light, perhaps?' she said in a low voice, but at the
beginning of the show she hadn't worried about waking him
up. I struck a match and held it out to her.

"Then I saw her hands. The fingers were long and shining
and her nails were enameled red. I saw her eyes too. Instead of looking at the end of the cigarette, she looked at

me. Her mouth was red, the same red as her fingernails. It did something to me to see them together, so close. As if she had hurt her fingers and her mouth and it was her blood I was seeing, a little of the inside of her body. Then I really wanted to sleep with her and I said to myself that I would follow them at the end of the show, I'd follow them in the B-12 to find out where they lived and if I had to, I'd watch and wait for her all the rest of the time I was in town. Her eyes shone in the matchlight and all the time it burnt they looked at me, free and easy.

" 'You're young,' she said. When she said that, I told her how old I am: 'Twenty,' I said.

"We began to talk in low voices. She asked me what I did. I explained that we lived near Ram, in muck up to the neck, on account of the concession they had palmed off on us. Her husband had gone hunting at Ram but she didn't know the place. She had been in the Colony only a short time, two years. I put my hand on hers, which was flat on the arm of the seat. She let me do it. Her husband, she said, had been in the Colony longer than she had, it was only two years ago that she had come out to him. First I began by putting my hand on hers. Before she had come out here, she had stayed two years in an English colony, I don't remember which. Then I began to stroke her hand, which was hot inside and cool outside. She was bored to death in this Colony, she said, very bored, she said. 'Why?' I asked, and she said, 'Because of the mentality of the people.' I thought of the cadastral agents of Kam and I told her that all the Colonials were swine. She agreed and smiled. I didn't see any of the rest of the show, I was busy with her hand. Little by little it was becoming burning hot in mine.

"But I do remember that a man fell dead on the screen, stabbed to the heart by another man who had waited for that from the beginning of the picture. I seemed to recognize those men but as if I had known them a long time. I had never felt a hand like that in mine. It was thin, I could put my fingers round it. It was limber, like a fish's fin. On the screen a woman had begun to cry because of the dead man. Lying down on him, she was sobbing. We couldn't talk any more. We didn't have the strength. I was kind of absorbing her hand in mine. It was so soft, so clean that hand, that you wanted to hurt it and I must have hurt her, for when I squeezed too hard she kind of pulled it away.

"The guy on the other side of her was still asleep. When the woman was sobbing on top of the dead man, she said to me in a low voice: 'It's the end of the show. Are you free tonight?' Ha, I'll say I was. She told me that all I had to do was to follow them. I don't know why, but all of a sudden I felt like a punctured tire. I was afraid of the light that was going to come on. I was afraid to see her after I had squeezed her hand like that in the dark. 'I'm going to clear out,' I said to myself. You can't imagine how scared I was. Yes, it was the light I was afraid of, as if we would stop living in the light, as if the light would make everything impossible. I even believe I let go her hand, yes I'm sure I did, for she took mine again. I had put it down on the arm of the seat and her hand came down on mine, then. She took my hand, she tried to cover it with hers, without being able to, of course. But she held me in a vise all the same, and I couldn't clear out. I said to myself that she must be used to picking up fellows like me in the movies and that she must be allowed to do what she wanted to.

"The lights came on. She took her hand away. I didn't dare to look at her right off. But she, she dared to look and I let her look, keeping my eyes down. The guy woke up suddenly then and we were already standing. He was a little older than she was, he was well dressed, big, hefty. I thought he was good-looking. He didn't seem to mind anything, he seemed to be feeling fine and not at all ashamed of having slept right through the show. You know, he's like those men you see pass by on the road at top speed, they ride in tremendous racing cars, they rent a *mirador* and they stay in the forest one single night, just long enough to kill a tiger, they have thirty trackers with them that they ordered by telephone from Pa Bart, telephoning down from a big hotel in the city. There, I said to myself, that's the kind of guy he is.

"'Pierre,' said the woman to him, 'this young man is a hunter from Ram. You know Ram?' He thought a while. 'I must have been there two years ago,' he said. I felt safe. 'Pierre, could we spend the evening with him?' 'Certainly,' he said. They must have said something else but since they talked with their backs turned I couldn't hear what they said. We went out of the show, following the crowd. I was behind her. She had a very straight figure, a little hefty, too, but with a small waist. Her hair was short, cut in a funny way, the ordinary color.

"Outside, we stopped by a magnificent car, a convertible 8-cylinder Delage. The guy turned to me. 'Will you get in?' he said. I said I had my car and would follow them. He was pretty nice. He seemed to think it natural for me to be there. For a minute she didn't pay any attention to me, as if we'd known each other forever. She said: 'Where's your car? Maybe you could leave it here and we can all go together in ours.' I agreed. I said I'd park the B-12 in the Place du Théâtre, because parking in front of the moving-pictures was not allowed during the shows. The B-12 was there a few yards away from their Delage. When he saw me going towards the B-12 the man came up and said: 'Good God, is that your car?' He said he had already noticed it when he arrived at the movies and that he had never seen a car like it. She came up to us, without hurrying. 'She saw the car too,' the guy said. They both looked at it, he with a serious look, she thinking about something. They could have laughed at it, really they could have laughed, for you should have seen what a sight the B-12 was, standing there beside their Delage. It looked like an old tin can. But they didn't laugh. And it seemed to me the guy was kinder after

he saw the B-12. I took it and parked it in the Place du
Théâtre, then came back. And then we all went off in their
Delage.

"Here begins the night that was the strangest in my whole
life.

"I was sitting in front and she wanted to sit in front between us. I didn't know where we were going or how it
would finish with her, from the minute he was there. But
I was sitting beside her, the car was speeding along, the
guy drove darned well. I told myself just to let go and drift.
I was in my shorts and sports shirt, with my sandals, but
since they didn't seem to mind I didn't let it worry me.
They had seen the B-12 and all the rest, for instance, how I
was dressed. They were people who must understand such
things.

"It was after we left the town that I began to want her.
The guy seemed to be in a hurry to reach some place,
I didn't know where. He drove faster. He didn't pay any
attention to us. I felt her body beside me, strained against
me. She had her arms stretched out, one around his shoulders, the other around mine. The wind blew her dress
against her and I could see the shape of her breasts almost
as if she was naked. She was a fine hefty sight. She had
good looking breasts, big, well set. A little after we left the
city lights, she squeezed my shoulder with her hand. I
thought I'd have to do it right away, I thought I was going
to fall right down on top of her, all at once. We were going
very fast, there was a lot of wind, everything seemed easy,
a little like the movies. She held my arm with all her
strength and when she was sure I wasn't going to do it,
she took her hand away. She behaved like that, on and off,
all evening long.

"We stopped at the first tavern we came to. 'We'll have a
slug of whisky,' the guy said. We crossed a garden and went
into a little bar. It was full. I thought we would eat there.
It was ten o'clock. 'Three whiskies,' said the guy. As soon

as he began to drink and the more he drank the less he paid any attention to us. It was when I saw him drinking his whisky that I began to understand. While we were drinking ours, he ordered two more for himself. He drank them one after the other, in a row. While we hadn't finished our first. He lapped it up like a sponge, that guy, he acted as if he hadn't had a drink for three days.

"She saw I was flabbergasted and she smiled at me. Then she said in a low voice: 'Don't pay any attention, it's his pleasure.' The guy was a nice fellow, he didn't go to the trouble to talk, he didn't give a damn for anything, for me, for her, and he drank as though he got a big kick out of it. Everyone was watching him drink, you couldn't help watching him. She was watching him, too . . .

"She was very pretty. Her hair was all messed up by the wind. Her eyes are very light blue, maybe gray, maybe blue, I don't know which. But they're so light you might think she is blind. Or you might say that with those eyes of hers she don't see what other people see but only a part of things. When she wasn't looking at me, she didn't seem to see a thing. When she was looking at me, her face lit up all at once, then almost at once her eyelids dropped as if it had been too much for her eyes. When she looked at me, while we were leaving the bar, I realized I was going to sleep with her that night, no matter what happened. And I realized she wanted it as much as the guy wanted drink.

"We went off again in the car. No one said anything, except herself, when sometimes she'd say to him: 'Be careful of this crossing,' or when he swore to himself because of the traffic. We crossed a part of the town again and he growled about it as if he'd been obliged to go that way, although I noticed afterwards that he needn't have gone that way.

"We came to another bar on the harbor side. He took two more whiskies and we, that time, took only one. But all the same, that made three I'd had and I began to feel a little tight. She must have been a little tight, too. She liked to drink. I thought, 'Every evening she must follow him like this in all the taverns, sometimes with a fellow she's picked up, and must drink with him.' As we left that bar she said to me in an undertone: 'We must stop drinking. Let him go on.' She must have wanted to sleep with me more and more.

"When the guy was having trouble climbing into the roadster, she managed to lean over to me and she kissed me on the mouth. Then I thought I was going to knock out the guy, take over the wheel, and go off with her. I wanted us to sleep together right away. But once more she must have guessed what was in my mind for she jarred against me and shoved me over towards the door.

"We went off. The guy was really beginning to be tight and evidently he didn't know it. He was already driving not so fast, leaning over the wheel to see better instead of sitting back on the seat. Once more we crossed the town. I wanted to ask him why he crossed the town like that all the time, but I think he didn't know why himself. Maybe it was to make the trip last longer. Maybe he didn't know the other routes, maybe he didn't know anything about the Colony but the center of the town and the bars around it. My nerves began to get a little on edge, especially now that he was driving so slow. Then, he was driving us around, like that, without asking us what we wanted to do. He ordered whisky and soda because he liked it.

"We stopped at a third bar. This time he ordered three Martel brandies, without asking if that was what we wanted. I said: 'I'm fed up, you can get outside your Martel if you want to, I'm not having any.' I felt like pitching into him. It was an hour since we'd left the Eden Cinema and honestly I didn't see when it would end. 'I'm sorry,' the guy said, 'I should have asked you what you wanted to drink.' I said: 'And I wonder why you don't take all your drinks at the same bar?' He said: 'You're a kid, you don't know anything.' It was the last thing he said that made sense.

"After he'd drunk two Martels he drank mine. Then, after that, he slumped down and waited. He seemed to be perfectly happy. I asked her to go away with me and leave him. She said she couldn't do that because she didn't know the proprietors of that bar well enough and she wasn't sure they'd bring him back home in the morning. I insisted. She refused. But she seemed to want to sleep with me more and more. Now it was as visible as if it had been written on her face. She went over to him, shook him gently, and reminded him we hadn't eaten yet, that it was almost eleven o'clock. He took some money out of his pocket, put it on the bar, and without waiting for the change he stood up and we went out.

"So then he began to drive very slow. She directed him, told him where to turn, what road to take. We drove as if we were going through molasses.

"As for me, while she was telling him what road to take, I lifted up her skirt and I began slowly to caress her. She let me. The guy didn't see a thing. He was driving. It was wonderful, I was making love to her there, right under his nose and he didn't see a thing. Even if he'd seen, I believe I'd have gone right on, because if he'd said anything I'd have knocked him out of the car.

"We reached a night club, a kind of bungalow built high on piles, where they were dancing and eating. The dance floor was at one side, on the other side there were stalls for the people who were eating.

"He had parked the Delage under the bungalow and we'd gone up the steps. She helped him up the steps, he leaned on her. He was absolutely dead drunk. In the light, she seemed to be done for, tired out. But I knew why, it was because she wanted to sleep with me so much and because of what I'd done to her in the car.

"As soon as I saw people looking at us in a funny way, kind of laughing at us, I no longer wanted to give him a punch. I was for him and against the others, everyone except her. At the same time I'd had enough, you can't imagine how fed up I was. She was so gentle with him and he was so slow, so slow, it had been at least three quarters of an hour since we'd left the third bar. And all that time I'd been making love to her. It wouldn't ever finish.

"She had chosen a stall by the dance floor, opposite the entrance. He had sunk down on the bench, glad not to have to drive any more, not to have to do anything, not even walk. For a second I asked myself what the hell I was doing there with these people, but by now I couldn't have left her. All the same, it made me wild to see how gentle and patient she was with him and he was so slow, so slow. We were going towards each other like people drowned in molasses. We'd never come out of it. For two hours, since the Eden, I'd been hunting her in a tunnel. She was at the end of it calling out to me, her eyes, her breasts, her lips were calling out to me, and I couldn't reach her. I think if no one had been on the floor I would have danced all alone to 'Ramona.' Up to then I'd thought I didn't know how to dance, but all at once I'd become a dancer. Maybe I could have danced on a tight rope. I thought, 'I've got to dance or I'll knock out the guy.' You know, 'Ramona,' that's a lot prettier tune than you think, in certain cases.

"I stood up and asked the first girl I saw to dance. She was pretty and small. While I was dancing, I wanted the other one so much that I didn't even feel the girl in my arms. I was dancing all alone with a girl as light as a feather in my arms.

"When I went back to the table, I realized I was terribly drunk. She was looking at me with her big eyes wide open and shining. Later she told me: 'When I saw you dancing with the girl, I called out to you, but you didn't hear.' I realized that she was feeling badly, that maybe she was unhappy, but I didn't know why. I thought it might be on account of him, that maybe, while I was dancing he had said something to her, reproached her for something. There

were three hard-boiled eggs in mayonnaise on the table.
The guy took a whole egg with his fork, put it all at once
into his mouth, and bit down. The egg ran down out of his
mouth, dribbled onto his chin, but he didn't feel it. I took
mine, like him, planted my fork in it and like him I put the
whole thing into my mouth. She began to laugh. The guy
began to laugh, too. He laughed as much as he could, and
it was as if we had all three known each other always. The
guy said, with his mouth full of egg: 'I like this fellow.' And
he ordered champagne.

"Ever since I'd danced with the other girl, she had
seemed determined to do something. I understood what it
was when the champagne came. I could tell by the way
she poured out the champagne for him, filling up his glass
to the brim, keeping the bottle in her hand, waiting till he'd
drunk it. He fairly fell on that champagne. So then, she
helped herself to it, poured some for me, and filled up his
glass the third time. Then again she waited, the bottle in
her hand, till he'd finished that glass. And again she poured
out champagne only into his glass. Four times straight. I
looked at her without being able to make a move. I realized
that the moment was coming when we'd be together, completely together.

"They brought us three fried soles garnished with lemon.
That, with the eggs in mayonnaise was all they would serve
us. It was midnight, the rooms were so full that they were
now serving only drinks. The guy ate the half of his sole,
then fell asleep. I drank my champagne and asked for more.
I ate all my sole, then hers that she offered me. From the
beginning of my life I've never been as hungry or as thirsty
or wanted a woman so much.

"All of a sudden her eyes opened very wide and her
hands began to tremble a little. She raised herself, leaned
across the table where the guy's head was resting and we
kissed. When she straightened up, her lips were pale and

in my mouth I had the taste of her lipstick, like almonds.
She was still trembling. But the guy went on sleeping.

"She leaned across the table again and again I took her
mouth. 'They're looking at us,' she said. I didn't mind.

"The guy woke up. You couldn't ever tell when he'd wake
up. He grumbled and shook himself, we had time to draw
apart before he raised his head. 'What the hell we doing
here?' he asked. 'Don't you worry, Pierre, you know you're
always worrying,' she said. She spoke very gently. He drank
and went to sleep again. We leaned over and kissed across
his enormous head with its closed eyes. I mean, while he
was sleeping we kept on like that with our mouths together,
without being able to get apart. Even her lips in mine were
trembling. He woke up. 'If at least we had something to
drink,' he said, in a slow, paralyzed voice.

"She poured out some champagne for him. He was really
completely drunk and when he was asleep you'd say he was
forgetting some terrible grief, a grief that went to sleep
when he did and began again the minute he opened his
eyes. I wondered if he didn't know what we were doing.
But I don't believe he did, I believe what he couldn't stand
was to wake up, what hurt him was to see the lights, to hear
the orchestra, and to see people dancing on the floor. He
raised himself, opened his eyes for ten seconds, swore a little, you didn't know who or what at, then let his head fall
on the table again. 'Pierre,' she said, 'you're comfortable
there, what more do you want? Go to sleep , and don't
worry.' So then maybe he smiled. 'You're right, Lina,' he
said, 'you're a nice girl.'

"Her name was Lina. I heard it from him. She spoke to
him with an extraordinary gentleness. Now that I know her,
I believe that it was not just so we could kiss without being
disturbed but also because she really felt friendly towards
him, maybe she still loved him. Every time he tried to wake
up, she poured some champagne into his glass. He swal-

lowed it down. It was like pouring it into sand. He didn't
drink, he poured the champagne inside him.

"Then he slumped forward. She bent over him towards
me and we kissed. She was not trembling now. Her hair was
in a complete mess, her lips were pale, she was not pretty
any more except only for me, I'd eaten her lipstick and I'd
messed up her hair. She was full of a marvelous happiness,
looked as if she didn't give a damn. The guy grumbled.
We drew apart. The guy raised himself up. 'It's whisky I
wanted,' he said. And she said, I remember very well:
'You're always asking the impossible, Pierre. I don't know
where the waiter is. I'll have to go look for him.' The guy
replied: 'Don't bother, Lina, I'm a bastard.' The people were
looking at us. I don't believe there was anyone, though,
who laughed. The people at the next table where the girl
was that I'd danced with had stopped talking and were
just watching us.

"The guy wanted to go to the can. He stood, with a great
effort. She took him by the arm and led him across the entire room. While he was crossing it, he yelled a lot: 'What a
whore-house!' he yelled once, so loud you could hear him
above the noise of the orchestra. She said something to
him, whispering in his ear, I suppose to calm him down.
While they were away I drank several glasses of champagne, maybe four, I don't remember. I was thirsty after
all that kissing. I wanted her so much I was burning hot.

"That's when, all by myself, I said to myself that I was
changing forever. I looked at my hands and I didn't recognize them. New hands had grown there, other arms than
what I'd had up to then. Honestly, I didn't recognize myself any more. It seemed to me I'd grown intelligent in one
night, that I understood at last all the important things
that I'd noticed before without really understanding. Of
course, I'd never known people like them, like her and like
him. But it wasn't because of them. I realized that the reason
they were so free, so full of liberty, was above all because

they had lots of money. No, it wasn't on account of them. I believe that it was first of all because I wanted a woman like I'd never wanted a woman before, and next because I had drunk and I was tight. All that intelligence I felt in myself, I must have had in me for a long time. And it was this mixture of sex and alcohol that had made it all come out. It was wanting a woman that had made me not give a damn for any other feeling, even the feeling you have for your mother. And it was that, too, that made me realize it wasn't any use to be afraid because, well, till then, I'd really believed I was up to my neck in fine feelings and I was afraid of them. And it was the alcohol that made me see the truth: I was a cruel man. All my life I'd tried to be tough and cruel, a man who would leave his mother one day and go off to learn to live, far away from her, in a town. But I'd been ashamed of it till then. And then I understood that it was the cruel man who is right. I remember I thought that when I left her I would be leaving her to the agents of Kam. I thought about the Kam agents. I told myself that one day I must get to know those agents. I told myself that one day I must not be satisfied just to know them as I knew them on the plain, through their dirty tricks, but that I must get into their plots, find out all about their dirty deals, but that I must do this without suffering, must keep my mean-ness, the better to kill them. The idea that I'd have to go back to the plain came to my mind. I remember I swore out loud, to be sure of myself, and I told myself that it was all over with. I thought about you, about her, and I said to my-self that it was all finished, you were finished, everything to do with you and her. Finished. I couldn't ever be a child again, even if she died, I told myself, 'Even if she dies, I'll go away.'

"They came back. She was holding him by the arm and he, worn out with the effort to cross the room and cross the room again, was staggering. If someone had cracked a joke about him or had said no matter what against him, I'd have smashed his face. I felt very close to him. He was so free even when he was drunk. Everyone seemed happy but him. She, she who'd got him drunk so we'd be left alone to kiss each other, she held him up as gently and understandingly as if he had been victimized by the others, the others who weren't drunk.

"When she came back she saw right away that the bottle was empty, so she got up again and went to tell the waiter who was standing at the other end of the dance floor to bring another bottle. The waiter didn't come for a long time. She began to tremble again. She was afraid the guy might sober up. I went to get the waiter. I walked as if in cotton. I brought back a bottle of Moët. Now I felt the time was drawing near.

"She gave him three more glasses of champagne. He went to sleep again and she woke him up to make him drink. The time was drawing nearer and nearer. When he had finished drinking, he fell forward again on the table. I said, 'Let's clear out of here.' She said: 'If he doesn't wake up in ten minutes.' So then I said: 'If he wakes up, I'll give him a sock in the jaw.' But it was impossible for him to wake up again. I think if he'd wakened up I'd have pitched into him, yes, for we'd reached the limit of what we could do for him, for anyone else but ourselves.

"When she was sure he'd not wake up again she took him by the shoulders and made him lie down completely on the bench. Then she opened his jacket and took out his wallet. Then she stood up and went to call the waiter. The waiter didn't come. I had to get up and go hunt him again. 'Let him sleep,' she said to the waiter. 'When he wakes up you will find a taxi for him. Here is the address you'll give to the driver.' She handed him some money and a visiting card.

"The waiter refused to take the money and said he'd have to ask the head waiter, that he didn't know if the guy could be left there lying on the bench for the rest of the night while so many customers were waiting for a table. You couldn't do a thing with that waiter, you couldn't force him to accept. So we had to wait for him to bring the head waiter. 'The room is full,' said the head waiter, 'we can't keep this table just for him alone.'

"I thought she was going to cry. Me, I could hardly keep my hands off the neck of that head waiter, I wanted to get my fingers into his neck. She drew out a lot of paper money from the wallet. 'I'll pay you for the table during the whole night,' she said, and put the money into the head waiter's hand. He accepted it. She threw a last look at the guy and then we went out.

"As soon as we were in the car under the bungalow I laid her down on the back seat and I took her. Over our heads the orchestra was still playing and you could hear the sound of the dancers' feet.

"Afterwards, I started up the Delage and we drove to a hotel that she chose. We stayed there a week.

"One night she asked me to tell her about my life and why we'd left the plain. I told her about the diamond. She told me to go get it right away, that she'd buy it. When I came back to the Hotel Central to get you, I found the diamond in my pocket."

13

THE TIME FOR JOSEPH'S DEPARTURE APPROACHED. SOMETIMES
Ma went to seek out Suzanne in the middle of the night to
talk to her about it. At last, after much thought, she wondered if it were not, after all, a solution.

"I don't see how I can stop him from going," said Ma, "I
don't believe I have the right to, because I don't see any
other way out for him."

She did not broach this subject except at night and then
only privately with Suzanne. After hours spent working on
her accounts in the company of the Corporal, she found
courage to talk about Joseph. During the day, she fooled
herself still, perhaps, but in the middle of the night she became lucid and could talk calmly.

"If he has something against me," she said, "then he must
have a reason. The only good thing that could happen to
you is for me to die. The land agents would have pity on
you. They would give the concession of the five hectares
outright to you. Then you could sell the land and go away."

"Go where?" asked Suzanne.

"To the city. Joseph would find work. You could go to
live with Carmen till you found someone to marry you."

Suzanne did not reply. Usually Ma went off at once after
having thrown out these suggestions, which were always
the same.

Decidedly, what she said had little importance to Suzanne. Never yet had Ma seemed to her so old and so insane. The imminence of Joseph's departure relegated her, with her worries and qualms, to a past devoid of interest. Joseph, alone, counted. The only thing that counted was what had happened to Joseph.

Suzanne rarely left his side now, since their return to the plain. When he went to Ram in the one-horse carriage, he took her with him most of the time. However, after he had told her his story, that is to say, after the first days following their return, he talked to her very little. But little as it was, he talked to her all the same more than he talked to Ma, to whom, obviously, he had not the courage to address a word. What he said required no response. He talked only because he could not resist the temptation to talk about that woman. It was only about her that he talked, always. Never had he believed you could be happy like that with a woman. He said that all the women he had known before her did not count for anything. He said that he was sure he could stay for days and days in bed with her. That they had made love for three whole days, barely eating, and that they had forgotten all else. Only, he had remembered Ma. That was what had made him go back to the Hotel Central—not the lack of money.

It was on the occasion of a trip to Ram that Joseph confessed to Suzanne that the woman was coming to fetch him. He was the one that had asked her to wait a fortnight before coming. He could not say exactly why.

"Maybe I wanted to see this hell-hole one last time, to make sure," he said.

Now she would not be long in coming. He had thought about what would happen to Ma and Suzanne once he had left the plain, he had thought about it a great deal. As to Ma, he could see no possible future for her except on the concession. It was her incurable vice.

"I'm sure," he said, "that every night she begins to build all over again her barriers against the Pacific. The only difference is that they are sometimes a hundred meters high, or two meters high, depending on whether she feels well or not. But little or big, she begins rebuilding them every night. It was too fine an idea."

He could never forget them, he said. He could never forget her, or rather, what she had endured.

"It's like forgetting who I am, it's impossible."

He did not believe that Ma could live much longer, but —and this was contrary to what he had formerly believed —he no longer thought this had much importance. When anyone had such a desire to die, you should not stop him. As long as he knew Ma was alive, he would not, moreover, be able to do anything worth while in life, he could undertake nothing. Every time he had made love to that woman he had thought about Ma, had remembered that she had never made love since their father had died, because she believed, like an imbecile, that she hadn't the right. She had believed that she must work and go without everything so that they, her children, would one day have the right to love. He told her that Ma had been very much in love with an employee at the Eden Cinema for two years, that's what she had told him, and that she had never slept with him once—always on account of the children.

Joseph talked to Suzanne about the Eden, about the horror of those ten years passed by Ma there, playing the piano at the Eden. He remembered better than Suzanne did, because he had been already a big boy then. And Ma had sometimes talked to him about it.

Ma had been forced suddenly to take that job as pianist at the Eden when it was offered to her. She had not played for ten years when she took it, not since she had left Normal School. She had told him: "Sometimes I cried when I saw my hands had become so stiff and awkward that they were incapable of playing the scores. Sometimes I wanted to cry, to close the piano and run away." But little by little her hands had got used to it. The more easily since the same scores were invariably played and the manager of the Eden let her practice in the mornings. She had lived in terror of losing her job. And if she had formed the habit of taking her children with her, it was not merely because she dared not leave them alone at the house; rather, it was the more to secure the sympathy of the manager as to her difficult life. She arrived a little before the show, covered up the children on two chairs, beside the piano, where they slept. Joseph remembered all that very well. The thing became quickly known and, as the theatre filled up, the spectators would come down to the orchestra pit to look at the pianist's children as they slept. It had soon become a kind of attraction —which did not annoy the management.

Ma had told him: "It was because you were so beautiful that they came to look at you. Sometimes I found toys and candies beside you, things people had left."

She still believed that. She believed that it was because they were beautiful that people had given them toys. He had never dared tell her the truth. They went to sleep immediately after the lights were put out and the newsreel began. Ma played for two hours. It was impossible for her to follow what was happening on the screen: the piano was not only below the level of the screen but it was well below the level of the audience.

For ten years Ma had not been able to see one single movie. However, at last her hands had become so expert that she no longer had to look at the keyboard. But she still could see nothing of the movie being projected above her head.

"Sometimes," Ma had told him, "it seemed to me I slept while I played. When I tried to look at the screen it was terrible, I got dizzy. It was just a blur of black and white dancing above my head, and it made me seasick."

Once, once only, her desire to see a movie had been so strong that she had pretended to be ill and staying at home. Then she came secretly to see the show. But at the end of it an employee had seen and recognized her and she had never dared to do such a thing again. Once only in ten years' time had she dared to do it. For ten years she had wanted to go to see the movies and had not been able to go except once, and secretly. During ten years, while she grew old, this desire had remained as fresh in her as it had been in the beginning. And at the end of ten years it had been too late, for then she left to go to the plain.

It was so intolerable to remember these things about Ma that it would be preferable for him and for Suzanne if Ma were to die. So said Joseph, adding: "You must remember these stories about the Eden Cinema, and you must always do just the opposite of what she always did." However, he loved Ma. He even believed, he said, that he would never care for any woman as he cared for her, that no woman would ever be able to make him forget her. "But live with her—no! That's not possible!"

What he regretted was not to be able to kill the Kam agents before he went away. He had read the letter Ma had written to them before taking it, as she had asked him to do, to the driver of the bus. After he had read it, he had decided not to give it to the driver, but to keep it. He had decided to keep it forever. When he read that letter he felt himself become what he wanted to become—capable of killing the agents of Kam if ever he met them. He wanted to stay like that for the rest of his life, no matter what happened to him, even if he became very rich. That letter would be more useful to him than it would ever have been in the hands of the Kam agents.

Thus, even if they were destined to make her suffer, Joseph's projects were made because of what Ma had endured. If he had become rough and mean with her, he said it was as necessary as to be rough with the Kam agents.

Suzanne did not get the full significance of Joseph's words, but she listened to them religiously, as to a hymn of virility and of truth. Thinking them over, she perceived with emotion that she herself felt able to conduct her life as Joseph said she must. She saw, then, that what she admired in Joseph was also in herself.

During the week that followed their return to the plain, Joseph was morose and tired. He got out of bed only for meals. He never washed himself. But then, on the contrary, he began once more to shoot wading-birds from the verandah and to wash himself carefully every day. His shirts were always very clean and he shaved himself carefully every morning. That was why Ma knew that his time for departure was approaching. Just to look at him, anyone would have guessed it and guessed also that nothing and no one could prevent him from going. Every hour of the day he was ready.

The waiting lasted, in all, one month. Ma, for a good reason, had no reply from the cadastral office nor even from the bank. But all this no longer mattered to her. Finally, she stopped waking Suzanne up to talk to her about Joseph. She may even have wanted to see him go away quickly, since he was going. Vaguely she must be thinking that as long as he was there she could not sell the diamond to Pa Bart. Because ever since Pa Bart had bought the Victrola she had not stopped thinking about him. She talked about him, talking only about him, about his fortune, the possibilities he had, the investments that she, in his place, would make, instead of going in for the traffic in Pernod, and so forth. Was it that she was trying once more to fashion some kind of future? She herself must not have known very clearly. Nor did she know what she would do with the money if ever she succeeded in selling the sparkler to Pa Bart, once Joseph had gone.

One of Ma's most constant projects had been to manage one day to replace the thatched roof of the bungalow with one of tiles. But not only had she never been able to do it, she had never been able, in six years' time, to renew the old thatched roof. And one of her fears, no less constant, had been that worms might get into the thatch before she had found enough money to replace it.

Well, then, a few days before Joseph's departure, her fears were realized and there was a gigantic hatching out of worms in the decayed thatch. Slowly, regularly, they began to fall from the roof. Worms squashed under their naked feet, fell into jars, fell upon the furniture, fell into the plates, into their hair.

However, neither Joseph nor Suzanne nor Ma, even, made the least mention of them. There was only the Corporal who did anything about it. Since idleness weighed heavily upon him, without waiting for Ma to give him the order, he began to sweep the floor of the bungalow all day long.

14

A FEW DAYS BEFORE HIS DEPARTURE, JOSEPH SHOWED SUZANNE
Ma's last letter to the cadastral agents of Kam. He wanted
her to read it before he went, and Suzanne read it one evening, out of Ma's sight. This letter only confirmed Joseph's
words. Here is what Ma had written:

"To the Cadastral Agent of Kam.
Monsieur:—
Excuse me for writing again to you. I know my letters
are a nuisance to you; it is obvious, for I have had no reply
from you for many months now. Please note, however, that
it is now more than a month since I last wrote to you. But
doubtless you have not even noticed this. Sometimes I tell
myself that you do not even read my letters, that you
throw them into the wastebasket without opening them.
You know, I have got that so much into my head that the
only hope that now remains to me is that one time, only
once, you will manage to read one of my letters, just one
of them. I can only hope now that one of my letters will
attract your attention, one day, for example, when you have
nothing very urgent to do. After which, it seems to me you
will read the others, the letters that followed that one. Because it still seems to me that if you really knew my situation
you could not remain completely indifferent. Even if, after
years of carrying out your horrible duties, your heart has

227

grown hard, surely it would not be too hard to take my situation into consideration.

"What I am asking you, as you know, is very little. It is merely to grant me definitely the five hectares of land around my bungalow. This piece of land is on the fringe of the rest of my concession which, as you well know, is absolutely irreclaimable. Please let me have this small privilege. Let me own outright these five hectares of land, that is now all I ask of you. Afterwards, I might take out a mortgage and make one last attempt at constructing a part of my Ocean-barriers. I will tell you why, later, I want to attempt to build new dikes, a thing not easy to do. I know all your objections to granting me this piece of land; although you hate to avow them and although it is even to your interest not to avow them. I know that the five upper hectares are, to you, a valuable part of the hundred hectares lower down, which they serve precisely to disguise. They give the illusion that the rest of the concession is equally good. And, in effect, during the dry season when the sea has completely receded, who would not be taken in? It is thanks to these five hectares that you have been able to allot the concession four times already to different settlers, to poor unfortunates who had not the means of getting something better out of you by bribery. I have often before reminded you of these things, in each of my letters. I can't help repeating myself, for I can't help dwelling on this tragedy. I shall never, never get used to your infamy, and as long as I live, until my last breath, I will keep on talking to you about it, shall repeat in detail what you have done to me, what you are doing each day to others—and doing it in all safety and honor.

"I well know that if you cut off these five hectares of upper land from the hundred hectares of lower land there won't be any concession left. There wouldn't be enough room for a settler to build a bungalow or even enough space

to grow a year's supply of rice. Again let me say: the rest of
the concession does not count. During the great tides of
July, the waves of the Pacific lap the cabins of the last village, where the concession begins, and when the waves
have retired, they leave behind them dried mud on which
the rain would have to fall for more than a year to wash
away the salt to a depth of 10 centimeters—a little longer
than the roots of rice at maturity. And where, tell me please,
where would you then settle your victims?

"I know all this, and I also know that you would risk not
having any settler at all. But in spite of the inconvenience
such a definite grant of the five hectares represents as far as
you are concerned, you must give in to me. You know why I
want them. You know that I worked for fifteen years and
during fifteen years I sacrificed every least pleasure to buy
this concession from the government. And for the savings
I put aside every day for fifteen years of my life, of my
youth, what did you give me? A desert of salt and water.
And you let me give you my money. That money I religiously carried to you one morning, seven years ago, in an
envelope. It was all I had. I gave you all I had that morning,
all, as if I brought you my own body as a sacrifice, as if from
my sacrificed body would blossom an entire future of happiness for my children. You took that money. You took the
envelope containing all my savings, all my hopes, all my
reasons for living, you took it in the most natural way. And
I went off happy. That moment was the most glorious one of
my whole existence!

"What have you given me in return for those fifteen years
of my life? Nothing. Wind and water. You have robbed me.
And if I could manage to make these things known to the
Colonial government, if I had the means to do so, it would
be of no use. The big land-owners would raise their voices
against me and I would be immediately expropriated. And
probably my complaint, before it reached the general gov-

ernment, would be stopped by your superiors, who are even more privileged than you are, since their rank merits them still higher bribes than yours.

"No, I could not attack you by these means, I realize it.

"How many times have I asked you for my sake to renounce your villainy? How many times have I asked you not to inspect my concession because it is useless, because no one in the world could make anything grow in the sea, in salt? For—and I could repeat these things tirelessly a thousand times—not only did you give me a nothingness as a concession; you also say, 'Haven't you done anything this year? You know the ruling,' etc. And you go away, having done your job, for which you receive a salary each month. And when I tried building my dikes, you were afraid that I might succeed in making something grow in this wasteland. You may have been less confident than usual.

"And, by the way, do you remember how you cleared out with your tail between your legs, as they say, when my son fired off his gun into the air? We will all treasure that memory, for to see a man of your kind in a blue funk, that's something and something we like to see. But reassure yourself: a barrier against the Pacific, a barrier that holds up, is easier to achieve than to try to denounce your infamy. To tell me to make no matter what grow on my concession is to tell me to do the impossible. And you well know it, for your inspections are limited to ten minute visits during which you do not even stop your car engine. Oh yes, you are in a great hurry. For the number of concessions is limited and other people are waiting, as I waited. And you are afraid of losing the profits on the misfortunes you sow, you are afraid that if I don't go quickly enough or if I don't die soon enough that you will be obliged to allot a concession that is cultivatable to unfortunates who are unable to bribe you.

"But as to that, please resign yourselves. After me, no one will come here. You might as well grant me what I ask at once. For if ever you succeeded in making me leave, when you came to show the concession to a new settler, that is to say, show the window-dressing, the five hectares of upper land, a hundred peasants would come to hem you in. 'Tell the cadastral agent,' they would say to the new settler, 'to show you the rest of the concession. Once there, stick your finger in the mud of the paddy and taste it. Do you believe that rice will grow in salt? You are the fifth settler on this land. The others are dead or ruined.'

"And you could do nothing against those peasants, for if you tried to silence them you would have to have an escort of armed militiamen. Can settlers be shown lands in such conditions? No. Then, now that I have warned you, grant me at once those five hectares of upper land. I know your power, I know that you hold the plain in your two hands by virtue of a power conferred upon you by the general colonial government itself. I know your villainy and the villainy of your predecessors and of those who will follow you, the infamy of the government itself, even. And the weight of this knowledge of mine is alone enough to kill me—no one could bear the burden.

"If I were the only one to have this knowledge, it would serve no purpose. Because the knowledge of one man as to the crimes of a hundred others is of no use to him. It is a thing I took a long time to learn but I know it now for the rest of my life. And so, there are now hundreds on the plain who share my knowledge, who know what you are, and maybe two hundred that know you as I know you, in detail, as to your methods, your ways of doing things. I'm the one that explained what you are to them, patiently and at length. I'm the one that fervently keeps alive their hatred for your kind. For example, when I meet someone of the plain, instead of saying good-day to him, and showing my friendship for him, I ask him: 'Well, have you seen those swine, the cadastral agents, this week?' And I know some who rub their hands delightedly in anticipation of an inspection day when, perhaps, they will kill you, the three agents of Kam. But reassure yourselves, I still hold them in check, I still calm them, I tell them: 'It wouldn't be much use. Of what use would it be to kill three rats when an army of rats is behind those three there? That's not what we must do first.' And I explain to them that when you come with a new settler, etc.

"I perceive that my letter is very long, but I have spent my whole night writing it. I cannot sleep since the misfortune of my broken dikes. I hesitated a long time before writing this last letter to you, before acquainting you with all the considerations, but it now seems to me that I was wrong not to write all this earlier and that these considerations alone are susceptible of making you take an interest in my case. In other words, to make you take an interest in me I must talk about you, of your infamy. And if you read this letter, I am sure you will read the others to see the progress I have made in the knowledge of your infamy.

"Maybe it would still be useless to them to kill you one inspection day, but it might be useful to me one day. I shall soon be alone. My son and my daughter will soon leave me and I shall be alone and so discouraged that nothing will be of further importance to me. Then, perhaps, before dying, I might want to see your dead bodies thrown to the stray dogs of the plain, give those dogs a banquet, finally. So then, at the moment of dying, I might say to the peasants: 'If any of you wants to give me one last pleasure before I die, let him kill the three cadastral agents of Kam.' But I would not tell them to do it until the moment had come to do it. For the time being, when they ask me, for example: 'Where do they come from, those Chinese planters who have taken the best of our lands at the edge of the forest for their pepper plantations?' I explain to them that you are the ones who, taking advantage of the fact that they have no title to the property, have sold it to the Chinese

planters. 'What does that mean, title to property?' they ask
me. I explain: 'You cannot understand. It is a piece of paper
which testifies to your property. But no more than the birds
or the monkeys at the mouth of the *rac* do you have a title to
property. Who would have given it to you? Those swine,
the cadastral agents of Kam, are the ones who invented that,
so as to be able to dispose of your lands and to sell them.'

"This, then, is what I have resigned myself to do on this
irreclaimable concession. I talk to the Corporal. I talk to
the others. I talk to all those peasants who came to build
the dikes. I never tire of explaining to them just who you are.
When a little child dies, I tell them: 'That will make those
swine, the cadastral agents in Kam, very glad.' 'Why should
they be glad?' they ask. And I tell them the truth, that the
more children die in the plain the more the plain will be
depopulated and the more your hold on the plain will be
reinforced. I do not tell them, as you see, anything but
the truth. And before a dead child I owe that to them. 'Why
don't they send us quinine? Why is there no doctor, why is
there not one hospital clinic? Why is there no alum to purify
the water in the dry season? Why is there never any vaccina-
tion?' they ask. I tell them why and even if this truth is beyond your understanding, beyond your personal claims on
the plain, this truth that I give them is none the less true
and you yourselves are the cause of the events that will follow.

"You may not know it, but so many little children die here
that they are buried in the very mud of the rice fields or
under the cabins. And it is the father who, with his feet,
stamps down the earth at the place where he has buried
his child. As a result, nothing here marks the trace of a
dead child, and the lands that you covet and that you take
from the plainspeople, the only fertile lands of the plain,
are swarming with the corpses of children. Upon which
fact, so that these deaths may at last serve some purpose

much later (You never can tell), I pronounce these sacred words as a funeral oration: 'This will please those swine, the cadastral agents of Kam.' Let them at least know it.

"I am really very poor now and—but how could you know it?—my son, sick to death of such misery, is probably going to leave me forever and I no longer have either the courage or the right to prevent him from going away. I am so depressed that I no longer can sleep. For a long time now I have been spending night after night thinking over these things. I have dwelt on these things so long and it has been so useless that gradually I begin to hope that the time will come when these things will serve some purpose. My son is going away forever, young as he is and instructed as he is in your infamous ways. Maybe that is already a beginning. I try to console myself by thinking so.

"Now, you must surely see for yourself that you must grant me those five upper hectares that surround my bungalow. You will tell me, if ever you happen to reply to me: 'What's the use? Those five hectares are not enough and if you mortgage them to make new dikes, they will be just as bad as the first ones.' Oh, people like you do not know what it is to hope, they would not know even what to do with hopes, they have only ambition and they always get what they want. I would reply, as to my dikes: 'If I can't hope that they will hold this year, then it would be better for me to hand over my daughter to a brothel, better for me to urge my son to go away, and then have the three cadastral agents of Kam assassinated.' Put yourselves in my place: if, in the coming year, I do not have even that hope, even the prospect of a new defeat, what better thing remains for me to do than to have you assassinated?

"Where, alas, is all that money I earned, that I saved, penny by penny, in order to buy this land? Where is that money now? It is in your pockets which are already heavy with gold. You are thieves. And just as those dead children cannot be brought back, so my money, my youth—they can never be recovered. You must grant me those five hectares of land or one day your corpses will be found in the ditches along the highway in which they buried alive the convicts who worked on the road. For, I repeat it once more, something is needed to keep life in us, and if it is not hope, even a vague hope for new barriers against the Ocean, then let us have corpses, even the contemptible corpses of the three cadastral agents of Kam. When people haven't a crumb to eat, they're not very hard to satisfy.

"Hoping all the same to have a reply from you,
                    I am yours very sincerely, etc. . . ."

15

THE PROLONGED HONKING OF AN AUTOMOBILE HORN SOUNDED
on the highway, in the direction of the bridge. It was eight
o'clock in the evening. No one had heard the car arrive, not
even Joseph. It must have stopped on the other side of the
bridge, otherwise it would have been impossible, for when
a car passed over the bridge you could always hear the clattering of the boards that had been loosened in the heat. And
since no one had heard the car arrive, you could suppose it
was there, just beyond the bridge, and had been there for
some minutes. Maybe the woman had not been sure at
once that this was the bungalow Joseph had described. She
must have looked at it a long time, outlined in the darkness, half finished, without a balustrade, and, in the group
of people gathered round the acetylene lamp shining within
the house, she must have looked for Joseph's form. Yes, that
profile was his, since beside it were two other figures, one
of which was an old woman. She must have waited before
sounding the horn. Waited again, then again pressed the
horn, giving the signal upon which they had agreed. It was
not in any way a timid call. It was a summons both dis-
creet and imperative. For a month and for eight hundred
kilometers, she had waited to sound that horn. And, arrived
in front of the bungalow, she had taken her time and had
waited before pressing the button, although sure she must
do so.

They were eating when it sounded. Joseph bounded up as if he had received a discharge of bullets in his body. He left the table, pushing back his chair, crossed the room, and went down the bungalow steps at a run.

Ma slowly rose from the table and, as if henceforth she would have to take very good care of herself, she went to stretch out in the chaise longue in the sitting room, facing the entrance door. Suzanne followed her and sat down beside her in an armchair. It was a little like the evening when the horse had died. That evening was beginning again.

"Well, that's that," said Ma in a low voice.

Her eyes half closed, she stared in the direction from which had come the sound of the horn. Except that she was very pale, you would have believed she was drowsing. She did not say anything, nor did she make the least movement. The highway was perfectly dark. They must be out there in the darkness, the two of them, in a close embrace.

Joseph remained away quite a while. But the car did not start up. Suzanne was sure Joseph would come back in, if only for a few minutes, to say a few words to Ma, maybe not to her, but to Ma, surely.

Joseph did come back. He stopped in front of Ma and looked at her. For a month he had not of his own accord addressed a word to her, for a month maybe he had not really looked at her.

"I'm going away for a few days," he said gently. "There's nothing else I can do."

She raised her eyes to her son and, for once without whimpering, without crying, she said:

"Go, Joseph."

She spoke clearly, but her voice was hoarse and unreal. After she had spoken, Suzanne raised her eyes towards Joseph. She barely recognized him. He was looking at Ma fixedly and at the same time his face was suffused with laughter which, manifestly, he could not contain. He had come in from the black night, but he looked as though he had come from a conflagration: his eyes were shining, his face streamed with sweat, and laughter burst out of him like a flame.

"God damn it, I'll come back, I swear to you, I'll come back."

He did not budge, but stood waiting for Ma to give some sign that she could not give. An immense beam of light appeared on the highway, stretching off to infinity. The headlights cut the highway in two and you would have said that the road sprang from the lights, that on the other side there was nothing, nothing but the suffocating heat of the dense night. The beam of light slanted progressively, by jerks, sweeping the bungalow, the *rac*, the sleeping villages in the distance, the Pacific, until a new highway loomed up in the opposite direction. The car had turned noiselessly, they had not heard it. A tremendous roadster, that 8-cylinder Delage must be! In a few hours they would be in the city. Joseph would drive like a madman to the first hotel, where they would stop to make love. Now the beam of light showed the direction of the city, the direction Joseph was going to take when he went away.

Joseph turned, the beam passed before him, he stiffened, dazzled. For three years he had waited for a woman who would come silently and determinedly to take him away from Ma. She was there. And henceforth they were as separated from him as if he had been ill, mad, or at least deprived of his right senses. And truly it was hard to look at this Joseph who was no longer any concern of theirs, this living dead man that he had become for them.

Again he turned towards Ma and remained waiting still for that sign of peace which she could not but give him. And he was still laughing. His face expressed so much happiness that it was no longer recognizable. Never had anyone before, not even Suzanne, believed that his face, so resolutely impassive, could ever be so open, so almost immodestly open.

"Hell," said Joseph, "I swear I'll come back. I'm leaving everything, even my guns."

"You don't need your guns any more. Go, Joseph."

Again she had closed her eyes. Joseph took her by the shoulders and began to shake her.

"I swear it, even if I wanted to leave you I couldn't."

They were sure he was going away forever. Only he still doubted it.

"Kiss me," said Ma, "and go."

She allowed Joseph to shake her. Joseph began to shout.

"In a week! When you've finished cursing me out! I'll be back in a week. You'd think you didn't know me!"

He turned towards Suzanne.

"Tell her, for God's sake, tell her!"

"Don't worry," said Suzanne, "he'll be here in a week."

"Go, Joseph," said Ma.

Joseph decided to go into his room for his things. The car was still waiting, the headlights were dimmed, now. She had not sounded the horn again. She let Joseph have time—her time. She knew it was hard for him. She would have waited all night, that was sure, without sounding the horn again.

Joseph came back, wearing his tennis shoes and carrying a bundle of clothes, evidently prepared beforehand. Flinging himself upon Ma, he raised her in his arms and hugged her with all his strength, his face buried in her hair. He did not go towards Suzanne but forced himself to meet her eyes. In his eyes she saw something of fear and maybe of shame. Then briskly he passed between them and went down the steps at a run.

The headlights lit up a little afterwards, headed towards the city. Then the car started up very gently, without their hearing it. The headlights shifted, lengthened, lengthened still more, leaving behind them an ever larger margin of night, and then nothing could be seen.

Ma, her eyes closed, was still in the same position on the

chaise longue. The bungalow was so silent that Suzanne could hear Ma's raucous and disordered breathing.

The Corporal came up, accompanied by his wife. They had seen everything. They brought hot rice and some fried fish. It was the Corporal who, as always, spoke first. He said the rice and the fish that had been on the table had gone cold and that they had brought fresh rice and fish. The Corporal's wife who, ordinarily, never stayed in the bungalow, squatted down by his side in a corner of the room. They had at last understood what events had been preparing since the return from the city, and already the exhaustion of anticipated hunger was in their eyes. They waited for Ma to give them some hope that they would have something to eat a while longer. It was doubtless for their sake that, an hour after Joseph's departure, Ma consented to speak. She looked at them, but addressed Suzanne.

"Go finish your supper."

She was red and her eyes were glazed. Suzanne brought her a cup of coffee and a pill. The Corporal and his wife looked at Ma in the same way that she, a month before, had looked at the horse. She drank the coffee and took the pill.

"You can't realize what it's like," she said.

"It's not as terrible as if he had died."

"I'm not complaining. There was nothing for him to do here any more. I try and try to think of something he could do here, but there's nothing."

"He'll come back now and then."

"What's terrible is . . ."

Her mouth twisted as if she were going to vomit.

"What's terrible," she repeated, "is that he has had no education, so I don't know what he can do, I don't see anything ahead of him."

"She will help him."

"He will leave her, he will always run away as he always ran away from all the schools where I put him . . . He stayed the longest with me . . ."

Suzanne helped her to undress and motioned to the Corporal and his wife to go. It was only when she was in bed that Ma began to cry, as never before. She wept as if she had at last discovered grief, real grief.

"You'll see," she cried, "you'll see that this will still not be enough. What he should have done was to fire his buckshot at me before he went, since he knows so well how to do it . . ."

In the night, Ma had an attack which almost killed her. But it, too, was not enough.

16

SUZANNE WAS THINKING ABOUT JOSEPH. IT WAS NOT, SHE DE-cided, through that woman or by his departure that he had become absolutely another man. She remembered what had happened two years before. To be exact, it had happened in the week following the collapse of the sea walls . . .

That day a small car, new and shining, stopped in front of the bungalow.

Joseph came out of the sitting room, followed by Suzanne, and stood on the verandah, looking down at the car. A medium-sized man, brown haired, dark eyed, whose face, shadowed by a cork helmet, seemed small and ordinary, got out of the car. He carried a briefcase under his arm. With resolute step he entered the drive leading up to the bungalow.

It was the time of the high tides of July, the period of the year when men like this one showed themselves, taking their car and going to inspect the concessions of the plain. For doing this work, they earned a big salary and were even furnished a car to facilitate things. Never did they ride in the bus.

"How do you do?" said the man. "Is your mother at home? I would like to speak to her."

"Are you the cadastral agent?" asked Joseph.

The man was at the foot of the verandah, and he looked first at Joseph, then at Suzanne, in a rather surprised way.

Suzanne surprised him because it was the first time he had seen her and he perhaps thought she was not bad looking; while Joseph's tough manner was always so evident that always and everywhere it nonplussed people, impressed and baffled them. Suzanne had never met anyone as rude as Joseph. When people did not know him, they could never decide how to tackle him or how to dissipate that brutality before which the most self-confident people lost their poise. Leaning on the balustrade, his chin in his hand, Joseph was looking at the cadastral agent, who had doubtless never before been looked at with such calm ferocity.

"Why do you want to see my mother?" asked Joseph.

The agent essayed a timidly kind smile. Suzanne recognized that smile: she had seen it used before on Joseph. She had afterwards often seen it on Monsieur Jo's face. It was the smile of fear.

"It's the period of inspection," said the agent agreeably.

Joseph laughed as suddenly as if someone had tickled him.

"Inspect? You come to inspect, do you?" asked Joseph. "Go right ahead, make yourself at home, hell, inspect all you like!"

The agent averted his face as if he had been hit over the head with a club.

"Go on," said Joseph. "What are you waiting for? You don't need my mother to do your job for you, do you?"

What Joseph said seemed very fine to Suzanne. She had often heard of the cadastral agents, of their fabulous fortunes, their almost divine power. This one, who stood at Joseph's feet, made you want to laugh. Suzanne had to restrain herself from calling Ma so she could see him and laugh, too. She wanted to put in a word, to talk like Joseph.

"Go on," said Suzanne, "since he's told you to."

"If you need a boat for the inspection we'll even go so far as to lend you one," said Joseph.

The agent raised his head without, however, meeting

Joseph's eyes. Then he essayed the effect of a serious piece of news.

"I would like you to realize," he said, "that I am here officially and that this year ends the next to the last delay accorded to your mother for the cultivation of a third of the concession."

At that moment, Ma appeared, no doubt alerted by the noise of the conversation.

"What's up?" she asked.

But as soon as she saw him she recognized the little man. He had made her wait at least ten times in the anteroom of his office in Kam and she had sent him perhaps fifty letters.

Joseph turned towards Ma, waved his hand as if to stop her and, in a changed voice, said to her:

"Let me manage this."

It was the first time he had ever taken a hand in business relating to the concession. And he spoke to Ma in a voice as self-possessed as if they had come to the common agreement that he should intervene. She had not yet been conscious of these first signs of Joseph's springtime, his new importance.

The cadastral agent had not removed his helmet before Ma, but had merely nodded his head and mumbled some kind of salutation. She looked tired. She was wearing one of the nondescript dresses, completely shapeless, that she was beginning to wear, a kind of dressing gown, very ample, in which she floated, a human wreck. For the first time since the crumbling of the sea walls, she had combed her hair and her tight gray braid, fastened at the end with a section of inner tube, hung down her back in a laughably silly way.

"Oh!" said Ma, "I was expecting you, I knew you couldn't put off coming much longer."

Joseph again motioned to her to be quiet. It was useless for her to go to the trouble of replying.

"Our dikes have held up," said Joseph. "We have a tremendous harvest, you never saw anything like it in your life."

Ma looked at her son, opened her mouth as if to speak, without, however, uttering a word. Then suddenly her expression changed completely and in a few seconds was one of pleasure, pleasure only, and all her weariness had gone.

Astonished, the cadastral agent looked at Ma, as if expecting some help from her, as if he thought she would surely not stand for all this fooling.

"I don't understand . . . They told me you had had no luck . . ."

"Well, that's the way things are," said Joseph. "You see, we're luckier than you are—for anyone can see you're out of luck!"

"Yes, anyone can see that, right away," said Suzanne.

The agent's face was scarlet. He passed his hand over his cheek as if to rub away a blow.

"I've nothing to complain of," said the agent.

"We haven't either," said Joseph, with a guffaw.

Suzanne remembered that moment perfectly well, for it was then that she had realized she would perhaps never meet a man she could admire as much as Joseph. Others might have thought him a little crazy. When, for instance, he had torn the B-12 to pieces, without reason, it really had looked as though he were. Ma sometimes thought so. But she, Suzanne, had known for a long time that he was not crazy. And from the way he stood up to that agent, she was very sure of it. How exactly he had hit upon the right thing to do! She remembered how he had looked standing there on the verandah, his body naked from the waist up, his face bedazzled, as if at his own cleverness. He had taken an indecent pleasure in tearing the B-12 to pieces. Now, he was doing the same thing to the red faced and well dressed agent, was trampling on him, tearing to shreds that man who had been so self-assured till then, so terrifying to everyone.

"I would like to have a serious talk with you," said the agent. "In your own interest . . ."

"In our interest? Just listen to him! He's talking about our

interest!" said Ma, turning towards them like an actress on
the stage, emphasizing a point. And she, too, laughed.
Joseph held her captive like a bird. Moreover, it was from
her that he had his capacity to laugh like that, to be able
suddenly to laugh for the very reasons that, the day before,
caused tears to flow.

"Hell," said Joseph, "we're talking seriously, and how! It's
you that's not serious. If you did your job right, you'd go to
see our sea walls. I'm going to tell the Corporal to get the
boat ready. You don't need more than six hours to see everything, and you are going to see everything!"

The agent took off his helmet and wiped his forehead. He
was standing in full sunlight, on the earth terrace, and no
one invited him to come up. He had always known, even
before they were begun, that the dikes would not stand, and
he knew they had not stood. This was not what worried
him. All he wanted was to stop their laughter, to stop, at
any price, this unexpected collapse of his authority which
their laughter represented. Surely they were not going to
force him to go down to the dikes. Vainly he tried to find a
means of escape, he looked in all directions for a way out.
A rat, that's what he was. Evidently he was unused to seeing
his authority put to the test. He could find no solution.

"Corporal!" shouted Suzanne. "Get the boat ready quick,
the agent needs it!"

The agent raised his head and smiled crookedly at
Suzanne, making an effort to look comprehending and even
indulgent.

"It's no go," he said. "I know you were unlucky. Things
get about. And anyway, I told you," he added, in a tone of
reproach, turning towards Ma.

"My dikes are wonderful," said Ma. "If there's a good
God, He's the one that made them hold up, if only to let me
have the opportunity to see you land agents pull a long face.
And here you are, you've come to let us see your ugly mug."

Suzanne and Joseph burst out laughing. It was wonderful,

inexpressibly wonderful to hear Ma talk like that. The agent did not laugh.

"Do you realize that your fate is in my hands?" he said.

This time he was trying threats. Joseph stopped laughing and went down a few steps of the bungalow.

"What about your own fate—don't you realize it's in our hands?" he said. "If you don't go down at once to the sea walls, I'll shove you into the boat and you'll die of a sunstroke before you get there. Now, if you'd rather, you can get the hell out of here. And I mean, get out quick!"

The agent took a few steps in the direction of the road, cautiously. When he was certain Joseph was not following him, he turned and said hoarsely:

"All this will be the subject of a report, be assured of it."

"Come up here to say that, come on," cried Joseph, stamping his feet as if about to go down the steps at a run, and the agent took four or five quick steps towards his car before realizing that Joseph had still not budged.

"Skunks!" yelled Ma. "Swine! Thieves!"

Beaming with wrath, freed and rejuvenated, she turned towards Joseph.

"Oof!" she said. "That does me good. They're worse than swine!"

Then she turned back towards the agent, she could not stop herself.

"Thieves! Assassins!" she yelled.

The agent did not turn. Stiffly he went with measured steps towards his car.

"That makes four," said Ma. "I'm the fourth on this concession. All of us either ruined or dead. And they—they fatten on it."

"The fourth?" said Joseph, astounded. "Cripes! The fourth! I didn't know. Why didn't you tell me!"

Joseph thought a second, then had an idea.

"Wait a minute," he said.

He ran into his room and reappeared armed with his Mauser. He was laughing again. Ma and Suzanne, transfixed, looked at him without daring to say a word. He was going to shoot the agent! Everything would change. Everything was going to finish, that minute. Everything was going to begin again. Joseph shouldered the gun, aimed at the cadastral agent, took a good aim, and, at the last split second, raised it towards the sky and fired it into the air.

A heavy silence fell. The agent began to run with all his might towards his car. Joseph guffawed. Ma and Suzanne roared with laughter. The agent must have heard them laugh, but he continued to run like a hare. Once he had reached the car he dived in and, without a glance towards the bungalow, started off at top speed towards Ram . . .

After that, the cadastral agent restricted himself to sending written "notices." He never again returned for an inspection. You would have thought he would have come back as soon as Joseph had gone away. But doubtless he was still unaware of that departure.

In any case, no one, not even the cadastral agent, stopped in front of the bungalow. The cartridges remained in Joseph's belt. Useless. And also his Mauser, innocent, without a master, hung stupidly on the wall of his room. And the B-12, too. "The B-12, that's me," Joseph always said. Slowly now it became covered with dust and, stored forever between the central piles of the bungalow, it rusted.

17

ATTRACTED BY THE SEEDLINGS, GAME CAME DOWN TOWARDS the plain and, consequently, at that time of the year there passed by quite a number of hunters' cars. During the past four years, moreover, there had been an increasing number of these, for Ram was becoming more and more famous as a center for big-game shooting. You began to hear the hum of their car-engines in the distance on the highway, then the sound grew and grew until the cars arrived in front of the bungalow, when you would have said the noise filled the whole plain. They passed, and soon you could not hear anything except the long echo of their horns as they traversed the forest of Ram. Sometimes you had to wait hours for them, and then Suzanne would stretch out in the shade of the bridge.

The doctor had returned to see Ma a few days after her attack. He did not seem to be very disquieted. He had prescribed doubling the dose of pills, had recommended that she remain quiet, but also had advised her to get up and take a little exercise each day. He had told Suzanne that what was needed was for Ma to think less about Joseph, to worry less, and to "regain a little her taste for life." Ma agreed to take her pills regularly, because they made her sleep, but that was all. She absolutely refused to get out of bed. During the first days Suzanne had argued, but it was useless. Ma was obstinate.

"If I get up I'll begin waiting for him again. And I don't want to wait any more for him."

She began to sleep almost all day long.

"For twenty years," she said, "I've wanted to sleep like this."

And she really slept for the sheer delight of sleeping, with persistence as never before. Sometimes she even showed a certain interest in things when she woke up. Most often it concerned the diamond.

"Must get up one of these days to settle that affair," she said.

She now regarded it with perhaps a little less distaste than formerly, but she still wore it on the string around her neck, along with the store-cupboard key.

Suzanne was soon allowing Ma to do as she liked, except for the pills which she willingly took and which Suzanne gave her every three hours. Since Joseph's departure, and for the first time, Ma was at last completely uninterested in the concession. She expected nothing more, either from the cadastral agency or from the bank. It was the Corporal who now had to take the initiative in regard to the sowing which would assure the cultivation of the upper five hectares of land. Ma let him do as he liked. It was, besides, also thanks to the Corporal that at mealtimes there was always food— hot rice and fried fish. Suzanne took it to Ma and often ate with her, sitting on the bed.

Except at mealtimes and some evenings, Ma not only went entire days without saying a word to Suzanne, but often when Suzanne entered the bedroom she neglected even to look at her. In general she did not talk to Suzanne except in the evenings, before Suzanne went to bed. Then it was almost invariably to tell her that one of these days she would have to get up and go to see Pa Bart.

"Ten thousand, I'll be satisfied this time with ten thousand."

Suzanne regularly replied: "That's not bad. That will make a total of thirty thousand."

And Ma would smile a timid, forced smile.

"You'll see, we'll manage somehow, after all."

"But maybe it's not worth the bother of selling it yet? There's no hurry," Suzanne sometimes said.

On that question Ma was vague. She did not know what she would do with the money. What she did know was that she would not again try to build the sea walls. Maybe the money would serve to take them away from the plain. Or maybe she wanted the money for no purpose, merely wanted to have ten thousand francs.

Every three hours, Suzanne climbed up to the bungalow, gave Ma the pills and then went back to sit down again near the bridge. But no car stopped in front of the bungalow. Sometimes Suzanne wistfully recalled Monsieur Jo's car and the time when it had been stationed every day in front of the bungalow. At least it was a car that stopped. Even an empty car would have been better than no car at all. Now it was as though the bungalow were invisible, as though she herself, near the bridge, were invisible. No one seemed to remark that there was a bungalow and, nearer still, a young girl waiting.

Then, one day while Ma slept, Suzanne went into her room and took out of the closet the package of things that Monsieur Jo had given her. She pulled out her prettiest dress, the one she had worn when they went to the canteen of Ram, the one she had worn a few times in the city and which Joseph had called a street-walker's dress. It was a bright blue dress that could be seen at a distance. Suzanne had stopped wearing it so that Joseph would stop bawling her out. But today, now that Joseph had gone, there was no more fear of that. From the moment he had chosen to go away and leave her, she could put it on if she liked. And by putting on that dress, Suzanne realized she was performing an act of great importance, maybe the most important of her life. Her hands trembled.

But the cars did not stop before the girl in the blue dress, the street-walker's dress. They passed by as they had done before. Suzanne tried wearing the dress for three days on end. Then, on the evening of the third day, she threw it away into the *rac*.

18

.EEKS PASSED LIKE THAT, WITHOUT ANYTHING HAPPEN-
..g. There was no letter from Joseph, no letter from the bank
even, and not even a notice from the cadastral agency. After
that, one morning, she saw young Agosti arriving, alone and
without a car.

He did not go directly towards the bungalow, but came
towards the bridge to meet her.

"Your mother sent us a note by the Corporal, she says she
has a service to ask of us."

"She's not well," said Suzanne. "She can't get over Joseph
being gone."

Agosti had a sister who had gone away, ten years ago that
was, with a Customs officer of Ram. But she, Agosti's sister,
had given them news of her.

"Any of us might clear out," said Agosti, "that's not the
question. What's lousy is for Joseph not to write. It wouldn't
cost him a thing. My mother almost died when my sister
went away, then after she wrote everything got better. Now
it's all right, she's used to it."

Once at the canteen of Ram, while "Ramona" was being
played, they had kissed. He had drawn her outside and he
had kissed her. She looked at him curiously. You might say
he resembled Joseph.

"What you doing here all day long by this bridge?"

"Waiting for the cars."

"That's crazy," said Agosti, disapprovingly.

"There's nothing else to do," said Suzanne.

Agosti thought about it for some time, then agreed.

"I expect you're right. But supposing some man offered to take you away?"

"I'd go away with him, even now, with her sick, I'd go right away."

"That's a lousy thing to say," said Agosti, with no great certainty.

Maybe he remembered having kissed her. He had a rather strange look in his eyes.

"My sister waited like this, too."

"If you want a thing bad enough," said Suzanne, "it finally happens."

"What do you want?" asked Agosti.

"To go away from here."

"With no matter who?"

"With no matter who. Yes. Afterwards, I'd see."

He seemed to be thinking about something which he didn't say, as he went off towards the bungalow. He was two years older than Joseph, he was a woman-chaser, and everyone on the plain knew that he sold contraband Pernod and opium. He was rather short, but terribly strong. He had big teeth stained with nicotine, closely set, which looked menacing when he laughed. Suzanne stretched out under the bridge and waited for him to come back. She thought with great intensity about him, his arrival had driven every other thought out of her head, she could think of nothing but him. All you had to do was to want something enough. He was the only man on this part of the plain. And he, too, wanted to go away. Maybe he had forgotten that they had kissed each other a year before, to the tune of "Ramona" and that she was now a year older. She must remind him of it. They said he had had all the prettiest native girls on the plain and

even some of the others who were not so pretty. And all the
white women of Ram young enough for that. All except her.
All you needed was to want something enough, and to have
enough courage.

"She gave me this to try to sell it to Pa Bart," said Agosti
as he returned.

He was holding the diamond, without any precaution,
tossing it in the hollow of his hand expertly, as if it were a
little ball.

"You ought to try to sell it, that would do her good."

Agosti reflected.

"Where on earth did you get it?" he asked.

Suzanne raised herself up and looked smilingly at Agosti.

"A fellow gave it to me."

Agosti began to smile too.

"The guy with the Léon Bollée?"

"Of course, who else could have given me a sparkler?"

Agosti studied Suzanne very attentively.

"I'd never have believed it," he said after a moment. "But
whore or not, you sure are a pretty one!"

"I didn't sleep with him," said Suzanne, laughing.

"Tell that to the next one," said Agosti. He looked at the
diamond unsmilingly and added: "I don't like the idea of
selling it, not even to Pa Bart."

"He believed I would sleep with him," said Suzanne, "but
it's not the same thing."

"You didn't do anything with him?"

Suzanne smiled more broadly, as if she were teasing.

"Sometimes when I took a bath I let him see me, naked as
a jay-bird. That's all."

Words used by Joseph came to her, delightfully, as in a
kind of drunkenness, and were uttered as of themselves.

"I'll be damned!" said Agosti. "That's the limit."

But he looked at her really very attentively.

"And only just to look at you . . ."

"I'm worth looking at," said Suzanne.

"You don't wait to be told, do you?" said Agosti.

"The proof," said Suzanne, pointing to the diamond.

He came back another day. That time Suzanne realized it was for her. He did not even go up to the bungalow.

"I think Pa Bart's going to come across," he said in a funny voice, "and if he don't, either I'll drop the Pernod or maybe I'll denounce him."

And almost at once he announced to her: "In a few days I'll come to get you. You ought to see my pineapple plantation."

He smiled at her and began to whistle "Ramona." Then, without saying goodby, he went off, still whistling.

19

TWO DAYS AFTER YOUNG AGOSTI'S VISIT, MA RECEIVED WORD from Joseph, a very short note saying that everything was all right, that he had found some interesting work. He was acting as guide to rich Americans hunting on the high plateaus, and he was earning a decent amount of money. He also said he would come to see them and to get his guns, in about a month. He was living at the Hotel Central, or at least that was where he told them to address him. Suzanne read the letter aloud, but Ma asked to read it again to herself. She discovered that Joseph made many mistakes in spelling, and she complained about this as though he had made the mistakes only to hurt her still more.

"I'd forgotten what a bad speller he is, he should have had her read the letter over before sending it to me."

All the same, that first letter from Joseph pacified her. She stuck to the question of his mistakes in spelling and, at the end of a few hours, she seemed to have found renewed vitality. She began to ask about young Agosti and to pester Suzanne to find out if he had come again. Twice a day she asked about him. Suzanne repeated to her what Agosti had said, that he hoped Pa Bart would buy the ring, and to urge him to do so Agosti had threatened to stop smuggling his Pernod. Suzanne added that he had said he was coming again in a few days and that by then he would surely have sold the ring. Ma said that if he did not come back he

must be sent for, because she needed the money. To go see
Joseph. He made too many mistakes in spelling for the son
of a schoolteacher. She must go to the city immediately, to
teach him the elementary rules of grammar, at least. Otherwise, he'd end up by being ashamed of himself. In the city
it was not like on the plain. She alone could teach him. She
had discovered what to do with her money, and so eager
was she to have it that Suzanne finally told her about
Agosti's intention to take her to see his pineapple plantation.
Then, surely, he would bring the money from the sale of the
ring, said Suzanne.

Ma forgot the ring for a few minutes. For a few minutes
she remained quiet and her impatience seemed to die down
all at once. Then she told Suzanne that it was a good thing
to go see his pineapple plantation, that it was a fine plantation.

"But you don't need to tell him you've talked to me about
it," she added.

Now the seedlings were already high and of a brilliant
green, ready to be reset. Already, from time to time, they
were beginning to pull them up and to put them in bundles
for resetting, which would take place in a fortnight. Suzanne
talked to Ma about it and Ma began to tell her that if the
Corporal thought it wise, he could do it, that she had
no opinion in the matter, that it was all the same to her. But
the day after having said this, she thought it over and said
it was better to reset them, that it was a shame to let them
rot in the shed.

"Even after we're all gone, he could still sell the harvest
on the spot," said Ma.

The Corporal therefore began the resetting of the seedlings with his wife. Once Ma rose and went out to watch
them from the verandah. When the thinning out had been
done, they waited until it had rained again for a few days,
then set out the upper five hectares of land. They worked
with ardor, like people upon whom idleness had weighed

heavily. And, also, they believed that, since Ma had got up
to watch them work, even though it had been only once, she
must not be as ill as they had thought up to then.

Every three hours, Suzanne climbed up to the bungalow,
gave Ma her pills and then went back to her place by the
bridge. She couldn't stand herself except there, with the
bridge nearby. And still the cars passed by the bridge and
still the children went on playing near the bridge. They
bathed in the water, they fished, or, sitting on the railings
and dangling their legs, they, too, waited for the hunters'
cars to pass and then ran towards them on the road. The
heat was so intense at this season that when it rained there
were more children than usual: they came out from everywhere, gathered round the bridge playing in the rain, frenziedly screaming. The filth and the lice in their hair, washed
out by the rain, flowed in long gray streaks down on their
little necks. The rain was a godsend to them. With their
heads tilted back and their mouths open, they thirstily drank
the rain. The mothers put their little ones out of doors, those
that did not yet know how to walk, placing them under the
eaves of the huts. The children played with the rain as they
played with everything else—the sun, the green mangoes,
the stray dogs.

Suzanne no longer enjoyed watching them, as she had
done in Joseph's time. She now looked at them playing, living, with lassitude. They played. They did not stop playing
except to go and die. To die of destitution. Everywhere, and
in all times. By the glimmer of the fires which their mothers
lit to warm their naked legs, their eyes became glazed and
their hands empurpled. No doubt children died everywhere
like that—in the Mississippi River Valley, in the Amazon, in
the cadaverous villages of Manchuria, in the Sudan, and on
the plain of Kam. And everywhere throughout the world, as
here, they died of misery. The mangoes of misery. The rice of
misery. The milk of misery, the too thin milk of their miserable mothers. They died, with their lice in their hair and it

was well known that as soon as they were dead the father said that, since lice left dead children, the corpse must be buried at once, otherwise lice would overrun them, and the mother would say, "Wait, let me see it," and the father would say, "What will happen to us if the lice get into the straw of the hut?" And he would take the dead infant and bury it, still warm, in the mud under the cabin. And although they died by the thousands there were still as many on the road to Ram. There were too many, and the mothers did not take good care of them. The children learned to walk, to swim, to delouse themselves, to steal, to fish, without the mother, and they died without the mother. As soon as they were old enough to walk, at once they joined the other children of the plain, who played on the road and on the bridges of the road, their rallying points. From everywhere, they made an assault upon the road. When they were not in the mango trees gathering the mangoes that were never allowed to ripen, they were to be found on the highway. And in all the Colony, wherever there were roads and highways, the children and the stray dogs were considered as the great affliction of automobile traffic. But never had any constraint, police, or punishment served as remedy. The road remained at the disposal of the children. When a motorist ran over one he stopped, paid a tribute to the parents, and went on. For a run-over dog or chicken or even for a pig, the motorists did not stop at all. It had to be a run-over child to make them lose a little of their scheduled time.

And as soon as the motorist had departed, the children again swarmed on the road. For the gods of the children were the Ram bus, machinery on wheels, the electric horns of the hunters' cars, metal on the march, and after these things the foaming mountain torrents, and last of all the deadly mangoes. No other god presided over the destinies of the children of the plain. No other. They lie, those who deny this.

The whites were not satisfied with this state of things. The children interfered with the circulation of their motorcars, damaged the bridges, tore up the stones from the roadways, and even created problems of conscience. "Too many of them die," said the whites. Yes. But they would go on dying. There were too many of them. Too many mouths opened in hunger, crying, demanding, avid of everything. That's what made them die. Too much sun on the earth. Too many flowers in the fields. There was too much of a great many things.

The prolonged honking of the horns of the hunters' cars, the murderers, could be heard afar off. The sound became clearer as they approached. And finally they passed in front of the bungalow in a cloud of dust and with an intolerable clattering of the wooden bridge. Suzanne no longer looked at them as she had formerly done. That highway was not exactly the highway she had formerly looked at and along which a man would come to stop before her and take her away. She had waited so long for this that the road could not be exactly the same. It was now rather the road along which Joseph had finally gone away, after years of impatient waiting, the road also along which had appeared Monsieur Jo's Léon Bollée, to Ma's amazement, the road on which came Jean Agosti to tell her he would come to fetch her in a few days. The Corporal was about the only one for whom the road remained eternally the same, abstract, intact, dazzling.

When it rained, Suzanne took shelter under the verandah, always facing the road, waiting for the rain to stop. When the wait became too long she picked up the old *Hollywood-Cinema* album and looked for the photograph of Raquel Meller, Joseph's favorite actress. Formerly that face had consoled her for many things because she found it of a surprising, mysterious, and fraternal beauty. But now, when she thought of the woman who had taken Joseph away, she imagined her with the face of Raquel Meller. No doubt it was the most beautiful face, said Joseph, the most beautiful face you could ever hope to see—perfect, definitive, superbly unattainable. But this no longer consoled Suzanne. Beside the enlarged photograph of Raquel Meller, there was another entitled: "The sublime actress walking in the streets of Barcelona." On the crowded sidewalk, Raquel was walking along with big and happy strides. With big and happy strides she walked through life, with disconcerting ease she absorbed, you might say assimilated every obstacle. But it was always of Joseph's woman that Suzanne was now reminded.

She closed the book. She had her troubles and Raquel Meller doubtless had her own, at least Suzanne was beginning to suspect it. And that Raquel Meller could solve her problems with so much facility, that she could walk like that in Barcelona, in no way set forward the hour of Suzanne's departure from the plain.

20

JEAN AGOSTI CAME FOR SUZANNE IN HIS CAR. IT WAS A
Renault, much less old than the B-12 and much swifter.
Joseph had envied him that car for a long time. Usually,
when Agosti came to see them, he came in a one-horse carriage or even on foot, hunting along the way. He did not
come in the car for fear that Joseph, if he saw the Renault,
might borrow it to go for a ride. He was afraid of this ever
since the time he had lent it to him and had had to wait
three hours for its return. Joseph had forgotten all about him
and had taken the car as far as Ram. Now, Agosti died
laughing when he talked about it.

"Joseph only behaved right with women—he was almost
straight with them. He must have hated your guy like poison
not to have asked him for the loan of his Léon Bollée."

They had driven slowly until they reached the height of
land where was the field of pineapples. Then he had left the
Renault on the road, long before reaching the Agosti bungalow, placing it behind a clump of trees so that his mother
could not see it. Ever since the departure of her daughter,
Ma Agosti spent the greater part of her time waiting for her
son or watching the road whenever he absented himself.
They had then walked for quite a while on a path which
climbed the hill where, at the very top, set back a little, was
their bungalow. It was on the side of that hill that was laid

out the field of pineapples. A great many rows of pineapples were dead, but other rows were still flowering.

"It's the phosphate," said Agosti. "We got to be modern and we tried it out. Another three years like this and I'm beating it, with some dough."

The field stretched out in the broiling sun, without a tree, at the edge of the tropical forest. All Agosti's rice fields were, like Ma's, invaded by the great tides of July, but he managed to get along with maize, pepper trees, and the pineapples which he planted on the sides of this hill. In addition, Jean Agosti dealt in contraband Pernod with Pa Bart. Pa Agosti was an adjutant living in retirement who, as veteran soldier and for lack of means to bribe the cadastral agents, had obtained an irreclaimable concession. It was five years since he had settled on the plain. Pa Agosti had taken to smoking opium and had completely lost interest in the land. From time to time he would disappear for two or three days and they would regularly find him in an opium den in Ram. Then Jean Agosti would tell the drivers of the bus and one of them would put old Agosti by force on the bus and bring him back to his bungalow. He always began all over again. Every two or three months he would clean out all the cash in the house in order, presumably, to return to Europe. But he always stopped off in the opium den in Ram and forgot his project. Father and son often had fist fights and always fought in the same place, below the pineapple field. Ma Agosti would follow them, scrambling down the hillside to try to separate them. Her two big braids flapping on her back, she ran, calling to the Holy Virgin to help her, jumping over the rows of pineapples, flinging herself upon old Agosti, knocking him down and sprawling on the ground with him. These scenes occurred so often that Ma Agosti had remained as slender and agile as a spider.

All the Agostis were practically illiterate. Every time they had to write a letter, to the cadastral agents or to the bank, they came to see Ma to have her write it for them. Thus,

Suzanne knew their affairs as well as those of her own house. She knew that if they managed to stick it out it was above all things thanks to the contraband trade in Pernod and opium which Jean Agosti carried on in collaboration with Pa Bart. The contraband trade enabled him not only to give some money to his mother but also to rent a room by the month at the Ram canteen. It was to that room that he usually took the women with whom he slept. Suzanne he had preferred to take into the pineapple field, she did not know why, but he doubtless had his reasons.

It was the siesta hour and on that side of the road, towards the forest, there was no one. It was towards the rice fields that the children, singing, led their buffaloes.

"I was the one you were waiting for beside the bridge," said Agosti. "Lucky I passed by. I knew of course that Joseph had gone and I wondered what you were doing. Even if your mother hadn't sent that note, I'd have come."

"I'd never thought of you since he went away."

He began to laugh, a little under his breath, as Joseph did sometimes.

"Whether you thought about me or not, it was me you waited for. I'm the only man in all this district."

Suzanne smiled at him. He seemed to know where he was taking her and what he was going to do with her. He seemed so sure of himself that she felt very tranquil, and was even more certain of being right in following him than the other day when he had asked her and she had decided to follow him. And what he said was true: he was a man who could not endure the idea that somewhere on the plain was a girl alone who was waiting and watching for the hunters' cars. Even if Ma had not asked him to come, he would have come one day or other to take her off in his Renault.

"Come into the forest," said Agosti.

Ma Agosti must be asleep, otherwise she would have called out long ago. And Pa Agosti must be smoking in the shade of the bungalow. They left the field of pineapples and entered the forest. By contrast, it was so cool that you could believe you had entered water. The clearing where Jean Agosti stopped was rather narrow, a sort of dark green abyss surrounded with tall thick timber. Suzanne sat down against a tree and took off her hat. Yes, of course; one felt secure here, more secure than anywhere within four walls, but if that was the reason he'd brought her here, to be safe, it was useless trouble. Joseph had gone away. Ma had agreed to her coming here. She had given her permission easily—far more easily than she had ever allowed Joseph to go to Ram for a woman. And doubtless Suzanne would have preferred the room Jean Agosti had at the Ram canteen. They would have closed the shutters and, except for the rays of sun that would enter the cracks, it would have been a little like the tremendous gloom in the moving-picture theatres.

Agosti let himself down beside her. He caressed her feet, which were bare and white with dust, like his.

"Why do you always go barefoot? I made you walk a long ways."

She smiled, a little constrained.

"That's nothing, I'm the one that wanted to."

"It's true you wanted to. Would you have followed no matter who?"

"No matter who, yes, I believe."

He stopped laughing.

"How hard up can you be!" he said.

He had had all of them except her. It was a glory and his face reflected his good luck. Button by button, slowly, he began to undo her blouse.

"I got no sparkler to give you," he said, smiling very gently.

"And really, it's on account of the sparkler that I'm here."

"I sold it to Bart. Eleven thousand, a thousand more than she wanted. O.K.?"

"O.K."

"I got the money here, in my pocket."

Her breasts were beginning to peep out at him and he opened the blouse to uncover them completely.

"It's the truth. You sure are worth looking at."

Then he added in a lower voice, mean, this time:

"It's the truth, you're worth a diamond and even more. You'll not have to worry."

When he had quite undressed her and spread her clothes beneath her, he gently laid her on her back. Then, before touching her, he stood up a little to look at her. She closed her eyes. She had forgotten that Monsieur Jo had seen her like this, for the phonograph and the diamond, she was sure this was the first time anyone had seen her. Before he touched her he asked:

"Now that you've got the money, what'll you do with it?"

"I don't know. Maybe, go away."

While he embraced her, she recalled the tune of "Ramona," as it had been sung on Pa Bart's radio-phonograph, when they had stood in the shadows of the wooden piles beneath the canteen, with the sound of the nearby sea covering it, immortalizing it. From then on, she was in his hands, adrift with the world, and she let him do as he would, as it had to be.

21

IT WAS ALREADY LATE IN THE EVENING. THE LAMP IN MA'S bedroom was burning. Agosti turned the car half around and stopped at the top of the driveway, near the bridge. But Suzanne, motionless beside him, seemed to be in no hurry to get out.

"It's no joke for you, I'll bet," said Agosti.

His voice recalled Joseph's, with its hard inflections, its straightforwardness. They had made love twice, lying at the foot of the tree in the clearing. The first time was when they first arrived, the second time was just before leaving. At the very moment when they had stood up to go, suddenly he had undressed her again, embraced her, and they had started all over again. Between times he had talked, had told her about how he also wanted to leave the plain but not as Joseph had gone, with the aid of a woman; he wanted to leave with money he had earned. What had happened to Joseph was no surprise to anybody, he said. Several times he had met Joseph at Pa Bart's during the last month he had been on the plain, and Joseph had said that a woman was coming to fetch him. He did not know Joseph very well— many people did not know him very well—but he talked about Joseph without any jealousy and with a kind of restrained admiration.

From Agosti's conversation you guessed that Joseph had always been a puzzle to him and that he was full of questions in regard to him that he could not answer. So, he had decided, as had many other people, that Joseph was a little mad and was capable of doing inexplicable things. They had hunted together and never had Agosti seen anyone hunt with such fearlessness. One time he had been a little jealous of Joseph. That was during a tiger hunt at night, about two years ago. Agosti had been very frightened but Joseph had not been, nor had he even noticed Agosti's fright. "Ever since that night, I've never been able to be exactly his friend," said Agosti. They had been pursued by a female panther whose cub they had shot. She pursued them for an hour. As he fled, Joseph shot her. He hid and from his hiding place he had shot at her. The sound of the shots betrayed their whereabouts every time and the beast became more and more enraged. At the end of an hour Joseph had got her. By that time there were only two bullets left and Agosti and Joseph had gone such a distance in their flight that they were two kilometers away from the road. Ever since that night, Agosti had gone hunting very rarely with Joseph.

Agosti told Suzanne that for a very long time, for months, Joseph had wanted to finish with this life on the plain, no matter how. He had said he could not stand living there, could not endure the rascality of the agents of Kam. One evening when they were coming back from Ram where they had been drinking a little, Joseph had confessed that every time he returned from the hunt or from the town or every time he made love to a woman, he felt so disgusted with himself and with everything that he wanted to die, simply because he had been able, all the same, to forget for a short time the dirty dealings of the Kam agents. That was in the year of the sea wall. His desire to kill the agents of Kam was so strong then that if he was disgusted with life it was because he felt he was a coward not to do it.

Suzanne had not talked about Joseph to Jean Agosti. She could not have talked about him to anyone, except perhaps to Ma. But Ma had lost her taste for talking about anything other than Joseph's mistakes in spelling and about the diamond.

No, what had counted had been his gestures with her, the attitude of his body towards hers and the new desire he had had for her after they had made love the first time. He had taken out his handkerchief and had wiped off the blood that ran down his thighs. Then, before leaving, he had put a corner of the bloody handkerchief in his mouth, without disgust, and with his saliva had cleaned away once more the dried blood stains. That love could abolish physical differences to such an extent she would never forget. He was the one who had dressed her again, when he had seen clearly that she neither had the wish to dress nor to rise to go. When they were ready to leave, he had cut off a pineapple to take to Ma. He had cut the pineapple from its base in a gentle and inexorable way, and the gesture had recalled his ways with her. What he had said about Joseph, on the side, was of no importance.

Suzanne did not budge from the Renault. Ten minutes had passed since they had reached the bungalow. However, he was not surprised to see how little she wanted to get out of the car.

He took her in his arms.

"Would you rather it happened, or would you rather it hadn't?" he asked.

"I'm glad it happened."

"I'll go in with you to see her."

She agreed. He entered the drive and stopped the car in front of the bungalow. It was almost night. Ma was in bed, but she was not asleep. In a corner of the room squatted the Corporal, waiting, as always, for a sign, always the same sign to assure him that she would go on living and that he would go on eating. He was there more and more often, now that Suzanne spent her days near the bridge and now that he had finished setting out the rice seedlings. The bungalow was terribly deserted.

Ma turned towards Agosti and smiled at him. Her face showed emotion and the smile contracted it. She saw that Suzanne was holding a pineapple in her hands.

"That's kind," she said quickly.

Agosti was perhaps a little ill at ease. There was no chair in the room. He sat down on the bed at her feet. Truly, Ma had got much thinner since Joseph had gone away. And tonight she looked very old, very worn.

"You worry too much over Joseph," said Agosti.

Suzanne had placed the pineapple on the bed and Ma ran her hands mechanically over it.

"I don't worry. It's something else." She made an effort and added: "It was kind of you to come for her."

"Joseph will always manage to get along. He's confounded smart."

"I'm really glad to see you," said Ma. "We might as well not be neighbors. Suzanne, go get yourself a cup of coffee."

Suzanne went into the dining room, leaving the door open the better to see. Since Joseph had gone away they lit only one lamp. Thanks to the Corporal, there was always coffee on the sideboard. Suzanne poured out some coffee into two cups and took them in, along with Ma's pills.

"We saw each other in Ram, all the same," said Agosti. "You were all the time with that Léon Bollée guy."

Ma turned towards Suzanne and smiled gently.

"Sometimes I wonder what ever happened to him."

"I met him once in the city," said Suzanne.

Ma paid no attention to this. It was as far away as her girlhood.

"He had some car!" said Agosti. "But as to him . . ."

He began to laugh softly, remembering doubtless what Suzanne had told him, things he alone knew.

"You talk like Joseph," said Ma. "He was certainly not handsome, the poor man . . . But that's no reason . . ."

"Joseph didn't hold his looks against him," said Agosti. "It was because the guy didn't understand anything about anything . . ."

"We understand what we can," said Ma. "And that's no reason either to hold anything against someone. He was not a bad fellow, not mean . . ."

"Sometimes we can't help not liking people. Joseph was like that. He couldn't help himself."

Ma did not reply. She gave Agosti a long look.

"I saw Joseph at Pa Bart's," said Agosti, "when he came to sell the phonograph the guy gave you. He said he was glad to get the phonograph out of here."

"It wasn't only because that fellow had given it," said Ma. "He'd have sold the bungalow if he could . . . You know how he is."

For a moment they had nothing to say to each other. Ma kept looking at young Agosti with increased attention, more and more apparent. It was certain she had just discovered a new interest in him. Only Suzanne remarked the fact; he did not, as yet.

"You are often with Pa Bart," Ma said at last. "Do you still carry on the contraband in Pernod?"

"Have to. My father's once again used up half the money from the pepper harvest. And then, I kind of like it . . ."

Ma drank her coffee and swallowed the pills Suzanne had brought her.

"And if they ever caught you?" she asked.

"You can always buy them off, the Customs people. They're like the cadastral agents. We got to forget all that, or we're sunk."

"Yes, better not to think. You're right."

She avoided talking to Suzanne. Agosti was still as embarrassed as if he were seeing Ma for the first time. Maybe, too, he was struck by the aspect of the bungalow. His mother had gone to great pains to arrange theirs. They had electricity from Ram, a roof, and even a ceiling. Their bungalow had been better built and the boards of the walls were not disjointed. Ma Agosti thought that the way to keep men at home was to make a comfortable, pretty house for them. To try to keep her son with her as long as possible, she had hung up pictures on all the walls, had put colored cloths on all the tables and handpainted cushions on all the seats. It was the first time Jean Agosti had come to see them at night. The last time he had been there had been one morning, very early, when he had come to ask Joseph, just returned from a night hunt, if he had not seen his father, who had once more disappeared.

"Suzanne told me you've had news of Joseph. I was right when I told you not to worry."

"You were right. But he makes so many mistakes in spelling that I'm sick over it."

"I make more than he does," said Agosti, laughing. "After all, I don't think it's so important."

Ma tried to smile.

"But I think it's important. I've always wondered why he makes so many mistakes. Suzanne makes far less than he does."

"If he needs to learn to spell, he'll learn. You worry all the time. Me, I reckon I'd learn spelling if I had to."

For the first time in months Suzanne looked attentively at Ma. She gave the impression of being finally resigned to all her defeats without yet having been able to control her old ferocity. However, with young Agosti she was making an effort to be amiable and conciliating.

"Sometimes," said Ma, "I tell myself that even if he wanted to, Joseph would have a hard time to learn. He's not made for that kind of thing. It bores him so, he'd never manage."

"You always have to worry about something," said Suzanne. "Now it's because Joseph makes so many mistakes in spelling. You always have to think up something to worry about."

Ma nodded her head in agreement. Even about herself she had nothing to learn, now. She mused upon what she would say, suddenly indifferent to their presence.

"If anyone had told me," she said at last, "if anyone had told me, when they were little, that when they were twenty they'd still make mistakes in writing, I'd rather have had them die. That's the way I was when I was young. I was terrible."

She did not look at either of them.

"Since then, of course, I've changed. But now sometimes it all comes back to me as it was when I was young and it sometimes seems to me that I would rather see Joseph dead than to see him making so many mistakes in spelling."

"He's smart," said Suzanne, "when he wants to, he'll learn to write. All he needs is to want to."

Ma waved her hand in denial.

"No. He'll not learn any more now. Now, no one will ever take charge of it. I must go to see him. I'm the only one that could make him learn. You say he's smart. I say I'm not sure he is. Now that he's gone and now that I get to thinking over these things, I say that maybe he isn't smart."

Anger thrust through her words, as strong as ever, stronger than herself. She seemed exhausted and was perspiring a great deal as she talked. She must be struggling against drowsiness, with all her anger. It was the first conversation she had sustained since her dose of sedatives had been doubled.

"Writing's not the only thing," said Agosti, who perhaps felt that Ma was aiming her words at him. Or maybe he was merely trying to calm her.

"What else is there? Nothing's more important. If you don't know how to write a letter you can't do anything. It's as if you lacked—I don't know what, lacked an arm, for instance."

"What good has it done you to write so many letters to the

cadastral agents?" asked Suzanne. "No good at all! When Joseph fired off his gun into the air, that did more good than all your letters!"

Ma was not convinced. And the longer the conversation about spelling lasted the more she despaired of ever finding an argument to convince them.

"You can't understand. Anyone can shoot off a gun into the air. But to defend yourself against those rascals you need something else. When you've understood that, it will be too late. Joseph will be cheated and fooled by every crook in the world and when I think of that it's worse than death."

"What do we need to do?" said Jean Agosti. "What do we need to do against the agents of Kam?"

Ma struck the bed with her hands, outside the covers.

"I don't know, myself. But something could be done, surely. And it will happen sooner or later. The agents there —at any rate they could always be knocked off. To see that done is the only thing that would do me any good. Nothing else. Maybe not even Joseph. Just to see that, I'd get out of bed."

She waited a little, then sat up, her eyes wide open and shining.

"You know it. You know that I worked fifteen years to be able to buy this concession. For fifteen years I thought only of that. I could have married again, but I didn't do it because I didn't want anything to take my mind off the concession that I wanted to give the children. And you see where it got me! I wish you would realize it so well that you'd never forget it."

She shut her eyes and, exhausted, sank back on her pillow. She was wearing one of her husband's old shirts. Around her neck there was no longer the diamond on the string but only the store-cupboard key. It had no sense there, now, for now she would let herself be robbed with total indifference.

"I think Joseph was right, but I'm not sure yet. If I stay in bed it's not on account of Joseph or because I'm sick, it's on account of something else."

"On account of what?" asked Suzanne. "On account of what? You must say it."

Ma's face wrinkled up. Maybe she was going to begin to cry in front of Agosti.

"I don't know," she said in a childish voice. "I like it here in bed."

She made a visible effort to keep back her tears in front of Agosti.

"I don't see what else I could do if I got up. I can't do anything more for anybody."

As she spoke she raised her hands and let them fall again on the bed in a gesture of impotence and exasperation.

"Up there," Suzanne said gently after a moment of silence, "they've planted pineapples. And they sell them. Maybe you ought to think about that."

Ma threw her head back and the tears began to flow in spite of herself.

"It's dry land that they have," she said, weeping. "Here we couldn't manage to do it."

No matter how you approached her now, you always touched something sensitive and hurt her. It was no longer possible to talk to her about anything. All her failures were held in an inextricable network and depended so closely one upon the other that you could not touch one of them without affecting all the others and making her despair.

"And tell me why I ought to grow pineapples? Why?"

Young Agosti stood up, came nearer her, and remained standing at the head of the bed for a long while. She spoke no more.

"I must go," he said. "Here's the money for the sparkler."

She sat up suddenly and flushed red. Jean Agosti took out of his pocket a wad of thousand-franc notes pinned together and held it out to her. She took it mechanically and let it lie in her half-opened hand, without looking at the money, without thanking him.

"You must excuse me," she then said gently. "But everything people tell me I already know. I'd thought about growing pineapples. I know that the fruit-juice factory in Kam pays very well for them. Everything people tell me I already know."

"I must go," Agosti repeated.

"Good night," said Ma. "Maybe you'll come again?"

He made a wry face. Without a doubt he suddenly had realized what they wanted of him, what they wanted him to say, what assurances, even vague, they expected from him.

"I don't know. Yes, maybe."

Ma held out her hand to him without replying, without thanking him. Agosti left the room with Suzanne. They went down the bungalow steps. He looked uncomfortable.

"Mustn't pay any attention to what she says," Suzanne said to him, "she's so fed up with everything."

"Come with me to the end of the drive," he said.

He still looked upset. He walked beside her, his mind off somewhere else. In the afternoon he had been very different, he had looked at her with such attention, he had said, "I like the way you're made." Suzanne stopped halfway down.

"I don't want to go to the end," she said. "I'm going back to the house."

He stopped, surprised. Then, smiling, he put his arms around her. Indifferent, she let him embrace her. What she must say to him was difficult to put into precise words. She had never yet made an effort of this kind, an effort which mobilized all her forces and kept her from realizing that he was embracing her.

"You don't need to be afraid," she said at last.

"What kind of craziness are you talking?" he said, releasing her and holding her away from him, looking into her face.

"I'll never marry a fellow like you. I swear it. We won't ever speak about it again and you mustn't pay any attention to what she'll say to you for I swear it, I'll never marry you."

He looked at her with a great deal of curiosity. Then, relieved, he laughed.

"I believe you're as cracked as Joseph. Why wouldn't you marry me?"

"Because what I want is to go away."

He became serious again. Maybe he felt a little put out of countenance.

"I never intended to marry you," he said.

"I know," said Suzanne.

"Maybe I'll never come back," said Jean Agosti.

"So long."

He went off, then came back and caught her.

"Even in the forest this afternoon, you didn't think you could live with me?"

"Not even in the forest."

"Not for a minute?"

"Live with you? Never, even less than with Monsieur Jo."

"Why didn't you sleep with him?"

"Didn't you ever look at him?"

He laughed and she, too, began to laugh, full of calm security.

"I'll say I did! At Ram everybody died laughing when he came in with you. Didn't you even kiss him?"

"Not once. Even Joseph wouldn't believe that."

"All the same, that's the limit."

She felt a calm triumph, not a wrinkle disturbed the calmness. Jean Agosti took her gently by the arm.

"I'm glad it was with me," he said. "But I believe you're as crazy as Joseph. So it's better if I don't come back."

She went off this time and Agosti did not try to stop her.

Suzanne softly entered Ma's bedroom. She was not asleep. When Suzanne came in Ma looked at her silently, her eyes brilliant. In her hand on her chest there was still the wad of thousand-franc notes that Agosti had given her. No doubt she had not even counted them. She was perhaps wondering what to do with all this money now.

"Everything all right?" asked Suzanne.

"All right," said Ma, weakly. "After all, he's not bad, that young Agosti."

"Go to sleep. He's just like everyone."

"All the same, you're hard to please. It's not that Joseph . . ."

"Don't you worry about it," said Suzanne.

Suzanne started to go and took the acetylene lamp.

"Where are you going?" asked Ma.

Suzanne drew near her, holding the lamp in her hand.

"I'd rather sleep in Joseph's room. There's no reason why not."

Ma lowered her eyes and again her face reddened violently.

"That's so," she said gently. "There's no reason, now he's gone away."

Suzanne went into Joseph's room and left Ma alone in the darkness, still awake, and with the wad of thousand-franc notes in her hand.

All that money for which she now had no use, in her inert and imbecile hands.

Joseph's room was as he had left it the day he had gone away. On the table, near his bed, there were some empty cartridges he had salvaged and which he had not had time to recharge. There was also a package of cigarettes, half smoked, that he had forgotten in the suddenness of his departure. The bed was not made and the sheets still bore the imprint of Joseph's body. Not a gun was missing from its nail.

Suzanne took the sheets and shook out the worms that had fallen from the roof, then she put them back carefully on the bed, undressed, and lay down. Had Joseph been there, she would have told him about what had happened between her and young Agosti. But Joseph was not there, and there was no one to whom she could tell it. Time and time again Suzanne recapitulated Jean Agosti's gestures, minutely, and each time they troubled her in the same way, reassured her in the same way. She felt serene, serene with a new understanding.

22

MA HAD HER LAST ATTACK ONE AFTERNOON WHEN SUZANNE was not there.

Agosti, contrary to what he had resolved, had returned the day after their excursion to the forest. "I couldn't help coming back," he had said. Since then, he had come every day in his Renault, at the time of the siesta. He did not go again to see Ma but immediately upon his arrival he and Suzanne went off to Ram, where they used his room at the canteen.

Ma knew about it. No doubt she thought it was good for Suzanne. She was not mistaken, for it was during that week, from the time of the first excursion to the pineapple field to the time of Ma's death that Suzanne at last unlearned her senseless waiting for the hunters' cars and abandoned her empty dreams.

Ma had said she could do without her, that she would take her pills all alone, that all Suzanne had to do was leave them on a chair near the bed. Maybe she had not taken them regularly. Maybe Suzanne's neglect was the reason why Ma's death occurred a little sooner than it should have occurred. It is possible. But that death had been preparing for so many long years, Ma herself had talked about it so often, that hastening it by a day or two no longer had much importance.

On coming back from Ram, in the evening, they perceived the Corporal who, stationed on the highway, motioned to them to make haste.

The great convulsive seizure had run its course and Ma no longer moved except for occasional jerks and tremors. Her face and arms were purple-splotched. She was strangling, and from her throat issued muffled, involuntary cries, a kind of angry barking, a yelping of hate and anger for everything and for herself.

Jean Agosti, after the briefest glance, went off to Ram in his Renault to telephone Joseph at the Hotel Central. Suzanne stayed alone beside Ma, with the Corporal who, this time, showed no sign of hope.

Soon Ma no longer moved at all but lay inert, completely without consciousness, yet still breathing. The coma was prolonged and, as the moments passed, her face assumed a stranger and stranger look. It was as if her face were torn apart with conflicting emotions, divided between an extraordinary and inhuman lassitude and a no less extraordinary and inhuman rapture. However, shortly before she ceased to breathe, the expressions both of rapture and lassitude vanished and no longer did her face reflect its natural and human loneliness. Instead, it was a face turned openly upon the world in a barely perceptible look of irony. "I certainly had them all. All—from the cadastral agent of Kam to that girl there who is looking at me and who was my daughter." Perhaps that was what the look expressed. But also it may have been a look of mockery at everything in which she had believed, of derision at the earnestness with which she had applied herself to all her wild undertakings.

She died shortly after Agosti's return. Suzanne clung to her and, for hours, she too wanted to die. She wanted ardently to die, and neither Agosti nor the memory still so recent of the pleasure she had had with him could stop her from returning, in her grief, one last time to the confused and tragic excesses of her childhood. It was not till dawn that Agosti dragged her away by force from Ma's bed and carried her in to Joseph's bed, where he lay down beside her. He had even held her in his arms until she went to sleep. And as she fell asleep, he had told her that maybe he would not let her go away with Joseph, had said that he believed he was beginning indeed to love her.

It was the honking of the eight cylinder Delage that woke up Suzanne. She ran out on the verandah and saw Joseph get out of the car. He was not alone; the woman followed him. Joseph motioned to Suzanne and Suzanne ran towards him. As soon as he saw her better he realized that Ma was dead and that he had come too late. He pushed Suzanne aside and ran towards the bungalow.

Suzanne rejoined him in the bedroom. He had sunk down on the bed, upon Ma's body. It was the first time she had seen him cry since he was a very small child. From time to time he raised his head and looked at Ma with a terrifying tenderness. He called to her, he kissed her. But the closed eyes were filled with a violet shadow, deep as water, the closed mouth was closed on a dizzying abyss of silence. And more than her face, her hands crossed upon each other had become hideously useless things which cried out the inanity of the ardor she had given to living.

When Suzanne came out of the room she found Jean Agosti and the woman waiting in the sitting room. The woman had cried and her eyes were reddened. When she saw Suzanne she made a movement of recoil, then reassured herself. She was doubtless afraid of seeing Joseph again, afraid of the reproaches he might make her.

Determined and patient, Agosti for his part also seemed to be waiting for something. Maybe he was waiting for Joseph, to talk about her to Joseph. That was possible. But it in no way concerned her now. Even if he had spoken to Joseph about her it could not be about her real self, he could not but mistake her present identity. All the same, they had made love together every afternoon for a week, right up to yesterday. And Ma had known it, had allowed it, she had allowed her to make love with him. But Suzanne was no longer, for the moment, in that part of the world where people made love. It would come back to her, of course. But for the moment she was on the other side, where Ma was, where the immediate future did not seem to matter, and where Jean Agosti had lost all meaning.

She sat down in the sitting room, near him. He had become as radically a stranger as the woman.

Agosti stood up and went to the sideboard where he mixed a cup of condensed milk.

"You must eat something," he said.

She drank the milk and found it bitter. She had not eaten since the day before but she was saturated with a nourishment heavy as lead and which, it seemed, would suffice her for days and days to come.

It was two o'clock in the afternoon. All around the bungalow there were many peasants who had come to watch over Ma. Suzanne remembered having seen them the night before, through the sitting-room door which was open, when Jean Agosti had carried her in to Joseph's bed. The woman looked at them without understanding what they were doing there. And, in her eyes, there was still the same horror.

"The Corporal's gone," said Agosti. "I put them on the bus to Ram and gave them some money. He said he had to find work and couldn't lose a single day."

Around the assembled peasants, attracted by the crowd, the naked children played in the dust of the terrace. The peasants paid no more attention to them than to the flies which flew around them. They, too, waited for Joseph.

The woman, not able to contain herself any longer, spoke.

"It's on account of him," she said in a low voice, "that she died."

"It's not on account of anyone in particular," said Agosti. "You mustn't say it's on account of Joseph."

"Joseph is going to believe that it was on account of him," the woman went on, "and that will be terrible."

"He won't believe it," said Suzanne. "You mustn't be afraid of that."

The woman seemed to be very humble. She was really very beautiful, very elegant. Without make-up, undone with the fatigue of the journey and with distress, her face remained very beautiful. Her eyes were exactly the eyes Joseph had talked about, so pale that you would have said they were blinded by the light. She smoked without stopping and stared at the door of the bedroom. From her look and from her whole being there emanated a desperate yearning for Joseph, from which you could see she could no longer escape.

Joseph at last came out of the room. He looked at all three in the same way, without looking especially at any one of them, but with the same expression of frightful impotence. Then he sat down beside Suzanne without saying a word. The woman took out a cigarette from her case, lit it, and held it out to him. Joseph smoked with avidity. A little after his return to the sitting room he perceived the peasants assembled round the bungalow. He rose and went out on the verandah. Suzanne, Jean Agosti, and the woman followed him.

"If you want to see her," said Joseph, "you can. All of you, even the children."

"Are you going away?" asked a man.

"Yes. Forever."

The woman, who did not understand the native language, looked from Joseph to the peasants and back again, at a loss, looking on from another world.

"They will take back the concession," said a man. "You must leave a gun with us."

"I'm leaving everything to you," said Joseph. "Especially the guns. If I was obliged to stay here, I'd stay with you.

But every one of you who can get away should get away. I
can, and I'm going. Now, see to it that whatever you do you
make a job of it. You must take their corpses into the forest, away up there beyond that last village, you know where,
in the second clearing. In two days' time there won't be
anything left of them. Burn their clothes in the brush fires
you light at night. Be careful about their shoes and the
buttons. Bury the ashes of the fires afterwards. Pitch their
car far off in the *rac*. Use the buffaloes, they will drag it to
the bank, you will put big stones on the seats, and you will
pitch it into the *rac* at that point where you dug the ditch
when we tried to make a sea wall, and in two hours' time
it will be sunk out of sight and nothing will remain. Above
all, don't get caught. And see to it that you don't any of you
confess. Or else, let all of you confess. Together. If you
are a thousand people that have done something together, no
one can do anything against you."

Joseph opened the door of Ma's bedroom which was on
the side of the road and he also opened the door which led
to the yard. The peasants entered the house. The children,
delighted, chased each other through the bungalow rooms.
Joseph came back into the sitting room and sat down with
Suzanne and the woman. Agosti addressed him:

"We got to think about the rest," he said.

Joseph ran his fingers through his hair. That was so. They
had to think about it.

"I'll take her to Kam tonight," he said, speaking low, "and
I'll have her buried there. Tomorrow."

Agosti said it would be better to put Ma's body in a coffin
here, and tonight. The woman thought so, too, and she and
Agosti went off in her car, going in the direction of Ram.

Joseph understood the meaning of Agosti's presence.
The minute that he was alone with Suzanne he told her he
was going back to the city and that if she wanted to go with
him she could. He asked her not to tell him what she had
decided to do until the last minute, when he was on the

point of leaving. After this, he went to his bedroom to get his
cartridges and unhook the guns from the wall. Then he put
all these things in a heap on the table in the sitting room.
And while the peasants argued among themselves as to how
they were going to hide these things, he went to sit on the
edge of Ma's bed. He wanted to look at her all the time that
remained to him.

When Agosti and the woman returned from Ram it was
almost night. The coffin was strapped to the top of the car,
a coffin of white wood, of native manufacture. The Delage
turned into the drive and stopped immediately in front of
the bungalow on the earth terrace.

Agosti took Suzanne down towards the bridge. He did
not want Suzanne to stay in the bungalow while Joseph and
the peasants put Ma's body into the coffin. Once there he
said:

"I can't keep you from going away, but if you want to stay
for awhile with me, before going to live with them . . ."

The muffled and regular sound of hammering came from
the bungalow. Suzanne asked Agosti to be quiet. Once
again, as she had done the night before, she cried.

She went back to the bungalow. In the sitting room the
woman was weeping silently. Suzanne went into Ma's room.
The coffin was standing on four chairs. Joseph was lying on
the bed in Ma's place. He had stopped crying and again
had that terrible look of helplessness. He did not seem to
be aware of Suzanne's presence.

Agosti made some coffee and poured out four cups. Then
he called Joseph and Suzanne. He was the one, too, who
remembered to light the acetylene lamp for the last time.
He brought each of them a cup of coffee. You felt he was
eager for Joseph to leave.

"It is late," said the woman softly and slowly.

Joseph stood up. He was wearing long trousers and beautiful tan leather shoes and his hair was cut short. He looked
elegant and clean. No one looked at Suzanne, not even

Joseph, but she on the contrary did not stop looking at him, not for a second.

"We're going," said Joseph.

"It's not important whether she stays with me or someone else, for the time being," said Agosti suddenly.

"No, it's not very important," said Joseph. "It's up to her to decide."

Agosti had begun to smoke and had turned a little pale.

"I'm leaving," Suzanne said to him. "I can't do anything else."

"I can't stop you," said Agosti at last. "In your place, I'd do the same."

When Joseph had stood up the others had also got to their feet.

The woman started the car and turned it abruptly round. Agosti and Joseph loaded the coffin onto it.

There was complete darkness now. The peasants were still there, waiting until they had gone before leaving. But the children had left when the sun went down. From the cabins came the sound of their sweet babbling voices.